INFINITY CHRONICLES
BOOK TWO

A PARANORMAL REVERSE HAREM

ALBANY WALKER

Infinity Chronicles Series

A Paranormal Reverse Harem Story
Albany Walker
© 2019

Cover art designed by Maria Spada of Maria Spade designs

Editing by Elemental Editing & Proofreading

Proofreading done by Tabitha Finch

✽ Created with Vellum

CHAPTER 1

The room is dark when I wake up. I can hear the slow steady breathing of someone behind me. Immediately, I know it's Ares. He has this way of wrapping me up in his arms while we sleep that I'm becoming familiar with. I let my eyes fall shut, enjoying how safe and warm I am with him beside me.

A creaking sound has my heart rate jumping, Ares doesn't like anyone in his room. He barely tolerates his brothers—the other three of our Infinity—in here, but with Mia still making excuses to stay here, we've been holing up in his room together.

I hold my breath, waiting for the noise to come again. Ares shifts behind me, his nose nuzzling my shoulder.

A shuffle, maybe a footstep, comes next. Reaching my arm back, my hand lands on Ares's upper thigh, and I push against him, trying to wake him up without speaking. He barely stirs, so I dig my short fingernails into him. Ares wiggles a bit, causing the fabric of the down comforter covering us to shift.

The room is too dark for me to see anything. Ares prefers it this way, he can see clearly even in the dark, so he keeps his room pitch black to help him sleep.

I think there's someone moving around in the room. It could be one of the guys using the bathroom, or getting a drink. But I don't get the sense it's one of them. Over the last week I've grown closer to all four of my guys, and I'm sure I would immediately realize if it were one of them. There's only one other person it could be.

Giving up on waking Ares, I lean forward and reach out for the other side of the bed. I remember Dante being next to me when I went to sleep. Keeping my movements slow so I don't make too much noise, my hand lands on an arm. I walk my fingers up to Dante's shoulder and give him a small shake. He grunts and scoots over a bit, giving me more room. Now I can barely reach him. Damn it.

I haven't heard anything, but I still feel like there's someone else here with us. Slowly I turn, first on my back, then I roll into Ares, tucking myself as close to him as possible. With my hands between us I reach up and tap my finger over his heart. My head is tucked up under his chin, so when Ares pulls me closer, my face is almost buried against his chest. I have the urge to bite him—why the hell isn't he waking up?

With more insistence I tap and rub over his chest. "Hmm," he groans rolling onto his back.

Angling my neck, I put my lips to his ear and breathe the words, "Someone in the room." Ares stops breathing, his head turns toward the door and then scans the room. His body goes rigid seconds later.

He flips the covers back, covering my head in the process. I don't move, I understand that he did it on purpose. "Mia, what are you doing?" Ares's voice shows no sign that he was deeply asleep just moments ago.

I knew it had to be her—there's no one else in the house—but I didn't want to believe she would come in here uninvited. And I know she wasn't invited.

In a whisper she replies, "I thought I heard a noise, and I got scared to be upstairs by myself." We've crossed paths a few more times in the last few days. I think she's getting suspicious of me being around so much. I've seen the way she watches the guys and their reactions to me. They've been careful to make it seem like I'm just a new friend from school, but I don't know if she believes them.

Ares lets out a huff, "It's an old house. I'll walk you back—"

"Can't I stay with you tonight?" Mia interrupts, her voice insistent, but she still manages to sound timid. I've never seen her flirt with Ares, but when she looks at him, especially when he doesn't realize she is, her eyes go all soft, and she gets a little smile on her lips. And she's always finding reasons to be close to him, to touch him.

"The guys are all in here."

"I don't mind," she tells him quickly. "I know you guys are a package deal." Her words come out like she's trying to make a joke, and maybe she is. But it feels like she's trying to imply much more, but that might just be my jealousy talking.

"How about we go get a drink, you'll see there's nothing to be worried about," Ares mutters, trying to sound consoling, and I feel the slightest bit of persuasion in his tone.

"Shut up already," Dante grumbles, reaching over to me so his hand lands on my lower stomach. I flinch at the contact then relax as he continues around to my hip. He makes a big deal of flopping around a bit to cover the noise he's making as he pulls me close to him.

"Scoot over," Milo fusses.

"See? There isn't even enough room," Ares adds. I know the others are making a bigger deal than it is, so she won't ask to stay. With the two king-size beds next to each other, there's plenty of room. Half the time we all end up on one bed cuddled together like a pile of puppies. Inevitably someone gets hot or uncomfortable at some point, and we spread out throughout the night.

A sliver of light penetrates the darkness of the room. I barely peek out of the covers enough to see Ares guiding Mia, his hand on her back, out into the hall. "Will you stay with me then?" Her question sends a spike of anger through me. My territorial feelings for the guys have only amplified.

"Come on, let's let them sleep," Ares replies without answering her question.

"He'll be back," Dante offers, rocking his head against the pillow.

"I don't understand why we can't tell her who I am, she's not even an Infinity." My tone is whiny even to my own ears.

The bed shifts, I hear a thud as someone bumps into the edge of bed. "Shit," Ollie curses. His hands slap the wall until he finds the panel for the bathroom door. He flips on the light, not even bothering to close the door as he pees.

"She's not one of us, but she's been working with Ares for years," Dante mutters, his voice even deeper than usual from sleep. I still don't get why that matters, but I'm going to ask Ares as soon as I get a chance.

The water runs for a second before Ollie stumbles back to bed, dropping down on Ares's side, leaving the light from the bathroom casting a dim glow into the room.

Ares has claimed dibs on that side of the bed and insists I sleep next to him. He says *his room, his rules*. The other guys haven't put up much of a fight, instead they shift around taking turns sleeping on the opposite side.

Ollie cuddles in close to me, spooning my back. His hand lands on my hip, if Milo were on the other side, he'd reach past me to him. There's a closeness between the two of them that exceeds the bond the four of them share.

I lie awake, waiting for Ares to return. Though I'm surround by the others, my thoughts are consumed with what he might be doing and wondering when he'll be back.

Eventually I fall asleep before he returns. When I wake up again, it's to the alarm from Ollie's phone. The room is dark again, and it seems Ares must have returned at some point. Ollie shifts. "Milo," he croaks, "snooze." Milo doesn't even acknowledge him as the light keeps flashing and the alarm keeps blaring. I climb over Ollie, knowing it will be easier to get past him for the phone than it would be to get past Dante and Milo. My feet hit the carpet, and I become chilled immediately. I've taken to sleeping in shorts and a t-shirt, otherwise I get way too warm. Shivering, I find my way to the phone, letting the flashing light be my guide.

Hitting the orange snooze icon, I drop the phone next to Ollie as I make my way to the bathroom. He's always in charge of waking up the others. Milo is usually the easiest, and Ares is the hardest with Dante falling somewhere in the middle.

I'm so happy I don't have to wake up Ares, much like my experience last night, he tends to ignore you or be a grumpy butthead when he's woken up.

With shuffling steps, I walk toward the bathroom. I've gotten over my hesitance to use the well-appointed room. Pushing into the door I squint and rub my hand over my eyes. The light is still on, and even though it's not bright, it's still too harsh on my eyes.

"Good morning, *Cara*," Ares purrs. I freeze, my back going rigid. I didn't even think about him not being in bed.

With my hand thankfully still over my eyes, I spin on my heels to face the door. "I'm so sorry. I should have knocked. I wasn't thinking."

Ares chuckles, his footsteps on the tile coming up behind

me. Ares is obsessed with my neck, and whenever he touches me it's usually there. So, it doesn't surprise me when I feel his palm on the column of my throat. Water drips from his skin landing on mine, he's just out of the shower. I swallow as Ares applies a scant amount of pressure, tilting my head back. "No need for apologies." My mouth falls open as he breathes the words into my ear. While I'm attracted to all the guys, Ares exudes an air of sexuality that makes my knees weak.

His front meets my back and the dampness from his skin seeps into my clothes, making me shiver hard. I feel the fabric of the towel around his waist brush against the back of my thighs. I sag with the knowledge, not sure if it's in disappointment or relief.

With his right hand still on my throat, his lips find the sensitive spot where my shoulder and neck meet. He traces the water droplets that have fallen from him onto me with his lips, pushing tiny pecks against my skin. My body goes pliant in his hold, my eyes falling closed as I let my arms drop to my side. Assuming my reaction is acceptance of his ministrations, Ares nudges my head farther to the right, exposing more of my neck to him. He plants open mouth kisses along the column of my throat until he's right under my ear. His breathing is a little ragged as he pulls in a deep breath.

"Can I kiss you *Cara*?" We haven't kissed since that day in my camper, and it feels like so long ago, but in reality, it's only been a few days. I nod, my mouth dry. I've wanted him to kiss me like that again for too long.

The feel of his teeth on my shoulder has me gasping, but

not in pain. It makes me shiver in a way that has nothing to do with being cold. Ares works his way over to my lips. I don't think it's possible for him to really kiss me, standing behind me like he is, but I'm proven wrong. Reaching for him, I tangle my fingers in his inky hair. Feeling the soft short hairs on the back of his head, I glide my hand up and grasp near the top where it gets a little longer.

Ares's hands move to my shoulders, and his lips leave mine as he turns me to face him. His eyes are heavy as he peers down at me, his lips still damp from our kisses. "Kiss me," he murmurs, not a demand, but I obey anyway. Lifting up on my toes, I close my eyes and brush my lips over his. Ares keeps his hands on my shoulders and arms, but his grip tightens on me. I let my mouth open a bit more and pull his full bottom lip between mine. A huff of hot minty air falls from his mouth. I have a second where I want to pull away, embarrassed I haven't brushed my teeth yet, but then his tongue licks under my top lip and I don't care anymore.

Pushing harder against his mouth I explore his lips with the tip of my tongue, kissing him deeper when he opens to me. I pull his tongue into my mouth and rub the underside in gentle strokes. The kiss slows, but my heart rate doesn't take the hint.

My eyes open slowly, dazed by his touch. I find Ares staring down at me, his eyes fully black and his lips parted. He leans down, capturing my lips again, and he controls the kiss this time. Nipping at my bottom lip, he plunges into my mouth and tangles his tongue with mine. Just when I think I'm catching on to his kiss he pulls back, coaxing my tongue from my mouth to kiss with the tips barely touching.

I sigh, leaning my chest onto his. Ares slows his movements, turning the fervent need into a low smolder as he releases my lips, going back to open mouth pecks punctuated with little bites. Eventually, he places his forehead on mine and takes a few deep breaths. I gulp a few lungsful of air also, trying to get my breathing and heart rate under control.

"Did you need to get ready?" Ares asks huskily, his voice deep.

I open my eyes. I'm not even sure how much time has passed, but it didn't feel long enough. "Yes, we have school," I answer dejectedly. I'd much rather stay here all day. He smooths his hand over my hair, giving me a kiss at my temple before pulling away. I can't keep my eyes from following his back as he fiddles with the black towel at his waist. The fabric pulls tight over his butt as he opens the sides, and then tucks them together, keeping his back to me. My mouth goes dry, and I wonder, if he turned around would I be able to see his mark?

"I'll let the others know you're getting ready." Ares pushes out the door, closing it behind him. My head falls back on my shoulders, and I let out a low groan. How can he seem so unaffected? My legs feel like jelly, and my lips are all puffy, but he's as cool as a cucumber.

I use the bathroom and wash my hands and face. I'm still a little flushed, so I keep the water cold to pull the heat from my cheeks. There's a knock on the door as I brush my teeth. "Come in," I call out around a mouth of foam.

Milo pushes into the room, his eyes sleepy and his hair all disheveled, looking terribly cute. "Almost done," I announce as he walks over to me and leans his shoulder against the wall. Holding my hair at the back of my neck, I put my mouth under the faucet, taking in water so I can rinse and spit.

When I stand up, Milo is watching me through the mirror as I use the washcloth to clean my face and wipe my mouth. "Everything okay?"

His lips turn down in a slight frown. "You were in here a long time." The heat I was hoping to erase from my cheeks flares back to life.

"I was? Sorry." I look away, unable to meet his eyes.

"It's okay." Milo shrugs, his frown disappearing, but his lips form a hard line instead. When I turn to leave, he stops me by placing his hand on my arm. "I don't mind." Milo's voice is soft. "Sometimes I get jealous, though." My head snaps up, and I see he isn't looking at me, he's looking at the floor. "Ollie and Ares make it look easy, but I never know if you want me around, or if… if I could touch you the way they do."

I get a pang in my chest. Reaching out to grab his hand in mine, I reply quietly, "This is all really new to me. I don't know what I'm doing most of the time. But I always want you… I mean, I always want you around, Milo." I want to slap my hand over my mouth for the slip. I didn't mean for it to come out so forward, but in truth it's what I meant. I want him to touch me, to be as close to me as the others—Dante, too. I just don't know how to show him that, or if it's acceptable to feel that way.

I think I have an understanding of what our relationship will be like, but it's so foreign to me I don't know how to deal with it yet. So, I just pretend that we're all just friends, even though I know it's more.

"You do?" Milo glances at me from the side, his head tilted.

I nod eagerly. "Always, Milo. I hate it when we're at school, and you guys barely talk to me. I feel so much lonelier than I ever did before, and back then I really was lonely," I confess. He's showing me a piece of himself and I feel like I should do the same in return.

Milo places his other hand over our already joined ones. "I don't like it either. I think we should just claim you."

My brows furrow. I've never heard any of them use the word 'claim' before regarding me. What does he mean?

"I mean, I know we haven't found your mom yet, but I bet Ares is close. He's been working on it every day. I don't think if the others knew we found you that it would make a difference at this point."

Wasn't I thinking the same thing about Mia a little while ago? Maybe we should just make the announcement—or whatever they call it—to the community that our Infinity is whole. Anybody really interested in us would already know anyway. I'm never far away from the guys, they've even taken to coming into work with me. And when I say they barely talk to me at school, it's a bit of an exaggeration. They do talk to me at school, we eat lunch together daily, but we can't be like we are at home and, most importantly, Ares isn't at school with us. I think that's part of the reason none of the guys fight him about our sleeping arrangements. When I finally get to see him in the evening after a long day of school and both of us working, he always looks a little run down. I feel it, too, but not nearly as bad as he does because I'm with one of the others several times throughout the day.

"Maybe we could talk to the others. I think I'm as ready as I can be at this point. I know there's still so much I need to learn, but maybe if we came out," the words feel weird, but I can't think of anything else that fits, "it might actually help find my mom. Maybe someone knows her or knew her."

"We'll talk to them tonight," Milo confirms his hands still holding mine as he leans down and give me a quick peck at the corner of my mouth. I don't even have time to return his affection before he turns and leaves the bathroom.

Should it feel strange that I was just kissing Ares, and Milo kissed me less than ten minutes later? My head is telling me it's not okay, that people would call me names, but the light feeling I have in my stomach and the grin on my lips says something else altogether. And what about the guys? Do they know that Ares has already kissed me? Would they be mad?

As my thoughts spiral, Ollie pokes his head in the door. "Almost ready?" His blond hair is pulled back in a low pony-tail near the back of his neck, but a few shorter pieces have already fallen out, framing his perfect jaw line. I know he'll end up taking the elastic out and redoing it several times throughout the day, maybe even abandoning the hair tie to let it hang down to his shoulders. His light green eyes run up my legs slowly. Ollie seems to have the same fascination with my legs that Ares has with my neck. I've noticed that every time I wear my sleep shorts, his eyes rarely meet mine.

"Yes. Just finishing up in here. I have to throw my clothes on."

A slow grin lights up Ollie face. "Want me to grab you something?" I'm shaking my head no before he even finishes. "What? There was nothing wrong with what I chose," he defends in mock outrage.

"Ollie," I warn, my tone full of disapproval. "If I had worn that to school, I would have been sent home on a dress code violation."

A low chuckle sounds. "We wouldn't have even made it to school, Ares would have killed us both." He leaves me then, returning to the bedroom. I follow behind him, tempted to hop on his back just because it seems fun.

Curbing the desire, I head over to the closet disguised as a wall and slide the partition back. Dante is lounging on the second bed. His arms are folded behind his head as he stares up at the ceiling. His mind wanders so easily. It's easy to see why he's such a magnificent artist. I think he spends half his time daydreaming. When I first met him, I labeled him *the bad boy*, but in truth, he's so much deeper than that.

I bite my lip and send thanks to whoever is responsible for my good fortune. Maybe it has something to do with my connection to the four of them, but I don't think I've ever seen a more handsome group than my guys. Dante's dark hair, though a few shades lighter than his brother's, is pushed back from his face. The beginning of dark stubble is visible on his chin and jaw. Some days he goes without shaving, today is one of those days. Though it only reaffirms his bad boy persona, I love the way it looks.

He tilts his chin down and looks at me. It's only then I realize I've been caught staring instead of getting dressed like I should be. "Okay?" he questions in that deep voice that always manages to work its way right into my blood stream.

"Just thinking," I reply, heading into the closet. I hear him shift on the bed, his footsteps nearing behind me.

"About?" Dante rarely wastes words. I find myself wishing he would go on and on just so I could hear him speak.

I've gotten better about always blushing, but I still feel a flush rise to my cheeks. "What I'm going to wear to school today."

I feel him over my shoulder as he leans in close to whisper, "Liar." His words hold no anger nor humor. "If you look at me like that when you're thinking about clothes, I shouldn't have anything to do with putting them on." I spin around with my mouth open in surprise. Dante doesn't even blink. He meets my stare and challenges me, raising a brow.

I snap my lips closed. I don't even know how to respond to that. I wasn't really going as far as thinking of him naked, but now that he's put the thought in my head, I can't get it out.

Dante reaches out, his finger and thumb snatching a chunk of hair, letting it run through his fingers. "You should get dressed, unless you need help?"

I narrow my eyes, now he's just trying to goad me. I turn away, my hair pulling from his fingers as I do. I jerk down the first pair of new jeans my hands land on. I've thanked them for all the clothes several times, and at first I was reluctant to take them, but it's been so nice to have more than two or three jeans to wear all week, and, man, does it save me from having to do laundry so often. Thankfully, the clothing they bought is pretty similar to what I've always worn. They are a lot nicer and fit so much better, but they're not trying to make me play dress up—well Ollie does, but that's not the point. Peering over my shoulder to watch his reaction, I snag the black t-shirt hanging farther down the line, it's Dante's. He stands back, his arms crossing over his chest, but his face is a mask of indifference. Pushing past him, I take my finds into the bathroom and, using my butt, I push the door closed.

Dante's shirt is too big, but I've already committed, so I'm going to make it work. I try tucking it in, but it's so long that it makes my hips and stomach look lumpy—not attractive. I settle with tying a big knot in the back. It pulls the waist tighter than I'm used to, but the top is still extra big, so I don't feel like it's too much. Turning, I check out my handywork in the back and have second thoughts. You can see a small triangle of my lower back, but I'm afraid to retie the knot, it was hard enough the first time.

"Time to go," Ollie yells as he bangs on the door.

"Damn this stupid idea," I mutter, and with my head held high I step into the bedroom, finding all four of them waiting on me.

My brow furrows, is there something going on? Usually Ares is running interference with Mia while Dante or Ollie start the car. That leaves me with one or two, tops, to get out to the car and then to school. Why are they *all* here? I forget about my shirt altogether.

Dante slaps his hand over his eyes. "Bad idea."

"What is?" My eyes skip from one to the other, while I wait for an answer.

"Nothing, Laura. Everything is perfect." Ollie is trying to suppress a grin but failing. He wraps his arm over my shoulder and leads me from the room. I hear Dante groan out a long sigh as we leave.

"Where's Mia?" I whisper, looking around like she might pop out from behind a corner.

"Ares said she wouldn't be up for a few hours. She was up pretty late."

My lips tighten in a thin line, and my muscles go rigid. "And what did Ares say they were doing up so late?" My voice is low, coming out pinched between clenched teeth.

Ollie stops and looks down at me. "Don't spark up on me now," he warns, his face serious. I pull away from him.

So far, I've only sparked up, as Ollie calls it, one other time on accident. It seems to be heavily tied to my emotions. That's another reason we keep everything friendly at school.

Touching Ollie always makes the connection flare. Lately

I've been feeling a different pull when Ares touches me, but now that I know I might light up like a firework, it's easier to push the feeling away.

"Give me a little credit, I've been practicing," I mutter, sulking down the hall. I make it to the car before the others. Ares didn't even say goodbye to me when I left. I'm not holding out hope that I'll be able to ask him in person what he was doing with Mia.

CHAPTER 2

*D*ante gets in the driver's seat, leaving Milo and Ollie to sort out which one of them will take the front seat. I've already claimed one in the back.

I've gotten used to arriving at school with the guys. The first few times I actually walked in with them, I acted like I didn't catch how many people stopped and watched. Now I don't have to pretend so much.

Delany hasn't even looked in my direction since that night at the diner last week. I've seen her around Dante a few times, but she acts like I don't even exist, which is strange, considering that's all I wanted in the beginning.

I walk into my homeroom with my backpack still over my shoulder. A lot of the bigger schools I've been to don't allow you to bring bags into class, but the teachers don't bat a lash at all the kids skipping their locker and toting their books around with them. I get a few head nods, and even a couple hellos as I pass by, making my way toward my seat. Mostly I still keep my head low. I don't like all the attention that comes with hanging out with the guys, but I'll deal with it because the rewards are worth it.

After a quick round of attendance, the teacher ignores us. I, like many others in the class, use the time to make sure I have everything I'll need for all my other classes. There's some talking, but it's still early; half the kids are sipping from insulated cups, getting in a dose of caffeine.

THE HALLWAYS ARE loud as we change classes, and I'm trying to make my way to third hour when someone taps my shoulder. Looking back, I find Charlie. I haven't seen too much of him since he came into the diner. We've passed each other in the halls, but he hasn't attempted to talk to me. "Hey, how are you?" I ask, the question just rolling off my tongue. I'm not really sure what he thinks after the encounter with Ares, but he has a small, sheepish grin on his face.

"I'm good. Been kind of busy." He looks away. "How about you?" he asks.

Slowing my steps but still walking in the direction I need to go, I nod. "Yeah, I've been kind of busy too. So, what's up?"

Charlie keeps pace with me, he's jostled a few times from oncoming students rushing to class. "Nothing really. I was just wondering how you're holding up. It's tough being the new kid and all."

Reaching up for my backpack straps, I run my hands across them few times. I don't really know him well. I realize he's making small talk, but I'm not great at it. "It's okay. I've been working a lot, and school isn't so bad."

"And hanging out with Dante and his friends?" Charlie adds.

"Yeah, I guess." I'm not sure what else to say about that so I just keep walking.

"So, are you dating one of them?" My steps falter. Am I? I don't really know what we are other than I think of them as mine, but if I told that to Charlie, he would assume I was crazy, because I wouldn't be talking about only one of them.

I shrug. "I have to go. I'm going to be late for class." I rush away before he can ask me any more questions.

I'm only a few steps from my classroom when Ollie pokes his head out looking left, then right, in my direction. His brow furrows, and he steps fully into the hall.

"Something wrong?" Ollie's eyes scan the hall behind me. "I was worried you might be late."

I don't want to tell him Charlie asked me a question that has me all flustered, so I just grab the sleeve of his hoodie and tow him with me to our seats. "No, nothing's wrong." Ollie eyes me with a tilted head. "Did you get your test results back in Bio?" Dropping into my seat with my bag on the desk, I try for a change of subject. Ollie is typically easy to distract.

He doesn't take the bait this time, though. "Was that Charlie I saw behind you? What did he want?"

I busy myself by taking my book and notebook out. "Nothing, he was just saying hi." I don't know what Ollie would think if I told him what Charlie asked me. I was afraid he or the other guys would assume I was the one asking about our relationship status. I'd rather ignore the topic altogether for right now.

Ollie stays quiet. I look over my shoulder, but his head is down. When he looks up, I watch as his shoulder lifts, and he shoves his phone into his front pocket. He meets my eyes and opens his mouth, but the tardy bell rings, cutting him off.

We don't have a chance to talk much in class, which I'm grateful for. I don't like not being honest with him, and by the way he keeps looking at me, I expect he knows I'm acting a little off. Giving him a wave and a smile over my shoulder as I walk out of class, I find Milo already waiting for me in the hall.

"Oh, are you meeting Ollie? He's coming."

"No, I'm here for you," Milo says and looking over my shoulder, he tilts his chin up, acknowledging someone behind me—Ollie, I'm sure.

"Why?" I can't keep the surprise from my tone.

Milo wraps his hand around the backpack strap high on my chest. I know immediately he's going to take it, so I shift my shoulder and turn so it slides off easily. "I'm walking you to class."

"Okay…" I let the word hang between us, he's never

walked me to class before. I barely see Milo throughout the day other than lunch. We don't share any classes. Once he has my bag, he lifts his hand in a go-ahead gesture. Shaking my head, I lead the way to my next class. Milo doesn't even speak to me on the way. He's stalking behind with his head on a swivel as he watches the surrounding kids. I slow down and he barely notices, bumping into me when I turn to face him.

"Milo, is something wrong?" I scan the halls much like he was doing, looking for whatever has him on alert.

"Nothing. We need to get to class." I recognize a brush off when I hear it, I just gave the same line to Charlie. I spin back around, my steps a little heavier than needed, and stomp away. Milo lays his hand gently on my shoulder.

"You don't need to run." He doesn't let go, instead he closes the distance between us, walking right on my heels. I navigate the halls until my classroom door becomes visible. When I turn to face him, he's already looking down at me. "You'll tell me if someone bothers you." I guess he meant for it to come out as a request, but he fails miserably. It's an all-out demand.

Narrowing my eyes at him I ask, "Why? What do you know that I don't? And please don't tell me…" I look around, making sure no one is listening to us. I lean up on my toes to get closer as I whisper, "…Delaney has remembered I exist."

When I drop back on my feet, Milo grins down at me. "I don't think she forgot about you. I think it's more like she wishes she could forget about you."

I roll my eyes. "As long as she keeps doing it, I don't care what she's telling herself." Milo's hand lands on my cheek seconds before I feel his lips on mine in a sweet peck. When he pulls away, he looks down at me. His eyes are blown wide, and his lips are parted. He looks as surprised by his actions as I am. A shy smile forms on my mouth. Milo just kissed me, and he looks positively freaked out, or scared. One or the other.

After a few seconds pass, his lips turn up with a self-satis-fied grin. "You need to go to class." His voice is a low whis-per. I nod, agreeing with him, but continue to stand there looking at him. Milo uses his hands on my shoulders to turn me, holding me in place. The weight of the backpack falls on my shoulders as he slips it on. A slight push toward my class gets my feet moving in the direction I need to go. I don't notice the people around me, I don't even care my teacher is about to close the door as I slip past her. All I can feel is the softness of Milo's lips on mine.

CHAPTER 3

*D*ante finds me a few seconds after my class gets over. Typically, we all meet in my stairwell and share lunch, but today he directs me toward the cafeteria. I want to drag my feet, to argue that our lunch spot is so much better, but it's like he knows me or something.

"Laura, Milo and Ollie are already waiting for us. You don't need to hide away in some corner. We should have been coming here to eat ages ago. I think we just liked having you to ourselves." I open my mouth to give him some reason why our private lunches are better, but he continues. "Milo told us he kissed you." That shuts me right up. What should I say to that? Will he be mad? "Probably wasn't the best idea considering we're trying to keep our relationship under wraps, but I wish I would have done it first."

My eyes snap up to his. Dante has a dark look. He's one of

the biggest guys in school, and before I knew him, I would never have wanted to tangle with someone like him. In reality, though, Dante is sweet and thoughtful. When he goes quiet, most people would think he's being all dark and broody, but nothing could be further from the truth. Yes, he is intense, and yes, he does have an edge, but that edge is buffered with a big soft spot for everyone he cares about.

"You're not mad?" My question comes out as a whisper, even though we're mostly alone in the hall.

Dante wraps his arm over my shoulder and squeezes me to his side. "Sometimes I wish you would have grown up like us, knowing what to expect when you found us." I open my mouth again to apologize, but he places his finger over my lips, shushing me. "But I know you wouldn't be *you* if you had. And you are perfect just the way you are." Dante's words are spoken just as softly as mine were, the deep timbre of his voice rolling over the syllables.

Something inside me melts with his words, and I find myself wrapping my arm around his waist. I want to lay my head on his chest, to pull the feeling of contentment he's exuding into me. But I know it's dangerous, it's not just his words but the closeness I feel to them when their gifts are connecting us. The last thing I need at school is for someone to see me sparking up.

"When are you going to shift for me?" I surprise myself by asking the question I've wanted to ask for a while. Dante releases me, and I feel the loss of his touch immediately.

Wrapping my arms over my stomach, I wonder if I've pushed him too far.

"You want to see me shift?" His words are hushed, and if I weren't waiting for his response, I wouldn't have heard him. He reaches forward and grabs the handle for the lunchroom door.

The noise hits me like a wave, but he hears my answer anyway. "I do. But I understand if it's private or something." I try to smooth over my blunder. If that's not something he's ready to share with me, it's okay. I can wait. I make a show of peering around the crowded room looking for Ollie and Milo. Dante brushes his fingers against mine as he passes. I know he did it on purpose. It takes away a tiny bit of the sting I feel at his rejection.

"They're over here." I tag along behind Dante, keeping my eyes on his back as he makes his way over to a corner table. It's a long, picnic-style table that looks rather full. It's clear this is where they usually sit, and there isn't any space for me. I shuffle my feet, wondering why they thought this was a good idea.

"Hey, took you guys long enough." Milo jumps up, pulling his legs out from under the table. "Here sit." He motions for me to sit down in the spot he just vacated. Not wanting to stand any longer I slide in next to Ollie. Milo puts one leg under the table before ordering the other side to, "Scoot down a little." His voice is rough, almost a yell as he makes the demand from the other end of the table.

Dante takes the seat across from me. When I meet his

eyes, he shrugs, tilting his head toward the right. It's then that I see Delaney in the spot next to him. I want to reach over and pull him to our side of the table, but when Milo places his hand on my arm, I stop myself from making a scene.

"I grabbed a few things from the hot line," Ollie pipes up, setting a tray of crunchy tater tots in front of me. My mouth waters just thinking about them. I qualify for free lunch, always have, but I rarely eat in the cafeteria, so it's not often I get anything other than the peanut butter and jelly sandwiches I bring. However, I love the school's tater tots. I've tried to recreate them at home several times, baking them and even frying them, but I can't manage to get the crunch just right, like the school convection oven can.

I peer up at Ollie, wondering how he knew. He gives me a cheeky wink but says nothing. Milo drops my turkey sandwich next. Suddenly, the noise at the table picks up; I hadn't even realized it had quieted with our approach, but now everyone is talking again, including Delaney.

"Are you still coming over tonight?" Delaney questions Dante. She has the straw to her cola poised at her lips.

Dante, digging into the turkey sandwich Milo also just gave him, huffs but nods his head. "We really need to get everything finished up this week. I have other things I need to be doing." He looks up, catching my eye, but looks away quickly.

"There are just a few more things to take care of," Delaney answers noncommittally. I pop a tot in my mouth and glance around. I'm trying not to focus too much on Dante and

Delaney across from me, but I have to admit my jealousy has me paying way more attention to her than I should.

Milo and Ollie lean past me a few times, talking about little stuff. I tune them out as I pick up a can of fruit punch to my right. I've grown used to sharing with the guys. All of them have offered me drinks from their cups at one point or another, so I think nothing about reaching out and taking a drink. The girl on Delaney's right leans over and whispers something in her ear with her eyes on me. I wipe my face with a rough white napkin, knowing they're talking about me, but unsure what I've done this time to warrant their whispers.

The lunch period seems to last way longer than usual since I'm crammed into the table with everyone else. I hope we can go back to eating in the stairway tomorrow. This sucks. I can't even enjoy my tater tots. I feel like everyone is staring at me.

Breaking away from the guys when lunch finally ends, I hustle to my next hour where I'm happily ignored.

DANTE MEETS me in the hall on the way to art. "Hey," I offer as I walk up to him, waiting a few steps out of my last class.

He gives me a chin jerk and starts walking. With anyone else I might think they were mad at me, or maybe even didn't like me. But I've come to realize it's just his way. Right before we make it to the art room door, he turns and faces me. "I'll show you tonight." I tilt my head, I'm sure he can read the confusion on my face. "After you get off work, I can show you." Dante shrugs. "The rest of me."

Realization dawns, he means that he'll shift, that I can finally see his power. I hop on my toes, excited at the idea. "Really, you don't have to, but I... I want you to." I stammer over the words. I hope I'm not being too demanding.

Dante lets out a low chuckle, "I didn't know you even wanted to. I thought it might freak you out."

I give him a light smack to his arm with the back of my hand. "Why would you think that?" I'm not really expecting an answer, so when he does, I'm a little surprised at the seriousness of his tone.

"It's not a common power—neither is Ares's ability—but mine scares some people."

I grab Dante's hand, linking our fingers together even though I know I shouldn't, not at school. "It's still you, right? So it doesn't bother me." I hope my words carry the truth, because it really doesn't bother me. He squeezes my fingers back and doesn't release me until we're about to enter class.

Now I have a whole new reason to be excited when I get off work tonight.

WE'VE FALLEN into a routine for the nights I work. Ares usually shows up a little after the dinner rush. Sometimes he helps me fold napkins and fill the salt and pepper shakers.

Sometimes he just sits and chats with Maggie. Either way, I feel so much more comfortable with him there.

Tonight when he comes in, he's dressed as casually as I've ever seen him, other than at home. His black t-shirt is just tight enough that I can see the definition of his upper chest. My mind immediately wanders back to this morning when all that perfect skin was on display. I bite the corner of my lip. Ares has this ability to steal my entire focus when we're together. He makes me forget I still have customers who want their refills and their checks.

Heat fills my cheeks when he saunters over, his head tilted to the side as he gazes at me, much in the same way I imagine I'm staring at him. "*Ciao, Cara,*" Ares purrs when he's just inches away from touching me. "*Mi sei mancato.*" Over the last few days he's taken to greeting me in Italian. I don't understand what he's saying, but he could recite a textbook in that language and I'd probably be a puddle at his feet.

"Hi, Ares." My voice is a little breathy. He doesn't seem to mind, though, leaning in to give me a slow kiss on my temple. I reach out for him, fisting the material of his shirt.

"You missed me, too," he mutters to himself. I nod anyway. I do miss him. Every day, when we're at school, I feel his absence like a sore tooth, an ache that doesn't disappear. "What can I do?" he offers when I don't release his shirt.

I want to drop my head to his chest, to soak in the comfort he surrounds me in, but I know I can't do that right now. "You could come to school with me, or maybe I could graduate early, but then that would leave me without the guys so…" My thoughts trail off as I try to think of a solution.

Ares places his hand on my shoulder and his thumb traces up my throat. "I meant, what can I do to help you with work, so we can get you out of here." His words are light, a small grin plays at his lips.

My face goes hot all the way to my ears. I back away from him, feeling very exposed and a bit foolish. "We've been pretty slow tonight. I've been keeping up." I adopt the cool tone I reserve for crabby customers. Smoothing my apron over my hips as I take a few more steps away from him. "I think Maggie wanted to talk to you." It's a complete lie, but it doesn't matter, Maggie always wants to chat with Ares. My eyes scan the few customers in their booths, there's one couple who has their plates pushed away—just the escape I needed. I don't say anything else to him as I make my way over to their table, a fake smile plastered on my face. I can feel the weight of his stare on my back.

About an hour has passed since I first talked to Ares. I've done just about anything I can to keep myself busy while he sits at the counter, nursing the coffee Maggie poured for him after he first sat down. It must be cold by now, but occasionally I see him lift it to his lips and take a sip. I'm done for the night; the only thing holding me back is my pride. I'm embarrassed he might laugh at me for what I'd said earlier. I know my reprieve won't last much longer because Maggie has looked at me a few times, then around the diner. I think she knows I'm stalling.

Ares, the sneaky bugger, comes up behind me as I'm wiping down the same table for the third time. "Ready?" he says, but I jump at the sound of his voice.

"Gah," I groan as the bleach towel in my hand goes flying.

"Maggie still wants the surface on this table for tomorrow, so I figured I better stop you now before it's gone." His tone is flat, bored even.

Collecting the towel, I hang it over the side of the sink. Maggie gives me a wave and a smile. She knew he was coming to get me, so it's time to go. When I turn, Ares is waiting with his eyebrow cocked up like he thinks I might make an excuse to stay longer. Untying my apron, I pocket the cash then roll up the fabric with the coins still inside, I'll sort through those another time.

"See you tomorrow," Maggie calls as Ares leads me out the door. I'm being a brat, but I feel stupid.

"See you," I mumble back.

He walks me to the passenger side but doesn't open the door. "Laura." My back stiffens. The flat tone is gone, replaced with what sounds like a trace of sadness.

"Yeah." I don't turn to look at him, but he has my full attention.

"I wish I could be with you all day. There are times when I want to drop what I'm doing and go to you just so I can see you, to feel you close to me." I look down at the ground, my lips in a tight line. Ares steps up closer and his front molds to my back. "It makes me happy you feel that way, too," he whispers, his chin resting on my head.

"I thought you were making fun of me," I confess, feeling even more like a brat for avoiding him.

Ares sighs. "I wish you knew that I would never make fun of you, especially for something like that. Now, if you manage to trip up the stairs again…" He lets the words hang, lightening the conversation.

· Jutting my elbow back I connect with his side, he grunts but I know I didn't hurt him. He's teasing me. Wrapping his arms around my upper chest he rocks us back and forth. "As much as I'd like to keep you to myself for a little while, Dante told me you asked to see him shift?" I nod, Ares's chin, still on the top of my head, follows along with the movement. "All right. I told him we'd meet him out near the house." A bubble of excitement flares to life in my stomach. I've been curious about what Dante shifts into from the moment I actually believed any of this was possible.

The car ride home seems to take longer than usual, I know it's from anticipation. "What does he shift into? What's it like? Does it hurt?" The questions burst from me as we get closer.

Ares turns his head, gazing at me. "You don't know? Why didn't you ask him?" His tone is full of curiosity.

"Well, he seemed so secretive about it, it felt like I shouldn't pry."

Ares chuckles. "This might be fun," he mutters under his breath before adding, "I'm not going to ruin the surprise."

Huffing, I cross my arms over my chest. "How come your

gifts are so different? It seems like since you guys are real brothers your abilities would be the same."

Ares nods his head a little. "We aren't as different as you might think. I have an ability to shift, but I don't become something else. I'm able to *shift* with the shadows. I can even shadow walk, but it uses a lot of energy, and I have to know the place I'm going very well. If I can't create an image up here," Ares takes his hand from the wheel and points to the side of his head, "I can't get there. Believe me, I've tried."

Curious about his last statement I ask him, "What happened when you tried?"

"It just didn't work, no matter how hard I tried." He doesn't seem bothered by the limitation, if you could call it that. "We're here." Ares stops the car, but leaves it running. When I reach for the door handle, he stills me by taking hold of my arm.

"Shifting to an animal form isn't very common, even in our world." I let my back rest against the seat, it seems like he has more to say. Ares runs his hand through the front of his hair. "Some people have a hard time reconciling the fact that Dante is the animal, and the animal is Dante." Scrunching up my nose I remember Dante saying something similar. "He wouldn't hurt you anymore in one form than the other." I feel a pang of sadness. Why does he feel like he needs to tell me this? Is he afraid of my reaction? Or is he thinking about the way someone else reacted to Dante?

"Ares," I say, getting his attention. When he looks over at

me, I continue, "I can tell you're worried about him, I wouldn't do anything to hurt Dante either."

"You might not mean to." His voice is pitched low as he looks at me from under his brow. "Just don't be afraid of him. It would kill him if he thought you were afraid of him." If I'm being honest, the warning frightens me a little. What could he turn into that would scare me? A snake? A giant spider?

My face goes white. "Oh my God! He doesn't turn into Aragog does he?" I can't keep the horror from my voice.

Ares head jerks back. "What the fuck is an Aragog?"

"It's the giant spider in Harry Potter." My arms go wide. "Like, as big as your truck big." I can feel the panic coming. "Please don't tell me he's some kind of bug."

"Christ no, he's not a bug. And let's not tell him you ever thought he might be," Ares mumbles under his breath as he turns off the car and opens his door.

I'm much more hesitant to get out, the nerves of excitement have morphed into something more akin to trepidation now.

Ares comes around to my side, and he waits for me patiently, standing at my side. "You're staying with me?"

"For now," he answers cryptically. Seconds later I hear the crunch of leaves and sticks. I take a moment to actually look around. We're near the entrance of the woods.

The headlights of the SUV turn off, plunging us into darkness. Reaching out I wrap my hands around Ares's arm. It has little to do with actual fear, more the possibility of what the darkness carries with it.

More footsteps and rustling of leaves. As my eyes adjust, I can make out a lightness near the ground several feet in front of me. Releasing my death grip on Ares, I take a step forward as my eyes try to focus. The animal slinks forward more. Head low, but still high enough to reach my hip. Squinting, I can't quite make out what it is, but it moves with a supple grace.

Clearing the edge of the woods, I get my first clear look at a huge tiger. I step back, my instincts telling me to run, but my foot gets caught and I end up on my butt. I sit there, eyes wide as the animal freezes, one bulky paw poised mid-air. "Dante," I say in a wonder-filled whisper.

Ares leans his rump against the car; he couldn't seem more blasé if he tried. The gigantic cat takes another step forward. Getting my legs back underneath me, I sit up on my knees with my hand outstretched. Slowly he lumbers over, his massive paws eating the distance between us. He stops a few feet away from me. I can just make out the tufts of fur on the sides of his face. Holy shit, he's a tiger, a huge-ass, beautiful tiger. "Dante, you're gorgeous." The words fall from me with no filter.

Walking on my knees I draw closer. The enormous cat freezes, his head held low, but his eyes remain locked on mine. One look and I know it really is Dante behind the amber irises. "May I…?" My hand reaches out, fingertips brushing against his fur. The animal doesn't move or make a sound, so I look back at Ares waiting for an answer.

"I don't think he'll mind." Ares waves a hand at the docile

beast before me. With his permission, I sink my hand into rough fur, not taking my eyes off Dante as I do.

"Oh, wow." I lick my dry lips, my thoughts swirling with amazement as I bring my other hand up to delve into the fur around his face and neck. Dropping his rear end, Dante sits and lets me run my hands all over him. I can't help but be fascinated with his ears. They're thick, and the fur is short and silky compared to the rest of him. When my hand runs down his side, he squirms under my touch and makes a chuffing sound.

I pull my hands back, thinking I've done something wrong, but he falls to the ground and rolls against my legs. Looking up at Ares to make sure it's okay, I run my hand down his side where his fur goes white. The hairs are a little shorter here, and the texture is finer; he rolls completely over on his back exposing his belly to me.

"Really?" Ares pipes up, stepping away from the truck. I look up at him, but he's staring down at the big cat under my hands. Dante, in cat form, opens his mouth in a wide yawn. Four huge pointed teeth are on full display as he makes a final chuff noise and rolls away from me before standing on four paws again.

He pushes his side against Ares, it's enough to make Ares takes a step back from the weight. Returning to me, he nuzzles his face against my ear. I giggle as his whiskers trail over my cheek, tickling me. "All right, you over-grown house cat, Laura still needs to eat, and I'm ready to get home. You going to meet us there?" Dante lifts his head, and I swear he gives

Ares a nod before giving me a quick lick along my neck and the side of my face with his rough tongue, then bounding away in the next second.

Ares walks over and, placing his hand under my arm, he lifts me until I'm standing in the same spot, staring after Dante.

Back in the car I finally manage to say, "He's a freaking tiger. A big ol' sweetie tiger that likes tummy rubs." I look over at Ares, still half in shock.

"I think you'd find there aren't many of us who wouldn't like a good tummy rub, as you call it."

I snort, "That's hardly the same. It's not like I would reach over and start stroking your stomach."

"Tell me, how is it different? That's still my little brother under all the fur—the bastard. And just so we're clear, you're welcome to stroke any part of me you'd like."

"Ares," I admonish, but now I'm left wondering if it really is the same as me rubbing one of their stomachs.

"Just saying," he responds, and I slap my hand over my forehead. Now my mind has gone to a completely different place.

CHAPTER 4

$\mathcal{D}$ante is already at the house when we get there. "He went up to take a shower," Milo informs us with a strange look on his face, like he's trying to figure something out.

"The furry asshole needed to cool down, did he?" Ares asks.

Milo looks between us, brows furrowed. "Something like that, I guess. Everything go okay?"

"Why don't you go check on how his shower's going, and you can tell me," Ares replies drolly.

"I think I'll wait until later," Milo tells him, fighting the grin on his face.

Ollie claps his hands together, getting our attention. "Children, let's eat." More than happy for the change of subject, I push past Ares, ready for dinner. I hope when Dante comes down, I can look at him without turning red. I think I have a pretty good idea of what Ares was alluding to.

At the kitchen island, we all dig into the dinner Gloria prepared. I've met her once or twice now, and she has always been nice. She reminds me of Maggie with her rounded tummy and softly lined face. Dante shuffles in, his hair still damp from the shower, his eyes seem to glow as he looks into the room from the doorway. It's like he is waiting for something. My worries of feeling self-conscious disappear when he seems unsure.

Putting my fork down, I slide off the stool and approach him slowly. "Dante it's so amazing that you can change like that. You were like a real tiger." His head bobs up and he looks at me, examining my face.

"When I shift, I am a real tiger," he tells me in that deep grumbly voice I've loved since the first time I heard him talk. I bounce on my toes, all my thoughts about his voice and his growl pull together to make a lot more sense. Staring into his golden eyes, I see the traits of his animal that I was completely oblivious to before.

"It's amazing," I say again, I can't seem to help myself.

"Really?" he asks, his voice quiet, shy even.

I nod my head vigorously. "Seriously amazing."

"Now I get it," Milo says from behind me. "He's a right bastard." His words are harsh, but his tone is light.

"Quit making googly eyes at her and come eat, Tom." Dante's head snaps up in his brother's direction.

"I'll show you a tomcat, you demon." Dante chuckles in

response. He walks past me, snagging my hand as he does and takes us both over to the island.

"Ah, but I'm only a demon to some," Ares adds with a grin barely this side of sinister.

I stop in my tracks. "What?" The two brothers look at me. Crossing my arms over my chest I glare. "Who says you're a demon?" I'm angry at the insinuation.

"You can calm down, Laura, no one really thinks he's a demon. That's just his moniker, a nickname to the people who don't like him," Ollie tells me while still shoveling bites of braised beef into his mouth.

I let my arms fall to my sides, but I still don't like the thought of someone calling him that name. It makes me think they believe he's evil, and Ares may be a lot of things, but evil isn't one of them. "Well, I don't like it. I better never hear someone say it." Ares chuckles, but doesn't respond.

Ares's bedroom—I guess I could call it our bedroom now, since it's been taken over by all of us—is filling up. The once open and severely minimalistic room has morphed into our hangout spot. The place we all relax and watch TV or play games. Occasionally, I'll see reluctant acceptance on Ares's face when one of the guys brings something else to add to the room. Tonight is the first time he's drawn a line. "No, absolutely not." Ares is standing in front of the door, blocking

Ollie's entrance, with his arms folded over his chest and his chin held high.

"Come on, please? Dante is watching that stupid TV show he likes, and I'm bored. I want to play."

"Oliver, we don't need another television in here. One is more than I wanted, you aren't getting two." Ares is firm, he hates the TV. It's obvious he'd rather not have anything but a bed in his room, like it was when we first slept here.

"Why do you even care? It's just a TV—I'll keep the sound muted," he offers in compromise. Ares's head falls back, and he lets out a heavy exhale, his whole body expanding with the movement.

"Fine, fine. You know what? Take the whole damn room." Ares turns, angling his body toward mine. I haven't gotten my jammies on yet, I'm waiting for my turn in the bathroom. At this rate, I really don't know why we bothered coming over to the main house at all. We'd have more room in the apartment over the garage.

"Laura," Ares barks my name, his voice full of frustration. I jump, not expecting him to address me.

"Yeah?" I stand up, waiting for his instructions. When he gets like this, it's all I can do to not either yell back or salute him.

"Come on." He beckons me, rolling his hand like I need to hurry.

My mouth falls open. "Where to, Mr. Costa?" I ask, already walking in his direction, even though he's being a bossy Ares.

His nostrils flare, "I just want some sleep. I was up half the night and away from you the rest of the day." The words are gritted out though his clenched teeth, but the sentiment is there. He's crabby and tired. That I can relate to.

"Okay." I soften my tone. Ares takes my hand, and his hold is gentle.

"Hey, we want her, too," Ollie adds, passing off a wide television screen to Milo.

"We're going up to her room. Come get us when you guys are ready for bed. I need sleep." Ares doesn't wait for anyone's reply. He tows me along behind him and I give Milo and Ollie a quick wave as he hustles us out the door.

On quiet steps, Ares treads up the stairs to the yellow room where I stayed my first night here. He places his finger over his lips and makes a soft shushing noise. Mia's room is at the other end of the hall, if she were to come out now, there would be no hiding. I kinda wish she would. I don't get why she's even still here.

Thoughts of her remind me that I want to ask Ares what they were up to last night, and maybe get an answer out of him about when she's leaving. If she weren't here, we'd be free to hang out in the living room. As it is now, they keep making excuses why I'm eating over all the time when she catches us. Then we have the big ordeal of one of them pretending to drive me home. It's a waste of time and energy.

The door opens with a barely audible click. He ushers me inside and follows quickly behind. The click of the lock engaging is louder than it should be, or maybe I'm overly

45

sensitized since I'm locked in a room alone with Ares. The atmosphere shifts. I can feel the moment he has the same realization I do.

"Come on." His tone so much softer than the one he used before, even though he's using the same words. Ares pulls me toward the center of the room, leading me to the bed. "I should have thought this through. You don't have any clothes up here."

"It's okay, I'm fine. I'll change when we go downstairs." I'm not sure I'll be sleeping anyway. My body feels way too keyed up for sleep right now.

Releasing me, he steps back, and the light coming through the curtain is enough to let me see him reaching his hand back behind his head. He pulls his t-shirt off and extends it out to me. I reach for it, gathering the fabric up to my chest.

"There, you can wear that. It will be more comfortable." Ares's voice has gone thicker, like the words are rumbling out.

I flee to the bathroom, leaving a tiny crack in the door so it doesn't make a sound. The last thing I want now is Mia coming to investigate the noise. Ares would leave me in here alone while he had to go play knight again.

With my heart beating a heavy rhythm in my chest, I strip out of my jeans, placing them on the counter. Biting my lip, I slip my shirt over my head and slide his on in one movement. It falls to mid-thigh, it's actually a little longer than the shorts I usually wear to sleep in. Killing time, I wash my hands and stare into the mirror. I can't really see much with the lights off, but I look anyway.

Gathering my folded clothes, I finally step into the room. It's darker than it was a few minutes ago. Ares is obviously at work on the shadows, or maybe it's just something mundane like he closed the shades. Reaching my arm out in front of me, I find the vanity to set my bundle on. Turning toward the bed, I rub the top of my foot with the bottom of my other one. I feel funny, like I should wait for him to say something. But he said he was tired—maybe he's already asleep?

The seconds tick by, and I'm still stalling. "Are you going to stand there all night?" Ares's gruff voice emanates from the darkness.

"I can't see in the dark the way you can. What if I trip?" I'm being silly; we both know it's not the thought of falling that has me hesitating.

"Close your eyes." Shaking out my shoulders I do as he says. "Now think about the room last time you were here, where was the bed, the chair?" Remembering the first day Ollie brought me up here, I think of the bright cheery bedspread, the soft billowy curtains on the tall windows.

His voice softer now as he commands, "Now listen to my voice, think about where I am, and how you will get to me." In my mind's eye I imagine Ares lying back on the pillows. His arms are folded behind his head. The blankets are pulled up to his chest, but his upper torso is bare. His dark hair is a little messy, and the scruff on his jaw is darker—he hasn't shaved today. I feel the pull to be beside him, to feel the warmth his skin would offer and the weight of his arm over my waist as he holds me.

"Laura!" Ares barks my name, his words frantic. I'm startled from my musings, and my eyes pop open to find Ares standing right in front of me, reaching out to grab both of my upper arms. "What the fuck?" Ares breaths, wrapping his arms around me. He runs his hands up and down my back like I might disappear any second.

"What's wrong?" I whisper, his reaction is scaring me. He gathers me closer, almost surrounding me with his body. It's then I notice his shirt is gone, and my face is plastered to his bare chest. Running my fingers around his side and down to his waist, I let the tips of my fingernails tickle along his spine.

I feel this edge of his power pulling me, it's not the same heat that dares me to take from Ollie, but more of a dark promise of something urging me to take the tendrils of shadow into myself.

"I couldn't see you," Ares confesses, pulling his face back to look down at me. My hands trail around to his front. I open my eyes and am surprised how clearly I can see him. I watch my fingers trace over his skin, fascinated with the inky tendrils I see reaching for me. A thick band coils up my finger and around my wrist.

I can actually see his ability, it doesn't manifest the way Ollie's does with fire, but in actual shadows. How come I've never seen this before? I expect a light show of sparks to begin any second as I begin to feel his power running over my skin.

My head falls back. His power is deep and vast, there is a darkness to it, but there's also something else: an awareness—of him, of myself, of everything around me. Oh, goodness! Is this how he feels all the time, full to the brim? As his power flows through me, my mind expands to include more of the house. I can feel Mia down the hall, the edges of her mind open to me, and I know that she's getting ready for bed, that Ares is on her mind.

Pulling away from her, I find myself searching through the house with a speed that isn't possible. Three sparks of light call me to the room I left a little while ago. Ollie's light burns a bright orange, almost as though he's bathed in a glow from a bonfire. The light surrounding Dante fluctuates, going from a gold to silver, sometimes swirling together. Milo is dimmer, his light pale compared to the others, but he glows a faint green.

I feel the pressure of Ares's head when it lands on my shoulder, bringing me back to this moment. "Oh, my God. What just happened? Was that real?" I know it was, but I have to ask anyway. Ares grunts in response, his breath hot on my neck. Is he tired? I feel like I could bounce off the walls, I'm so keyed up. "I thought I was the human sparkler… how did that happen?"

"No clue. What'd it feel like to you?" Ares nuzzles behind my ear, and I feel his whiskers tickling the sensitive spot where my shoulder meets my neck.

"It felt…it felt…big. Like anything I could think of would be possible," I stammer, not knowing how to articulate what it felt like. "I could feel you. I feel like I could have crawled inside your head and known your every thought. Is that what it's like for you?"

"No, not all the time. I've learned to control it. And some people have a natural barrier." Ares takes my hand, pulling me toward the bed. My vision isn't as clear as it was when I was sharing his power, but it's better than it was before.

"What did it feel like for you? Were you with me? Did you see what I saw?" I can't keep the excitement from my voice as I climb into bed.

"I don't know, it's never happened before. I think I was—or could have been—with you, but I was also here. I could feel you on my skin, all over me, inside me. Turn over." I do it without thought, curling my knees up. Ares scoots in behind me, wiggling his arm under my head.

"Did you see Milo? Why was he so dim?"

Ares grumbles, "Later." His other arm snakes over my waist, securing me to him.

My body relaxes against his. "Why are you so tired?" I whisper into the darkness.

"I didn't get much sleep last night," he answers on a sigh.

"Why? Did you stay up with Mia? What were you guys doing?" I try to sound causal, but probably fail.

"I took her to the kitchen. We had a drink, but she still didn't want to sleep alone." My body stiffens. Did he sleep with her, did he hold her like he holds me? "Whatever you're thinking, stop," he orders. "I sat with her until she was finally ready to go to bed. By that time, I was already too awake to go back to sleep, not to mention there was someone in my spot." I feel the blunt ends of Ares teeth as he nips my shoulder. "I got a few things done in the office, and then it was almost time for you to get up. So, I decided to get ready for the day. I had a nice start to my morning."

Ignoring his comment, I ask, "So that's it? You're just normal tired?"

"What other kind of tired is there?"

I flick my fingernail over my thumb. "You know, just more tired for other reasons. I guess."

"You'll have to tell me about those reasons, or show me." Ares's voice takes on an edge.

"I think you would know those reasons far better than I would," I rebut. I'm being petulant, and I know it.

"No, I don't think I do." Ares's tone is light and airy as he sighs.

I snort. There is no way he doesn't know what I'm alluding to. "I thought you were tired, go to sleep," I demand. His bicep is under my neck, with his forearm pillowing my head. I turn and bite the inside of his arm—not hard, just a nip like he's given me.

Ares's body coils behind me, and I have a moment where I think I've hurt him. He drags his arm out from under my head and I roll toward him in the process. An apology is poised on my lips as his face hovers above me. "I'm—" That's all I get out before his mouth drops to mine. His lips push against mine heavily. He pulls back, but only long enough to lick the seam of my mouth. He takes a stuttering breath, and when he leans in again, it's painstakingly slow. With a slight tilt of his chin, his lips land on mine with a scant amount of pressure. Following his lead, I let my lips barely graze his, pulling back the moment his lips pucker to return the kiss. Ares's palm lands on my lower stomach. I suck in a breath when I feel the heat of his hand through the fabric of his shirt.

He nips my top lip, pulling enough that I push myself closer to him. Ares's palm travels up past my navel, and slowly continues while I'm chasing his lips with mine. Our mouths are open now, but neither of us has deepened the kiss yet. Ever so slowly his fingers reach the bottom of my bra. My nipples tighten, he hasn't even touched me there yet, but my body knows he might, and it's already ready.

Ares's nose bumps with mine in a deliberate caress. I feel his warm breath as he pants, his breathing becoming shallower. "Laura." I hum in response, my hand reaching up to tangle in his hair. "This okay?" The tips of his fingers glide over the bottom of my bra between my breasts, his palm still flat on my sternum. My back arches, and his forehead rocks on mine. My body seems to think it's ready, but I'm not so sure. Taking my hand from his hair, I guide his hand up between my breasts until his fingers are at the base of my throat. Ares's whole body rocks against mine, his hand trembling as his palm glides up my neck.

I'm not sure I trust myself to let him touch me too much more. With the way my body reacts to his, I'd probably ask him for more than I'm ready for. His fingers tighten under my jaw and he turns my head away from him, his nose nuzzles my ear. His breath has gone almost ragged. I feel the tip of his tongue stroke behind my ear, and a soft whimper comes from me as I shift, feeling restless.

Ares turns me back to face him, his mouth descending on mine as he controls me and our kiss. His tongue traces over my lips slowly before he delves into my mouth. A groan of satisfaction leaves me when I can finally brush his tongue with mine. Turning my hips so I can get closer to him, I find myself almost covered by his body. Reaching under his arm, my hand lands on his bare back, sliding down until I encounter the fabric of his sleep pants.

Ares always asks me before he takes things to a new level of intimacy, even the first time he kissed me. Why don't I want to give him the same courtesy? I want to let the tips of my fingers explore what's just on the other side of that barrier. He rocks against me again, and my body follows his, my hips rising off the bed as I arch into him. "Oh, hell," Ares rumbles, nipping at my lips. I pull back, my eyes slowly opening as I lick my lips.

"Aren't you supposed to be sleeping?" I ask huskily, feeling brave knowing I'm affecting him.

Ares makes a sound somewhere between a grunt and a groan, and his forehead drops to my shoulder. "You started it." His voice comes out mumbled from between us.

"Me? How did I start it?" I'm completely baffled. He's the one who kissed me.

I feel his teeth on my shoulder as they scrape my skin— just enough where I can feel the pressure. I gasp as his tongue licks over the bite. Oh goodness, how can I feel that in places he wasn't touching? "Oh," is all I have to say after.

Ares pulls my back into his chest and tucks me into his

side again, spooning me. His lips and nose push aside the fabric of my borrowed t-shirt so he can kiss his way all over my back, neck, and shoulders. A few spots he hits have my body arching into his; he gives those spots a little extra attention before moving onto the next areas. I'm almost panting when his fingers flex on my hip, drawing me back into the crook of his body.

His kisses slow until he settles with his mouth near my ear and his scruffy chin against my shoulder. I'll probably have stubble burn all over my neck tomorrow, but I can't even pretend to care right now. My body is languid next to his. My shirt has ridden up with all of my movements, so I can feel the softness of his sleep pants on the backs of my thighs.

The weight of Ares's body behind me slowly increases. He's relaxing, his muscles loosening as he drifts off. I close my eyes even though I feel like I'm way too keyed up to fall asleep, letting the comfort of his embrace lull me.

As my body relaxes, the thoughts I've been trying to keep at bay begin to circle in my head. We still haven't found my mom. Ares installed a fancy security system in my motor home—it's probably worth more than the whole vehicle—but he's able to monitor if anyone comes or goes from his computer; even his phone has the app. She hasn't been back—not that I expected her to, at this point. I just wish I knew where she was, how I could find her.

I stopped by and paid the lot rent for another month at the end of last week. Michael, the camp host, gave me the side eye when he noticed Dante in the car out front, but he didn't say anything as he took the envelope of cash from my hand.

I feel like I'm spinning my wheels. Ares is hesitant about telling their community we are a true Infinity until he knows what my mom was hiding from me, and what she was hiding me from. So, I still feel like a dirty secret. I understand the reasoning behind his motives, but every time there's someone around, I'm unsure how to act. It's not just at school, either. Mia is always here, and then there are the other people coming and going all the time who either work with or for Ares. He mostly holes up in his office when I leave for school—running interference so we can get out of the house with no one knowing I'm with them. It's all way too cloak and dagger for me.

Secretly, or maybe not even so secretly anymore, I hate that Mia is still in the house with us. I've grown used to the idea that my place is with them, and my instincts tell me she has no place among us. The thought of her alone all day with Ares invokes a feeling of territorialism I was completely unfamiliar with until I met my guys. It is even worse than it was with Delaney because I've seen Ares with Mia. As badly as I felt for Delaney when I thought she and Dante were together, he was always so dismissive of her, and still is. It's the opposite with Mia and Ares, he has a genuine fondness for Mia—it's as clear as day when they're around each other. He listens when she talks, and he's relaxed when she's around.

Though I see the differences in the way he behaves toward Mia and toward me, I know she has feelings for him that go far beyond friendship. It's in the way she always finds a reason to stand next to him, in the way her eyes follow him even when there's no real reason for her to do so.

I can't say I blame her. Ares is darkly attractive. He has a way about him that makes you crave his attention. I think it has something to do with his powers. I've felt the way he influences feelings and emotions since we first met. I don't think he's even aware of the fact that his secrets pull you in, so you want to know more about him.

Wiggling a bit, I take a deep breath and blow it out my nose. There's nothing I can do to solve anything right now. It's not like lying in the dark will give me some answers to where my mom is; nor is it going to help fight my new territorial behavior.

Clearing my thoughts, I pull forward the ritual I use to fall asleep when my mind won't shut off. I build my forever home. I start with a large piece of property. It's nothing I've ever seen in real life—more like an amalgamation of several places I've seen or wanted to see over the years. There's a wooded area that offers cool shade during the hot months. A running creek that leads to a large pond just past the view of an older farm house. In the background, I can see waves of green corn stalks taller than my head. I take myself to where I know the house should sit.

Every time I build it, I change it a bit. The past few times I've done this, the house has taken on a striking resemblance to the house I'm sharing with the guys. I used to change it to fit my mood, sometimes I'd have a super modern interior, filled with high-tech gadgets, others I'd stay true to the exterior and keep it rustic. In my mind's eye, I slowly craft a wide front door. The wood is dark with two matching windows on either side, framing it. The front porch is next, it spans the whole front of the house. As I collect rooms to add to my imaginary house, I let the thoughts keeping me awake fall away.

CHAPTER 5

With blurry eyes, I stumble to the bathroom when Ollie's alarm sounds. I barely remember being woken up last night to come back downstairs. I don't think I even walked. I remember the feel of Milo's t-shirt against my cheek and his fresh-from-the-shower smell, but not much else.

I had to climb over Ares to get out of bed, but he barely stirred—he sleeps so deeply. He says it's new, somehow related to sharing a bed with me. I'm happy that he sleeps so well now, but honestly, it freaks me out sometimes, too. I feel like there are times when he might not wake up at all.

I flip the shower on and handle my morning business, and by the time I'm done brushing my teeth, the water is piping hot when I get under the spray. I revel under the water for a long minutes before soaking my hair, so I can wash and condition it. I love the way the products smell, it's the same scent all the guys use, so all day long, even when I'm not with them, I get subtle hints of them.

A few sharp raps on the door tell me I've been in here longer than intended. "Sorry, almost done." I shut off the water immediately and towel dry. I'm not sure who else will need the shower this morning. After wrapping the towel around my body, I realize much too late that I didn't grab my clothes this morning in my haste to get into the bathroom. "Damn it," I curse under my breath as I poke my head out the door, hoping the room has miraculously become empty in the last few seconds.

Ollie and Milo are in various stages of readiness. Ollie is tugging a tight, fitted, grey thermal over his head, his flat stomach still visible. The sight gives me pause. He's leaner than the other guys, but no less appealing. A throat clears to my right, and my cheeks blaze red having been caught staring. Milo raises his brows, but he has a light smirk on his face.

"Did you need something?" Ollie offers when the shirt finally falls into place.

Turning my attention back to him, red face and all, I bite my lip. "I forgot my clothes again," I say as a way of explanation. I've done this several times. When I used to shower at the campsite, it would always be such a big ordeal. I'd plan my showers depending on the lighting situation, plus I always had to take my shower caddy with me. Here it's just so convenient I've gotten kinda lazy and indulgent.

Ollie rolls his eyes good-naturedly. "Just wrap up in a

towel. I'm almost done. You?" he asks as he turns to Milo, who nods his head.

"I am."

I tighten the towel over my chest, the cold air from the room making me shiver.

"Come on," Milo beckons with a wave of his hand while he turns to gather something from the bed.

Pushing the door open, I tiptoe over to the wall of closets. I know my rump is covered, but that doesn't stop me from pushing my hands over the towel back there anyway. A low whistle rends the air. I know it's Ollie before even turning around. He couldn't pretend to be a gentleman if his life depended on it.

With narrowed eyes I peer over my shoulder in his direction, but his hands are raised in innocence, and he points to the door where Dante is standing, unapologetically staring at me. "And to think I could have missed this." He leans on the doorframe, ready to take in a show that I'm not planning to give.

Still surprised the whistle came from him, I move into the closet. My whole body is warm now, and it has little to do with the temperature. A small place inside me likes the way it feels to know all three of them had their eyes on me.

Putting those thoughts out of my head, I grab a silky pair of black panties from the built-in dresser. When the clothes first started coming, I objected. I didn't like the thought that they felt the need to take care of me, but after talking with them, and seeing that they do treat any need as a whole for the group, acceptance came much easier. A few times a week I'll find a new shirt or dress hanging with my clothes. I don't know who keeps buying the dresses and skirts, but there's no way I'm wearing them to school. I tried to tell them it's a waste, but no one even admitted to buying them.

When I turn to grab a pair of jeans from a hanger, I see all three guys have situated themselves outside the closet door. Huffing, I walk the few steps between me and the door and slide it closed. I was planning on taking my stuff back to the bathroom, but this will work just as well.

SADLY, I don't get to see Ares before we load into the car. I'm glad it's Friday, because I'll have a few hours with him tomorrow morning before I need to go into work. As soon as the day registers, I realize today is the day we find out who won the scholarship. I know Dante is hoping he will, even if he won't outright admit it. His artwork is so amazing, but he's almost shy about it. I lean forward, my arms perched on the back of the seat, and murmur, "Good luck today, Dante."

He turns to face me, his eyes soft and a small grin playing on his lips. "Thanks," he whispers back, looking down at his lap. Ollie slides into the back with me, and his brow furrows when he sees me leaning toward Dante. I fall back into my seat, twisting my lips with a shrug. He can be curious; I like to tease him.

"I have the year-end banquet tomorrow," Milo announces. "I only have two tickets." It's the first I've heard of any banquet. I glance over at him and he meets my eyes. "My mom and my dads are coming too." I haven't met his or Ollie's parents. Sometimes I forget they still see them. My relationship with my mom has always been so consuming, and now that she's not around, I forgot their parents are actually still in their lives.

"That's awesome. What's it like?" I ask, curious about the event.

Milo shrugs, looking out the window. "It's just a dinner thing. So, I won't be around tomorrow. My parents are getting a couple rooms in the city."

"Oh." Trying to cover how sad I sound, I ask, "Where is it?"

"Columbia. It's about forty minutes away." Milo sounds completely dejected. "That's why we're getting rooms, the guys were going to…" His words trail off.

"What, the guys were going to what?" I prompt when he doesn't seem like he'll finish.

Ollie puts his hand on my leg. "We were going to go up with him, make a weekend out of it, but—"

I interrupt, "But me, right? That's what you were going to say." Scooting forward so I can reach Milo's shoulder, I place my hand on him. "You still should. I don't need a babysitter. They should go with you. I don't really know what a football banquet is. But it seems pretty important."

Milo drops his head. "It's just some stupid dinner. I don't even want to go."

"And awards," Dante adds.

63

"You're getting an award?" Now I feel terrible, how did I not know this? I fall back into my seat feeling like shit. Have I been so wrapped up in my stuff that I don't know what's going on around me, or do they not talk to me? Both options are equally shitty.

"Milo, you're going to that banquet. And taking the others with you." I cross my arms over my chest, my words ring with an order.

"Ares isn't going, we didn't even know he was going to be back when we planned it." Milo puts his elbow over the seat staring at me. "So, he'll have you all weekend." I scrunch up my face, he sounds aggravated. "My parents won't understand if the guys don't come. They'll think we're fighting or something, and they already worry about us because they don't know we found you. And Ares won't let us tell them." Flipping back around, he slams into his seat, frustrated with the entire situation.

"Milo, why don't we just go for the day, make an excuse that we need to be back here. They know Ares is back. Tell them he's throwing you a party—he didn't know we were going to stay in Columbia for the weekend. Your parents won't care, especially if they think it will keep Ares around," Ollie, the voice of reason, appeals to Milo.

Milo lets out a long sigh.

"It's okay if you want to stay, Milo. Don't feel like you can't because of me. I don't want to hold you back." I hope he can hear the sincerity in my voice. I want him to celebrate his accomplishments; I just wish I could be there with him.

"It's not like that, Laura, but I don't like hiding you from my parents. If Ares would just let me tell them, we could all go, including him."

Dante pulls into the lot at school, he cuts the car off but makes no move to get out. "We can talk to him again tonight. He doesn't like keeping it from our parents either, Milo; he just thinks it's safer this way."

"Come on, guys, we'll talk to him tonight. It's Friday: last day to be at the hellhole this week. Perk up. We'll figure it out," Ollie presses, trying to lighten the conversation.

I'm still feeling a little out of sorts about this weekend when lunch rolls around. Ollie did his best to distract me in the class we share, but I feel like I'm the reason Milo won't have a great weekend with his friends and family.

What else don't I know about? I mean, this is our senior year, are they planning on going to college? Ares is obviously past that point, but what about the others? In the back of my mind I always knew college wasn't an option for me, unless I went to a community college while working, but even that was just a pipe dream. Will they go off to school? Will they even be able to go without me? I know I feel like utter crap when I'm not around them for a few hours, I can't imagine what it would be like if we went weeks, or months, without seeing each other. Maybe it'll get easier, maybe after we've been together for a while the bond will grow, allowing us to be separated for longer periods of time without suffering the effects of being apart.

I need to ask them more questions. Like, what is the purpose of our gifts? It seems that if we're blessed with these great ability's, then there should be a reason for them. Do they ever help people? There has to be more to this than parlor tricks.

"Laura," Milo waves to me from the down the hall. He's not as tall as the other guys, but it's still easy to spot him in the crowed hallways. I pick up my pace and head in his direction. I know I can't talk to them about all the things I've been thinking about right now, but I'm determined that I will, starting tonight, when I get off work.

"Hey," I greet him when I'm close enough for him to hear me. "We eating in the lunchroom again?" The tone of my voice clearly tells him I'd rather not.

"Yeah, Ollie is already waiting for us. You okay?" I shrug. What can I say? I'm not okay. I have a lot on my mind. I thought things would get simpler after I accepted that I was truly a part of them, that I had a place among them. But it opened up so many more questions about what the future holds for us.

Milo intertwines our fingers together. I probably should just give him a quick squeeze and let go, but I find myself clinging to his fingers. We pass through the double doors into the large cafeteria. I expect everyone to be staring in our direction, but we go in mostly unnoticed. He leads us over to the same table we sat at yesterday, and Ollie is, in fact, waiting for us.

A hush falls over the table as we walk up hand in hand. Ollie offers me a wide, toothy grin with a wink. Finally, releasing Milo's hand, I climb onto the beach seat next to Ollie. Milo joins me right after, so I'm sandwiched between them. My eyes scan the table. "Where's Dante?"

"He'll be here a little late. There's some other project Delaney is trying to rope him into." Ollie rolls his eyes, handing me a sandwich from his bag. Milo reaches over to snag his own.

Feeling a little self-conscious, I peel back the bag and take my first bite. I don't make eye contact with anyone else at the table, and mostly they just ignore the fact that I'm even sitting among them. It feels strange eating in here when I've spent every day since elementary school avoiding the lunch-room. I've gone so long trying to be forgotten that I don't really know how to be any other way while at school.

"I can't believe the season's already over, man," a guy I don't know states as he starts chatting with Milo.

"Yeah, it's crazy." Milo doesn't even seem very interested in the conversation. He's barely paying attention to the guy.

"I can't believe you're not going to play ball in college." That piques my curiosity. How does this guy already know Milo isn't playing football in college?

"Nah man, never really been my plan," Milo adds.

"I know, but I think it's crazy. I'd kill to be at your level." The guy doesn't sound resentful, more like he's just making a statement. "Oh, man, did you see Miller drop the ball?" He laughs, continuing with the story about one of Milo's teammates, I'm assuming. Milo chuckles along with his friend.

Feeling a tap on my shoulder, I turn in Ollie's direction. He extends an open bag of chips toward me, offering me some. I shake my head in refusal. He likes spicy chips, and if I had one, my mouth would be on fire. I do take a sip of his soda, though.

"Won't Dante be hungry? Did he have any breakfast this morning?" I ask, walking out of the cafeteria.

Milo looks over my head at Ollie. "I'm not sure. I grabbed a protein bar."

"I don't know either, but I'm sure he'll be fine. Delaney probably ordered a pizza or some shit, knowing her," Ollie adds as he spins so he's walking away from us. "I'll see you guys in a little bit."

"Bye," I call back to him while Milo waves.

"Only a few more hours and we can get out of here. I can't wait for this year to be over." Milo drops his arm over my shoulder and guides me toward my next hour.

"You don't have to walk me to class, you know." I definitely don't mind, but I'm always worried they're going to be late to their own classes.

"I'd rather be with you anyway."

A small smile splits my lips, I'd rather he be with me,

too. He leaves me at the door to my class, and our fingers pull apart as he backs away.

I've only just sat down at my desk, when the intercom buzzes to life. "Good afternoon, students," a disembodied male voice says, and it cracks with static. "We have a special announcement this afternoon." I edge forward in my seat. "I have already notified the recipients, but this year's big winner for the countywide art exhibit is our very own senior, Dante Costa." A round of applause sounds in the room. "Dante's winning portrait will be on display in the front trophy case as soon as it's returned from the art exhibit. We're proud they recognized Dante's talents with such a prestigious award. Go, Hornets!" The intercom falls silent, but the classroom erupts with noise.

"All right, settle down, settle down. You can congratulate Dante after school. Please return your attention to your books and continue." Mrs. Bonnie is a short, round woman. She has short, dark hair that only emphasizes her round face and small beady eyes. She's one of those teachers who doesn't really do much teaching. She assigns work from our textbooks and that's pretty much it.

The smile doesn't leave my face as I return to my work. Dante will be so happy! I can't wait to see him in art. I check the clock on the wall for what feels like the tenth time, it's going way too slow.

I RUSH FROM FIFTH HOUR, butterflies of excitement swirling in my tummy. I'm sure I won't be the first to congratulate him, but I'm excited, nonetheless. I drop my bag on the floor next to my stool. I'm practically bouncing as I wait for him to walk in the room. "Yeah, I got it." I hear Dante's gruff voice before I can even see him. He rounds the art room door with his head down. My excitement deflates, he's not happy. He storms over to the stool, kicking it out with his foot before plopping down. He doesn't even acknowledge me.

The old me would keep my mouth shut, let him ignore me. But I can't, not now. "Dante," I place my hand on his forearm, but he doesn't look up at me. "What's wrong?"

"It's just been a shitty day." His shoulders are rounded down.

Leaning my face down to glimpse his, I whisper, "What can I do?"

He peeks over at me, his eyes hesitant to meet mine. "I just want to get out of here."

I peer up at the clock, class hasn't even started yet. We have fifty-five minutes left. "I'm sure Mr. Adams would excuse you if you told him you weren't feeling well."

Dante sighs. "No, I need to be here, it's just..." He rolls his lips together not finishing.

"Just what?" I ask, concerned about the way he's behaving.

"Something happened when they came to tell me about winning the fair." Dante pulls his arms out from under mine, using his to push his hair back. He's still not really looking at me. I fold my hands in my lap, getting a bad feeling. "I was with Delaney, working on the poster for the FFA Halloween event coming up."

I nod, my throat not wanting to work. Why is he acting so strangely? "They came in with a photographer from the local paper. I thought it was so they could talk about the Halloween bash the high school does for the elementary school, to put an announcement in the paper."

"It wasn't?"

Dante shakes his head and looks forward. "They wanted a picture of me because I won first place. It surprised me." The final tardy bell rings cutting Dante off. "When they told me, Delaney, she threw her arms around me. She hugged me… and kissed me."

My stomach drops from my belly. I lean forward over the desk.

"I think I kissed her back," Dante adds; his voice is quiet, but I have no problem hearing him. "It will probably end up in the paper."

CHAPTER 6

The hurt and pain of betrayal hits me first. How could he do that? Shame lands on me seconds later. What right do I even have to be upset? I was just kissing his brother last night, for fuck's sake. Anger blooms next; I don't know if I'm really mad, or if I just can't process what I'm truly feeling.

"Let's hear it for our local celebrity!" Mr. Adams announces to the class. Everyone hoots and claps, calling out his name, but I'm frozen. I can't pull my eyes up from the desk. I realize that our teacher is standing on Dante's right side, patting his back. "Dante has put a lot of time and hard work into his artwork. I'm pleased his determination has paid off. To celebrate his—and everyone in the class's—effort, I'm giving you guys a free period." More happy shouts erupt.

Mr. Adams yells over the noise, "Make sure you pick up a copy of the *Independent* tomorrow. This guy is making front page news." He shakes Dante's shoulder.

As soon as Mr. Adams retreats to his desk so everyone can come over and congratulate Dante in person, I slide off the stool. I haven't spoken to Dante; I wouldn't know what to say to him anyway.

Making my way up to the front of the room with my backpack in hand, I tell Mr. Adams, "I'm not feeling well. I need to go." I don't even give him a chance to object before walking away from the room.

"Laura," Dante calls my name, but I ignore him. I can't be around him right now. The pain in my chest says I'm hurting, the lump in my throat is dying for me to scream *how could you?* But the shame I feel is rolling around like a lead ball in my gut, telling me that I don't even have a right to feel those things.

I make my way through the empty halls until I reach the side exit door. I draw in a deep breath as I push past the metal door to the parking lot. School won't be over for a while, so I skirt the front of the building. I don't want someone to come out, trying to find out why I'm out of class.

I don't really have anywhere to go other than my camper, and it would alert Ares the moment I walked in the door. So, I walk in the diner's direction. I almost wish I could call off work, but where would I go anyway?

I'm so focused on my own emotions I can't even examine

why Dante would let her kiss him, let alone kiss her back. He acted like he didn't like her. Before I even make it to the diner a car idles up next to me. I peer over to see Ares's black SUV. Stopping on the sidewalk, I shake my head, how the hell did he even find me?

The passenger window slides down, revealing Ares. He leans down so I can see his face. "Need a ride pretty lady?"

I snort, but stalk over to the vehicle, leaning on the window I ask, "What are you doing around here?"

Looking out the front window he answers nonchalantly, "I was in the area, saw a beautiful girl." He lets the sentence hang. "Come on, get in, I have something I want to show you."

I sigh, looking in the diner's direction. Do I really have the emotional energy to deal with him right now? But there's no way I'd refuse him, so I get in the car without a fight. "I have to be at work in a little while, so I can't go far."

"Seatbelt," Ares orders while turning the dial to D to put the SUV in drive. "Ollie's going to cover your shift tonight," he adds while making a U-turn. I open my mouth to argue, but snap it closed. Isn't that exactly what I wanted, to not go to work tonight?

"You talked to Ollie? He knows?" I wonder if he's talked to Dante, too; if that's why he's really here? Ares pulls back into the school parking lot, and I scrunch down in my seat. "What are we doing here?"

"I'm picking up Dante, he's coming with us."

I turn my head to face out the window. "Careful what you wish for," I mutter under my breath. I could have spent the evening busy at work, now I'll be stuck with the guy who just admitted kissing another girl, and his brother that I've kissed several times. Fucking fabulous.

"Why weren't you in school anyway? Shouldn't you be in art class with Dante?" Ares turns to face me, his eyes narrowed in my direction. "You were skipping school?" Ares scolds, his voice going dark, "That's naughty." He parks the truck in the back lot.

"Dante won the scholarship, it's going to be front page news." I'm still staring out the window when Ares drops his hand on the back of my neck. His fingers knead the muscles, forcing me to relax.

"What's wrong, were you hoping to win too?" Ares questions me softly. I shake my head no.

"No, nothing like that," I offer just as softly. Ares is part of the reason I feel so torn. I know they grew up knowing that their future relationship would be different, but how do they deal with the jealousy?

"How do you do it?" I look over at Ares, his brows are drawn.

"Do what, exactly?" Ares prompts, his fingers still rubbing my neck.

"How do you deal with the jealousy, or do you not have it? Are you like programmed differently? If that's the case, I think I'm broken." My voice is laced with heartache.

Ares's palm slides up to my cheek and, looking into my eyes, he urges, "Tell me what happened?"

I look away, what do I even say? Dante kissed another girl, I'm hurt, but I want to kiss all of you? "If you don't tell me, I'll ask him. He'll be out in about five minutes," he warns.

I hold off for a few seconds, but eventually break down and tell him. I need to talk to someone. "It's just hard. I don't like thinking about you guys with other girls. How are you guys okay with me being with other people?"

"What other people?" Ares's voice takes on a disbelieving edge. "Is that Charlie kid still sniffing around?"

"What? No. I'm taking about Dante and Delaney." Why is he even bringing up Charlie?

"Delaney? Dante told you he wasn't with her. She was just trying to mark territory."

"Yeah, well, he also just told me he kissed her." I wrap my arms over my stomach feeling the need to protect myself.

"No, no, he didn't," Ares objects, like I'm crazy for even suggesting it.

"Believe me, I know what he said. But how can I be upset with him when I kissed you last night?"

Ares places his finger under my chin, turning me to face him. "Listen to me, Laura. I have no idea what this shit with Delaney is about, but that isn't anything like what happens between us." His eyes search mine.

"How isn't it? Do you know Milo has kissed me, not like you kiss me, but he has? And you're okay with that?"

Ares's eyes close, when he opens them a long blink later his lips twist. "I am okay with it, because I've always known that's the way it would be for me. I didn't know I would be lucky enough to be paired with my best friends, but I knew I would have to share the affections of our woman."

I shake my head. "I can't do it. Not if it makes you feel even the tiniest bit like I do right now."

"It's not the same. If you were to kiss anyone else—Charlie, for example—I would give him nightmares so bad, he would kill himself within a week."

MY MOUTH FALLS OPEN. "You, you could do that?" I whisper, my voice betraying my horror.

Ares chuckles darkly. "That, and so much more."

"But… but," I stammer, trying to find the words to explain what I'm feeling.

"No buts, Laura. It's not the same between us. And it's not just because we grew up expecting to *share*. I see the way you smile at Ollie, the way you hang on every word Dante says to you. I also see the way your cheeks flush when I touch you, the way your eyes darken when you look at me. I wouldn't take that from you or them."

Something inside me softens with his words, but then the realization dawns. Dante still kissed another girl. Told me he kissed her.

The sounds of car doors slamming and of kids being

released from school on a Friday afternoon filter into the car. I know I only have minutes, maybe seconds, before Dante arrives.

"We'll figure out what happened today, but I know my brother. It's not what you're thinking," Ares offers.

CHAPTER 7

"It's not what I'm thinking, Ares; it's what he told me." My voice is flat. I want to believe him, but I'm still struggling to wrap my head around what I'm feeling and what Ares just told me about his willingness to share our relationship with the others. Could I really do that to them: expect them to share me without sharing them? It's what I want, but it's not fair to them.

The back door opens, and I pull myself from my thoughts. When I look up, I see Milo and Ollie waving from Dante's car. I give them a tight smile and wave in return. I know Dante is in the car with us, but I can't bring myself to look at him. He hasn't spoken either.

"Hey, man," Ares greets him.

"Hey," Dante mumbles back.

The car begins a slow roll forward, getting in line with all the other people trying to escape school for the weekend. "So," Ares prompts looking from me to the rearview mirror. "Laura said you had an interesting day." Dante makes a scoffing sound but doesn't elaborate further. "Well... do you want to tell me why she said you told her you kissed Delilah."

"Delaney," I correct automatically.

"Whoever," Ares counters.

"I didn't tell her I kissed Delaney, I told her Delaney kissed me..."

"Ah. See now, that makes more sense," Ares adds, nodding his head.

"But I kissed her back," Dante adds before Ares is even done defending him. He sounds nearly as dismayed about it as I am.

Ares hits the brakes a little harder than necessary. "What the fuck?" He turns to face his brother in the seat behind me, with the car at a full stop.

"It just happened. They came in to announce I was the winner. She jumped up to hug me. She kissed me before I realized what was happening. It was just a little kiss. But before I pushed her away... there might have been a second where... I kissed her back. I don't know, it happened so fast. And the photographer for the *Independent* was snapping pictures. I didn't mean it. It wasn't a real kiss." His words are rushed together in a mess of information.

Ares turns back to face the windshield, and he lets his foot off the brake, so we inch forward again. His head shakes back and forth a few seconds later, like it took him that long to digest the information. His lips in a tight line, he opens his mouth like he might say something, but he looks in my direction and snaps his mouth closed and shakes his head again.

"It didn't mean anything," Dante whispers, sounding completely dejected. I've sat in silence the entire time. I don't know what to say. I really don't think I have the right to say anything considering the situation, but that's not what my heart is telling me. That, and my head keeps telling me I can't expect something from them that I'm not giving myself.

"It's okay Dante, I'm not mad." I cross my arms over my stomach, my own shoulders rounding down, making myself smaller.

"Well, I am, and even if you're not admitting it, you're something—mad, hurt, something." Ares huffs repositioning himself in the seat.

"You don't care, but you left school?" Dante leans forward, sounding skeptical, maybe even a little sad.

"I didn't say I didn't care. I said I wasn't mad. How can I be? I could do the same thing to any of you." I shrug my shoulders looking down at my lap.

"Thanks for making this even harder, you dipshit," Ares grates. "Laura doesn't think she has the right to be pissed because she gets all of us, and we only get her. She thought that she would have to share us in the same way, and you just confirmed her assumptions."

"But that's... no. That's not how it is. It's just us," Dante adds, his voice more urgent.

"I know that, but this is all new to her, she doesn't fully

understand the bond yet. And we've been doing a piss-poor job of explaining it to her, if she thinks she can't be pissed off because you kissed another girl. Which can I just say again, what the fuck, Dante?" Ares ends on a shout.

I duck my head instinctively, he can be scary. His big palm returns to the back of my neck with gentle fingers, massaging my stiff muscles.

"If I hadn't been caught off guard, it never would have happened," Dante pleads.

I snort. "That sounds like the same kind of excuses I've heard guys at school say to girls. 'I was drunk, it meant nothing.' 'My hand wasn't down her pants, I was falling.'" I mean, really; do guys think girls are that stupid? They only believe that shit because they *want* to. They don't want to see the truth in front of their faces, so they believe the lie because it's easier, and it hurts less."

Angry now, I turn in my seat, dislodging Ares's hand. "What happens the next time when she does more than just kiss you? That won't be your fault either? You'll be so caught off guard that the next thing you know, you'll be having sex?" My voice is rising with my anger. "How would I ever be able to trust you?"

Dante shrinks away from me, turning his head so his neck is bared. He won't even look at me. I flip back around facing the front. We're out of the school lot and on the road that leads to Turtle Creek. "Where are we going?" I bark.

Ares clears his throat and says, "I got a hit on the security system, I wanted to go check out the camper and see if anything is out of place."

"Well, what did the video show?" I focus on Ares's profile as he grips the steering wheel.

"Nothing—there was interference. Whoever was there knew there was surveillance equipment, or they took precautions in the event there was. That's why I wanted you to take a look around, to see if you notice anything. And I want you to talk to Mark, learn if he saw who was there."

I nod my head and bite my lip, eager now that I have something to focus on other than Dante and Delaney. It's not long before Ares turns into the front drive of Turtle Creek. I haven't been here in a few days, but everything looks exactly the same.

There are a few long-term trailers parked around the pond, along with Mark's mobile home. We creep past the front area slowly, taking the narrow drive toward the back where my mom parked. I didn't complain—never did—when she wanted to be as far away from others as she could be. I was just happy we weren't too far from the bathhouse.

We pass by the storage lot where local people stow their trailers and campers for the cooler months, or if they don't have the room at home, and I spot our old motor home. The yellowish paint has faded into an off-white, but the stripes of orange and brown are still vibrant. I notice nothing out of place as we slow to a stop a few feet from the rear end of the RV. I never mastered backing the thing into these narrow spots, but Mom didn't care.

"You good?" Ares asks when I make no move to get out of the SUV.

"Yeah, it feels like it's been longer than a few days since I've been here. The RV feels empty, like it's been out here for years." A few weeds around the blacktop pad we parked on are rising up to the underside of the motor home. Usually they'd be matted down with my comings and goings, between trips to the grocery store and the laundromat, but the motor home hasn't moved in at least two weeks. That only adds to the abandoned feel.

Grabbing the door handle, I purse my lips. Should I ask Dante to stay outside? It makes little sense to deny Ares entrance. He's been in there several times already, but Dante hasn't. There's no real reason he needs to now. I also don't want to issue him an order, especially after what we were just talking about. I don't really want to talk to him at all. Not to mention, Ares has probably already told all of them or showed them the inside of the camper with his cameras.

Dante opens the rear door and exits, so I do the same. Ares comes around to our side, and we all just stare at the only home I've ever known. When I take a step forward, Ares grabs the back of my neck. "We go in first, but I want you to really look around. Someone has been here—we need to know who it was, and what they were doing here."

I nod, falling back behind them as they approach the door. "Dante, anything?" Ares asks, looking over the screen door like it might be booby-trapped. Dante's shoulders hunker down low as he closes his eyes and inhales deeply. His nose pinches up in a sneer as his head moves to the left, and then to the right.

"There's something there, but it's just on the edges—like I get a hint of it, but not the entire profile. I'd know it if it were someone familiar, or if I smelled it again." Dante opens his eyes; they're more golden than normal, and the pupils have shrunk down to a tiny pinprick. "Whoever it was tried to cover their scent, and I'm only getting one," he adds letting his eyes fall closed again.

"Maybe it was my mom?" I ask, a hopeful note in my voice.

"I would know if it were her; she's all over everything inside," Dante answers, taking a few steps closer to the door.

"Wait, you've been inside?" I shuffle my feet. My worries about him seeing how I lived are needless now that I know.

Dante looks over at me, his eyes squinting a bit. "Yeah, we helped Ares with the camera setup."

"Oh." I nod my head, looking away. They were all here, what were they thinking? Did they all talk about my tiny, little house on wheels and feel sorry for me? I can't stand the thought of them pitying me. My back straightens, and I walk over to Ares who's still examining the door.

He's completely absorbed in his task, and he barely notices my approach. "What are you looking for?"

"Anything. I want to make sure nothing has been tampered with. My equipment is still functioning, but I need to make sure it isn't compromised." Ares stands and, looking over his shoulder, he tells Dante, "See if you can get anything else, walk around the trailer."

A few seconds later Ares produces my key from his pocket, and until that moment, I hadn't even realized I didn't have it. Something that was so vital to me such a short time ago, and now I didn't even know, or care, where it was.

"Let me have a quick look around, wait here for a second. I'll call you when I'm ready for you," Ares announces as he steps into the camper without waiting for my response. I look over my shoulder, noting Dante isn't in sight. Inching up on my toes, I peer into the open door, watching Ares and his ever-present shadow move around the small space. I don't know if I'm more aware of his shadow, or if it actually takes on a life of its own.

"Come on in," Ares calls from inside. Entering, I take a quick look around. Nothing looks out of place, but something feels off. Glancing over, I see Ares coming from the back area, my bedroom. His brows are drawn down as he peers around. Crossing my arms over my stomach, I rub the exposed skin of my forearms. "What do you think?" he asks as he looks around.

Scanning the room again I narrow my eyes. There's some-thing here, something that isn't supposed to be, but I don't know how, or where to find it. "It feels…" Dante hops up into the RV before I finish, and his head jerks back like something hit him.

"Fucking weird." Dante begins to shake, the quivers starting at his head and working down his body.

"Off," I finish. "Something feels off, but I don't know what. It's like I can hear something—a whirring sound—or feel a buzzing vibration." I spin around slowly and close my eyes.

"That might be my surveillance equipment," Ares offers. Stepping over to the kitchen area, he feels along the top of the built-in cabinet and retrieves a small black object. Moving in his direction, I shake my head in denial before even reaching him. The feeling isn't coming from what he's holding. I didn't even know I could pinpoint it until he offered the little device.

"That's not it." I turn toward the front of the motor home. The driving area has been sectioned off for ages. Mom hung those heavy drapes and kept them closed all the time, but the weirdness is coming from up there. "It's something up there." I point to the curtain, uncertain if I want to go up there. The buzzing feeling is intensifying, making my ears ring with pressure.

Dante slinks up beside me, his head tilting in different directions like a dog. "I can feel it too." Making his way past me, he finds the part in the center of the drapes and pulls the heavy fabric back. Holding my breath, I expect to find a big machine, like a computer network or something, instead I see a small, white, ornate box, very similar to the one my mother kept her ring in.

Dante is still staring at it as Ares brushes past me to get a better look. When he reaches down like he might grab it I shout. "Don't touch it!" I don't know why I don't want him touching it, but I don't want any one of us near that thing. There's no way that thing is just a simple box.

Dante and Ares both turn to look at me. "Do you know what it is?" Dante asks, his eyes already back on the box.

"No, I don't. But it looks a lot like a box my mom had, though hers never felt like that. At least it never did to me before." I back away from the box without any real reason other than I feel like something about it is wrong.

Dante backs away, coming over to stand near the door with me. Ares picks up a pencil from the dinette table and gets closer to the box. "Are you sure this isn't your mom's box? What's different?" Ares questions, taking measured steps near the box.

Wringing my hands together, I watch as he uses the pencil eraser to open the lid of the box. "I know it's not the same box. Hers was round with a little gold bow painted on top. Is there anything inside?"

The lid swings back on tiny gold hinges, but I can't see inside. Ares's shoulders fall and he turns to face us. "It's empty."

I take a few steps toward him and look around him. It's not that I doubt him, but how could a small marble box be causing this feeling of dread in me? Dante wraps his hand around my fingers. I look back at him, and there's a small part of me that wants to shun his comforting touch, but a bigger part of me wants to grab onto him with both hands and not let go.

Keeping my hand in his, I make my way over to Ares where he stands to the side so I can get a better look. True enough, the box is empty. The smooth bottom is lined with thin grey veins, the fake marble giving off an iridescent sheen.

"You said your mom had a box like this. Where is it?" Ares asks after giving me a few seconds to look over the trinket. There's no way I'm touching it though.

"I think it's in the bathroom or maybe my room. I can't remember if I put it away or not after I took it from her hiding spot." Glad to have a reason to get away from the box, I turn and head into the minuscule bathroom. I have to lie on the floor halfway into the hall so I can check the underside of the sink cabinet. Mom's box isn't wedged back into the usual spot. Getting to my feet, I slide the thin curtain aside so I can see the bedroom area. I glance around the room quickly, there isn't much to see other than a few odd pieces of clothing that I never took, still piled on the bed, and a couple sheets of loose paper. Dismissing all that, I head over to the built-in shelves and drawer. This is the only other place I would have put it. Digging into the back of the drawer I feel around expecting to find it. Eventually I pull the entire drawer out, there isn't any box, just a few mismatched socks.

Spinning, I pull the covers off the bed and turn the pillows over. I close my eyes, thinking back to the moment I took the box out from under the cabinet. I remember thinking if the ring was gone, then so was she. Asking myself how long it had been gone. But I don't remember what I did with it later. Did I put it away or leave it lying on the bed, the counter?

I search through the room, coming up empty-handed. "I can't find it," I finally admit.

Dante has been helping me sort through everything, and he drops the blanket back on the bed, bracing his hands on his hips. "When was the last time you remember seeing it?"

Dropping to the bed in defeat, I mumble, "Right after Mom left, a day or so later. She kept a ring in there. I secretly always thought it was from my dad. She loved that ring, but it was gone, so I figured she took it with her. No one else would have known where to look, she'd stopped wearing it years ago and hid it under the sink."

Dante sits next to me, his thigh touching mine. His nearness reminding me that nothing between us has been resolved. "Why did you kiss her?" I surprise myself when the question comes out. Dante peeks down at me, his face already in a grimace.

His eyes dart away from mine almost immediately. "I didn't kiss her," he says with little conviction. "She kissed me."

I scoff. "Does it really matter at this point who initiated it? You kissed. Why?"

Dante hangs his hands between his thighs and sighs. "I turned to look up when the principal came into the room. I saw the photographer come in behind him. As soon as he made the announcement, Delaney…"

I growl when I hear him utter her name, Dante looks over at me and his mouth droops into a frown.

"She hugged me." His words are spoken in a softer tone.

"The next thing I know, she kissed me. I pushed her away within a second, but I was so shocked that it happened, I didn't push her away fast enough." Dante admits while lowering his head and slowly leaning it toward my shoulder. I lean away, wondering what he thinks he's doing. He just admitted to kissing another girl, but he wants to lay his head on my shoulder.

At my rejection, he tilts his head to the left exposing his throat to me. It's the second time today he's done this. His eyes are nearly closed, and he swallows, a quick bob of his Adam's apple. He stays in that position, waiting for something. Mad that he isn't explaining himself more, I have a fleeting thought that I want to bite his neck, teach him to think before he acts, but the thought dies the moment it forms. How would that teach him anything? Worse yet—how would that be any better than his childishness not responding?

"Dante." My tone is firm, and his head snaps around in my direction, at least he's looking at me again. "I need a better explanation." I soften my tone, but my words are still a demand.

He leans his head back closer and bumps his forehead against my shoulder. "I don't have one. The second I realized what happened, I pushed her away. Delaney has been desperate since you moved here. She was the one that who left the panties in the apartment."

My back goes ramrod straight. I had forgotten about those damned red panties. "You acted like you thought those were my panties," I seethe.

93

"I knew they were hers the moment I saw them, I just didn't want to admit it. I didn't know she had left them there."

Shoving him away with my shoulder, I stand up. "You made me feel like you thought I was a whore when you accused me of having panties in my bag."

Dante peers up at me, his eyes wide and lips parted. "I didn't mean to. I just didn't want you thinking I had a girl over."

"But you had a girl over—obviously. You had Delaney over if she left her panties wadded up on your floor," I shout, getting close to his face. I've never felt so aggressive in my life. I feel like I could shake him silly.

"She came over, but not because I invited her. Delaney and two of her friends showed up after you left. She must have left the underwear on purpose, because she didn't take them off for me," Dante counters, his hands still hanging loosely between his legs.

I roll my eyes to the ceiling, putting my hands on my hips. "Like I should believe that. You just admitted kissing her, you probably slept with her and she left her panties behind. That part probably was on purpose, I'll give you that much."

I hear a thud from the front of the trailer, reminding me we aren't alone. I snap my mouth closed. I've been shouting loud enough for neighbors—if I had them—to hear my yelling. I take a deep breath and look at Dante, he's slumped forward, and his knees almost touch the floor. "Jesus, what am I doing?" I spin around so my back is to him. Seeing him looking so contrite makes me want to keep yelling at him. But I know that reaction isn't just mine. There is something fueling that need to dominate him.

"Ares!" I shout, my voice full of worry. He steps into the walkway like he's been waiting there the whole time. I feel Dante brush his head against my thigh. My hand goes to the top of his head and I stroke my fingers through his dark hair. "Dante is acting weird, and… and I feel weird. I think we should go. That box is making us act funny," I stammer with my hand still in his hair as he nuzzles his face and cheek against my leg.

"I don't think the box is affecting you the way you think. But yes, I agree, we need to go." Ares takes a step in the room and Dante turns his eyes in his direction. He bares his teeth in a sneer, a low growl leaving his chest.

Ares steps back, his face a mask. "He'll follow you, *Cara*."

My hand tightens into a fist in his hair and Dante peers up at me. "Don't growl at him," I snap.

Dante's face softens, and he rubs his face on my stomach, coming up into a kneeling position. Shocked at my own demand and his easy acceptance, I release my hold and run my hand down his shoulder and back. "We're leaving now," I tell him just above a whisper. I don't know where the authority is coming from, but right before walking away, I add, "If you ever kiss another girl but me, I'll… I'll…" My threat dies off when I don't know what else to say.

"Never," Dante comes to his full height, towering over me.

He takes my cheeks in his palms with a sweet gentleness and brushes his nose against mine. His lips hover over mine like he's asking permission. Stretching my neck, I capture his lips with mine.

There's no peck, no sweet start. I bite his top lip in a quick nip then shove my tongue in his mouth. I have a burning desire to erase any traces of Delaney's kiss with my own. Dante freezes, and his deepening breath is the only cue I have he's interested. I want to punish him for allowing Delaney to touch him. I nip him several more times while stroking his tongue with my own—little bites of pain to go with the euphoria of the kisses. I pull back the moment his lips begin to chase mine, leaving him panting and his eyes squeezed shut.

Snatching up Dante's hand, I pull him from the room. Ares is standing near the door, his back to us, as I hustle over to him. Ares pushes the door open, waving his arm to let me know I need to go first. With Dante trailing behind me, I release his hand and get into the front seat of the car. I need a few seconds alone. I don't trust myself to sit in the back seat with Dante right now.

Dropping my eyes to my lap, I get my breathing and heart rate under control. I feel edgy, like my skin is crawling, and I have an itch that I can't scratch. Balling my hands into fists, I can feel my nails digging into the flesh of my palms. Peeking out the windshield, I see Dante and Ares standing a few feet from the car. They turn their backs to me, and Dante's shoulders are rolled down, his head dipping while the set of Ares's shoulders is rigid. I can see his hand gesturing wildly as he talks with Dante.

Is Ares yelling at him? Why? With a quick movement, Ares turns so I can see his profile. He reaches over, almost slapping Dante on the back with a few quick pats. Dante nods his head and his back rises. He lifts his head, and I watch as he comes to his full height, his shoulders rising and falling several times while he takes deep breaths. They stand together for a few more moments before Dante eventually turns to face the car. His eyes land on mine immediately. He bites the corner of his lip and heads in my direction.

Ares follows, going over to the driver's side and getting in. I roll my lips in, worried what they will say to me. Is Ares going to yell at me, too? Will Dante say anything about how bossy I was, or how I basically assaulted him with my kiss?

"Well…" Ares pauses still staring out the front window, before he settles on asking, "Were you guys able to find the other box?"

I shake my head but answer anyway. "No, I looked everywhere. I didn't find it."

Ares's eyes narrow. "You're sure your mom didn't take it with her originally?"

"I'm positive. It was there." The memory of finding the empty box is still fresh. I know it was there. I just don't know where it is now.

CHAPTER 8

e pull up to the house, and I see Mia's car parked right in front of the garage. I heave a sigh, wondering just how long it actually takes to find a place to stay. Considering this is her hometown, you'd think she'd have any easier time than she seems to be having.

"What's the plan this time? Do I need help with my homework? It's too early for my shift at the diner to be over." I'm so tired of acting like it doesn't bother me. That's probably part of the reason I lost my shit on Dante. How am I ever supposed to feel confident as their Synergist if they're always hiding me?

Dante opens my car door and reaches in to grab my hand. His amber-colored eyes meet mine. "No." That's all he says before pulling me from the car and walking us to the door. He enters holding my hand and doesn't let go as he makes his way toward the kitchen.

It's still early, but Gloria is standing at the stove stirring a pot. The whole room smells of garlic and onion. My mouth waters. God this woman can cook. If I were around more during the week, I'd be over her shoulder watching her every move so I could learn from her.

"Hey, Glory," Dante calls, towing me to the sitting room just off the kitchen. He drops into the sofa, pulling me along with him. I'm indecently close, almost in his lap. When I try to pull my hand from his and put a little distance between us, he grunts out a small growl. Snapping my head in his direction, I see his face is a calm mask. Making me question if I heard the sound at all.

"Whatchya makin?" Dante lifts his feet, dropping them onto the low table in front of us.

"Dante," I whisper his name, a warning. He plops our joined hands down on his thigh, grinning up at me from under his lashes. He's pleased with himself, that much is clear.

"Just some spaghetti, dear; how was your day?" Gloria calls back, not looking up from her task.

"Eventful." Dante waggles his brows at me.

"Oh well, tell me about it?" she says, finally turning and noticing Dante isn't alone. Her eyes take in how close we are on the couch, moving over our joined hands, and finally landing on Dante's cheeky grin.

She doesn't say anything for a long moment, then she looks in my direction. I start to pull my hand free from his, worried about what she's thinking, but a smile splits her lips as her eyes get all crinkly at the corners. "About time, wouldn't you say?" Her head tilts to the side. "Good for you, standing up to your brother. He's not always right, you know; none of us is perfect."

"Just in time I see. You were saying?" Ares adds drolly, moving into the kitchen from the doorway.

"Nothing, dear, just telling Dante how victory favors the brave. How was your afternoon?" Gloria moves past the topic seamlessly.

"Entertaining, to say the least," he answers glibly, making his way over to the opposite side of me, sitting nearly as close as Dante. My cheeks grow red at his words and nearness.

It doesn't surprise me too much that Dante is apparently done hiding our relationship. They could probably play it off that I'm his girlfriend. I know he's had others, especially since it seems like Gloria already knew about us anyway. But Ares is moving in too close when there are plenty of other places for him to sit, unless Mia isn't here, and he already knows she is.

I relax. Her car was in the drive, but that doesn't mean much; she could be out with friends or be using someone else's vehicle. Leaning my head onto Ares's shoulder, some of the tension in my body falls away. He adjusts, scooting in even closer, so I'm surrounded by their warmth. My eyes close as the television clicks on. I have no intention of sleeping, I'm just relaxing in the normalcy of the moment.

This is what I've been needing—to experience this

connection in a way that doesn't feel like I'm doing something bad. That's how it was starting to seem, always cooped up in the bedroom, like we were doing something wrong, even when touching.

"Seriously, again?" Ares groans. Peeking my eyes open, I look at the TV screen and see Bill Murray thrusting his hips while wearing a back brace. A small giggle escapes. I know, scratch that, I knew before I opened my eyes what it would be. King Pin is one of Dante's favorite movies.

"What? It's on TV, this isn't a recording," Dante defends.

"Yeah, but we've seen it a hundred times already."

"Here, you pick something then." Dante tosses the remote to Ares, a small pout on his lips.

Ares turns on the guide, scrolling through the channels for something to watch. I don't close my eyes again, but I ignore the TV altogether. "Where's Milo?" I question, as Ares settles in, having found something he wants to watch.

"He's working with Ollie. I didn't expect us to be back so early." Ares reaches over and places his hand on my upper thigh. His thumb makes lazy circles on the top of my leg while his fingers slide under my thigh. Having his hand on me while my other hand is still wrapped around Dante's sends a thrill of excitement to my stomach. Both touches are completely casual, but they cause a rise in my body temperature.

I know Gloria is in the other room, maybe that's why I feel so at ease with them both touching me. I know nothing will come of it. There's no pressure to pick one or the other. I can just be in the moment and take the comfort they're offering.

I'm so caught up in my own thoughts that I jump when Dante lets out a roaring laugh. His head turns to Ares. "Did you see that guy? What a baby." Ares's hand squeezes my leg, he knows Dante startled me. "He's an idiot. Who gets their first tattoo on their neck? She tried to warn him," he continues as he shakes his head, still engrossed.

"Gloria, have you seen Ares? His car is here, but…" Mia's voice trails off. I had lifted my head from his shoulder and tried to scoot even closer to Dante the second I heard her voice, but Ares's hand keeps me locked in place. Making it even more obvious, his hand moves up and down, stroking my inner thigh. "I knocked on your door," Mia finishes, her eyes bouncing from Ares's hand, up to my face, and then over to my hand held in Dante's grip.

"What did you need?" Ares sounds so casual.

"Oh… Mr. Albertson returned your call. I know you've been waiting to hear from him, so I… I wanted to let you know." Her head tilts to the side as her eyes narrow on me. "Hi, Laura." Her lips lift, but it looks nothing like a smile. More like she's pretending to smile. "No work today?" Mia walks over, taking a seat on the back of the sofa, her hands laid demurely on her turned out knee.

"No," I croak, and clearing my throat I amend, "No, not today. Are you still working?" I tilt my head in much the same manner she did, my brows raised in question.

"No," she scoffs, elongating the word. "Did we even work today, Ares?" Mia chuckles a little.

"Oh, Ares told me you're looking for another place to stay." Looking at her, I add, "Still having a hard time?" I fill my voice with mock sympathy, and she knows it.

Brushing imaginary lint from her perfect black sweater she answers, "Ares invited me to stay as long as I need to. Truthfully, I haven't really been looking very hard. I'm used to Ares's whims, who knows how long we'll be here before he moves us back to the city?" Mia shakes her head with a happy little grin on her face.

Ares's hand pauses for only a millisecond. "Mia, I told you. I'm staying here. You can go back to the city. Working remotely shouldn't pose a problem."

Her eyes dart over to Ares like she's surprised to hear him say that. "Yes, but we've been working together as a team every day for four years. I think you're seriously underestimating how vital your involvement has become." Mia stands, making her way around to the front of the couch. Her eyes leap to the vacant spot at Ares's side, but she settles on the sofa opposite us, straight across from Ares.

Dante squeezes my hand, seemingly still engrossed in the TV show, like this type of shit happens every day. I squeeze his back, but mine isn't a show of support; it's a cry for help. Why is she sitting down, is she going to stay? There goes my time to relax. Maybe we should have just gone into the bedroom.

"So, Laura, you're still in high school, right." Her eyes evaluate me quickly. "A junior?"

"No, I'm a senior like Dante."

She nods her head, her eyes crinkling a bit. "I remember those days. Seems like forever ago." Mia leans forward dramatically. "Everything felt so serious, like it would all last forever." She sits back into a prim position with her legs folded off to the side.

"Yeah, it must have been a while ago. What are you, like twenty-nine, thirty?" I know damn well she isn't even close to thirty, but I can play her insult game, no problem.

Ares makes a choking noise next to me, covering it quickly with a cough. "Gloria," Ares calls out, "did you say dinner was ready?"

"Oh no, dear, it'll be a while yet. You just enjoy that show you're watching." Gloria's voice is sugar sweet, but I know she's not talking about the television program.

"Twenty-three," Mia grates through a tight smile. "I'm twenty-three."

"Really?" I jerk my head back acting surprised. "Huh." I shrug looking back at the TV. Mia has been nothing but a little chilly to me. I know her more direct approach has more to do with Ares sitting next to me than it does anything else.

The conversation dies off until the next commercial. Dante finally looks over at me, his eyes wide as he shrugs his shoulders, like he's asking *what should I do?* I tilt my head to the left in Mia's direction. I don't want to look at her if I don't have to. Who knows what would happen if I decide it's time to go all bossy and demanding again? Somehow I know that Ares wouldn't ever react the way Dante did, but I want Ares to do something. Hell, I'd rather just go into the room instead of sitting out here with her.

It's like Ares knows exactly what I'm thinking, because his hand wraps around my thigh again, holding me in place. I glare over at him, but he ignores the laser eyes I'm trying to burn him with.

"Really, I don't know what would possess a woman to cover her body in tattoos," Mia says, trying to initiate a conversation.

"I don't know about tattooing, but I'd like to paint a woman's body." Dante's eyes smolder as he stares at me. "I can just imagine the colors." He bites his full bottom lip, still not looking away.

I swallow, thinking about how that would feel to have his hands all over me as he brushes my skin with strokes of paint. I break the stare, if I don't, I might lean over and kiss him. I'm not sure I'm ready for that step yet, not with Mia watching us so closely.

Mia is looking at her lap, using the back of her fingers to inspect the front of her thighs. Ares lifts his hand off my leg. I think he might move, or stand, but he wraps his arm around my neck. I lean forward pulling my hair out from under his arm enough so that it's not pulling.

"Any plans after dinner, after you take Laura home?" Mia fishes, directing her question at Dante. I think she would ask just about anything to get off the topic of body painting she'd inadvertently started.

"She's going to stay over," Dante answers casually.

"Your parents allow that?" Mia sounds positively scandalized at the thought. I shrug with indifference. I don't owe her an answer even if I had one. "Ares?" Mia looks to him for an explanation.

Ares rolls his eyes. "Come on, Mia; you were at Cole Castle's house more than your own in high school."

Mia's face goes bright red. "You had a revolving door of girls in your bedroom," she accuses.

Ares looks at me then, his lips twisted up in a grimace. "That was years ago," he adds, shaking his head in denial.

"Oh hardly, it's not like that behavior has changed over the years," Mia huffs.

"Dinner!" Gloria shouts unnecessarily loud. It doesn't escape my notice that hardly any time has passed since Ares last asked if it was ready.

INSTEAD OF EATING in the kitchen like we've been doing lately, Ares carries his plate to the dining room with Mia following behind him. I wait until Dante has his plate piled high instead of going with them. Mia is already seated to Ares's right, so I take the seat on his left. I don't really want to be directly across from her during the whole meal, but I'm not letting her cow me, either.

Dante takes the seat next to me, digging in as soon as he sits down. I pick at my full plate, noticing Mia has a much smaller portion, and she didn't even take any bread when Gloria offered. I took two pieces.

The first few minutes are painfully awkward. None of us really knows what to say to each other with the new group dynamic. Mia has come down a few times while we were all eating, but it's usually later in the evening so she doesn't eat with us, and then there's Ollie. Ollie is always so good at distracting her with an easy conversation, he always knows how to lighten the atmosphere, even with her around. I wish he were here right now.

Dante leans over and orders, "Eat." His mouth is still half full of bread, making the demand a little mumbled. I take a bite to appease him. He sticks his fork in my plate of noodles and twirls up a bunch of spaghetti, lifting it to my lips for me. Narrowing my eyes at him, I open my mouth and accept the bite.

Ares clears his throat, drawing my attention to him. I look over, expecting him to reprimand either Dante or myself, but instead I find him staring at me with a curious expression on his face I can't decipher. Reaching over without thought, I swipe my finger across his forehead, pushing away a few messy tendrils of hair that have dared to fall across his brow. Ares's eyes close on a long blink before he opens them back up, his pupils larger than they were moments ago.

Movement from across the table draws my gaze. Mia has her napkin at her lips blotting her mouth, but her eyes are volleying back and forth between Ares and me. I realize my mistake instantly. Well, I can't call it a mistake, I wanted to touch Ares, so I did, but I probably should have waited until she was gone to give into the temptation.

"How long have you and Dante been..." Mia pauses, looking for the right words I suppose.

"Friends?" I supply when she doesn't finish. "Not that long." I look over at Dante, then question, "But it doesn't feel that way, does it?"

Dante switches his fork to this left hand and wraps his arm over the back of my chair. "Sometimes it feels like you've always been with us," he answers, still shoveling food in his mouth. Dante has an appetite. He usually eats twice as much as the others. Now that I've seen him in his shifted form, it's easy to understand why.

Mia makes a slight scoffing sound. "Ah, to be young," she dismisses us and focuses on Ares. "I got an email from Randell this afternoon, he's ready to show you the new prototype." Ares gives his full attention to Mia. "He mentioned he would be in the lab late tonight. I know you've been eager to hear from him, I can set up a video conference when we finish up here."

Ares's lips twist and his head tilts. "It can wait," he finally answers, after giving the idea some thought.

"But..." Mia looks over at our side of the table, then back at Ares. "It's Friday." Her voice holds an edge of disbelief.

Ares picks up a short glass filled with water, his eyes not focused on anything. "I know, Mia." Ares's voice is soft, consoling almost. The atmosphere shifts, and I suddenly feel like I'm intruding on a private moment. I lean my side closer to Dante, but my eyes are glued to Ares and Mia.

She reaches out her hand, laying it on top of Ares's. He pulls his hand free the moment hers settles, picking up his fork again and pretending like it didn't happen. Mia tugs her fist back slowly, dropping it to her lap.

The tension in the room doubles. I can't think of anything to say to save my life, apparently neither can Dante nor Ares, because the only sounds are the clank of silverware against porcelain and the whirr of the heating system somewhere deep in the house. Mia seems to have finally given up on small talk. Her eyes are a bit glassy as they dart around the room. She can't manage to keep them off of Ares for long though, because her stare always returns to him.

I swirl my fork in my noodles, picking up a bite if for nothing other than to have something to do. The food that I know should be delicious tastes like sawdust in my mouth. But within minutes, my plate is mostly clean. I push it away, leaving one piece of bread untouched. Dante snags it from my plate immediately, using it to sop up some of the red sauce on his plate. "I'm going to grab some more, you need anything?" he asks, already half standing.

I plead with my eyes for him not to go, not to leave me alone with Ares and Mia. "I can get it for you," I offer a bit too eagerly.

Dante pats my shoulder, barely looking in my direction. "I got it. Ares, you want anything? Mia?"

"No, thank you," Mia replies demurely, her lips pursed in my direction. "Dante, you should let Laura get it for you. Girls like doing stuff for our guys." Mia sits back in her chair acting like she's being helpful, but I can hear the note of sarcasm in her tone. She either thinks she's embarrassing me by saying I like him, or trying to get rid of me.

"Laura, stay, Dante, I'm good," Ares answers, his voice level.

Dante's steps falter like he might have changed his mind about leaving the room. "You sure?" Dante looks between the three of us, his eyes falling lastly on his brother. Taking a deep breath, he continues out the doorway.

"Mia." Ares's voice is low he looks over in her direction. Her eyes jump to meet his, but she looks away instantly. When she doesn't respond he starts again, "Mia, there's something I need to tell you—"

"Right now? You need to tell me with her here?" she interrupts.

"I do. I wasn't trying to hide anything from you, but Laura, she's—"

"Don't say it!" Mia pleads, her eyes wide with a sheen of tears already visible on her lower lashes. I drop my head. I shouldn't be here for this.

"But it's truc. I should have told you sooner, Laura is our Synergist," Ares rushes out before she can interrupt again.

"But it's been years. You said you might never find... the person," she stammers. I know Mia isn't like them, she doesn't have any abilities, no identifier marking her as a

Synergist. I also know she and Ares have known each other for a long time, apparently through high school, and she's been working with him for years. I don't know what kind of personal relationship they've had. When I first met her, I assumed that they were together, but over the last few weeks Ares has never let on that was the case. It's plain to see she wanted to be with him, but I don't know if they were ever together in that sense.

She knows all about them though, about their abilities and the way an Infinity works. Hell, she probably knows way more than I do.

I chance looking up, and Mia's red-rimmed eyes dart to me. "No." She shakes her head in denial, turning to face only Ares like she's blocking me out because she can't see me. "She's nothing, just a stupid, high-school girl." I bristle. I know she's hurting right now, but I won't let her act like I don't exist.

"Mia." Ares's tone is full of rebuff.

"Don't you see? She's not who you think. She's just trying to worm her way in. I knew she was trouble the first time I saw her," Mia's voice raises, but she's not shouting.

Ares looks over at me, his eyes scrunched up he shakes his head like he's dumbfounded. "Mia, that's not possible, she is exactly who I think she is. I know you aren't one of us, can't understand what it means, but I can promise you, Laura is ours."

Mia's face blanches, then goes red. "You're going to say that to me, after all these years? Act like I'm some naïve girl who can't possibly understand you? I've been by your side for years. I've watched you grow darker, seen the things you've done," Mia bounces a hand off her chest, "and I'm the one still here. I followed you when you had to get away from your brothers. Stayed with you even when you scared me at times, and you're going to act like I can't understand what being with you is like?"

Mia's eyes turn to me. "But you think she can?" Doubt and anger drip from her words. Dante comes back through the door, his hands empty. He moves behind me, his hands landing on my shoulders.

"For fuck's sake, Mia, I never asked you to." Ares's voice booms through the room. Dante's hands tighten on my shoulders.

"You might not have asked, but you never turned me away, either, did you?" she seethes, her face splotchy with red spots.

"You knew from the beginning that this could happen, I made no promises to you about a future." Some heat leaves Ares's voice, but he's no less vehement.

Mia wipes a tear from her cheek with a quick swipe of her finger. "I can't believe you would do this to me, and in front of her. Are you truly that heartless, Ares?" Mia shakes her head, her mouth opening and closing several times before she adds, "Don't you know I love you?"

I reach up and wrap my hand around Dante's wrist. My immediate thought is to get her away from Ares—she loves him. What if he loves her too? All the sympathy I had evaporates when I begin feeling threatened by her proclamation.

Pushing my feet against the floor I begin to rise from my seat, only Dante's hands prevent me from standing. He bends his mouth close to my ear and he makes a noise that might come close to a hushing sound, but it sounds more like a low growl.

"I'm sorry, Mia; I should have never let that happen." Ares's large frame shrinks, taking the weight of the emotions. My back falls onto the chair behind me, he cares for her.

I already knew that, but this hits me harder because before it was an abstract notion. Now I can see it in the way his shoulders have fallen, the subtle way his eyes are watching his hands on the table before peeking up at her, like he's afraid of what he's going to find.

It's hard to watch. Ares has been bigger than life from the first moment he ghosted into my world. Never one to back down or bite his tongue, he says what he wants, when he wants, and expects everyone to yield to him without exception. Seeing him in that chair looking unsure, maybe even a little regretful, causes something in my chest to tighten. I try to draw in a breath, but my lungs feel constricted.

"We could work, Ares. I can be what you need—I *am* what you need." Mia's voice grows steady as she speaks, conviction filling her tone. Ares looks back down at the table, shaking his head no. "Why not?" she demands.

Finally, meeting Mia's stare, he tells her, "Because I don't love you. I don't want to hurt you Mia, but I don't love you."

Mia's eyes well up with tears again, and with a shaking voice she asks, "What does she have that I don't? I tried to be everything for you. I was never good enough, but I tried. I watched you with countless other women because you always came back to me. It may have taken a while, but in the end you always came back. So tell me, Ares, what does she have that will stop you from doing the same exact thing to her?" Mia's arm points at me from across the table.

"A piece of my soul." Ares turns to look at me then, some of his confidence returning as his eyes meet mine. "But it's not just that." His eyes still staring into mine, he adds, "I can't see anyone but her, I feel her on my skin when she's not with me. I smell her in the air, taste her on my tongue when I breathe. She is what I've been looking for my entire life. The feeling I get when we touch, it makes every moment I spent without her worth it. I love her."

CHAPTER 9

*J*didn't notice Mia leaving the table. Hell, the world could have been on fire, and I probably wouldn't have noticed. Emotionally, I'm a wreck. I don't know if I feel bad for Mia, or if I'm happy that Ares admitted how much I mean to him. Both, I suppose. Seeing how devastated she was and how hard it was on Ares isn't something I'll soon forget. I still have questions about their relationship, but I know now isn't the right time to voice them.

Hesitantly, Ares reaches over for my hand. I lay my palm in his, wrapping my fingers around his thumb. Dante drops a kiss on the top of my head and leaves the room, giving Ares and me some time alone. "That was my fault." Ares looks down, then back up at me. "I didn't realize she would be that upset."

My eyes go wide. "You really didn't know she was in love with you?"

Ares's shoulder rises, and he grimaces. "I know it makes me an asshole, but I had no idea." He looks away again, staring over my shoulder. "I thought it was a relationship of convenience for both of us. We haven't been together in almost a year." I see him peek at me from the corner of his eye.

I swallow, taking in that information. Can I trust him, is he being truthful? "Why won't you look at me then?" Slowly Ares turns his head, his eyes reluctantly meeting mine. My gaze roams over his face, looking for deception, but in truth I don't know what that would look like on him.

"I should have known something like that." Ares leans back in the seat, his eyes going unfocused, before he continues, "Should have seen the signs that something was up with her; she hasn't been acting like herself since we came back here."

"Why didn't you tell her?" I ask the question that's been bothering me for a while. Then rush out, "I mean what was the point of her not knowing who I was?"

His head swivels back in my direction. "Just a preventive measure, really. Several of my clients are in Infinities or will become one. I was trying to keep everyone in the dark." Ares's free hand moves to his forehead, his thumb at one temple and his fingers on the other, he squeezes like he's trying to rid himself of a headache. "I wasn't thinking about anyone but us, to be truthful. I was protecting us," he admits on a sigh after running his hand over his face.

"What should we do now?" I ask once he falls silent.

"There's nothing to do. I feel bad that I hurt her, Mia has been a good friend to me, but I'm not willing to do anything that would make this better for her. I'm a selfish asshole like that." He tries to make it seem like a joke, but I think his words hit a little closer to home than he intended.

I squeeze his hand, which is still wrapped around mine. "I'm sorry she's hurting too, but…" I pause, trying to find the right words to say without sounding like a bitch. "I'm so happy that you don't feel the same way about her." I look down at the table, guilt souring my emotions.

Ares releases my hand and, making a fist, I slide my hand back, dropping it under the table onto my lap. Out of the corner of my eye I see him stand, and I feel his footsteps on the floor as he comes to my side. "Hey." His fingers glide under my chin and lift it. Ares bites the corner of his lip and asks, "May I kiss you?" His words are spoken on a whisper. Just loud enough for the two of us, even though we're alone. I lick my bottom lip on instinct, nodding my answer.

Ares's fingers glide down from my chin to my neck, caressing as he goes. He leans in, and I close my eyes, expecting the feel of his lips on mine. He hovers his lips mere millimeters away, but I need him closer. Stretching upward, I try to close the distance, but he retreats, making a satisfied hum when I resume my original position. Eyes still closed, I wait until he's ready. I know that's what he wants, Ares always wants control.

Eventually he presses the lightest of kisses on my lips. The sigh that leaves me should have me feeling embarrassed, but it doesn't. I'm too eager for more. With a gentleness you'd never expect from him, he attends to my mouth—soft damp kisses mixed with swipes from the very tip of his tongue.

Reaching up, I twist my hand in the fabric of his shirt. Ares's clothes are always tailored, so every heavy pant he takes has my knuckles brushing his chest. He reaches for me, his hands wrapping around my waist as he guides me to stand, pulling me against his body roughly.

I feel every inch of him pressed against me, his hand flows around my waist, over to my hip and down my leg. Using one arm he lifts me, his arm wrapped under my butt. The air in my lungs heaves out and I gasp into his mouth. Ares wastes no time sliding his tongue inside.

He turns, setting my bottom on the dining room table. Spreading my legs with his body, he moves in close before breaking away from my lips to kiss the underside of my chin and jaw. The gentleness is gone as he devours me with open-mouth kisses. I feel the slight pressure of his teeth on several spots and the warmth of his mouth when he sucks at the skin on my neck. My hands go to his waist, my fingers tugging at the fabric of his shirt as my knees raise, trying to get him closer.

The tip of his tongue makes a lazy lap from my collarbone, all the way up my neck, and only stopping when he reaches my ear. Ares makes a groaning noise in the back of his throat that sends a shiver of awareness down my spine. His forehead meets mine, both of us struggling for air as we try to catch our breath. The tips of my fingers graze the bare skin of his side. I've pulled his shirt free, and the reward of feeling his skin against my own makes the effort so worth it.

I open my eyes and watch as my hand delves farther under his shirt. My palm connects with his side as I run my fingers around his back. Every touch leaves me greedy for more. Ares doesn't move, and I can feel the rigidity of the muscles in his back as my hands move slowly up and down.

His breath is shallow and, lifting just my eyes, I see him watching me with his bottom lip pinched between his teeth. Ares leans his hands on the table just beside my hips, crowding me even more. I love every second.

His voice a mere rasp, he says, "Keep touching." Ares buries his face in my neck, and I wrap my other hand over his shoulder in an embrace. His chest brushes against mine as he winds his arms around me, lifting me off the table. My legs encircle his lower torso, and the center of my body presses up against him. This is new, this feeling of having him right where I need him, all to myself. My arm over his shoulder tightens around his neck, helping me balance.

Coming to his full height, he walks me slowly from the room. I have the briefest moment where I almost tell him to put me down, worried someone might see us, but I ignore the nagging thought. I'm exactly where I want to be. Needing to touch more of him, I slide my hand down the neck of his shirt.

Every step he takes has the muscles of his back moving under my hands.

Turning my face into his neck, I pepper him with tiny kisses before becoming brave enough to use my tongue and teeth. Ares freezes mid-step, his breath panting. I pause with the tip of my tongue just below his ear. His body shivers, starting at his neck and working down. I did that. I pull in a deep breath, feeling powerful in a sense I've never experienced before. I want everything he's willing to give me. I've gone so long with just my mom and me, and she never showed me affection. I feel like I've been craving his touch my entire life.

He hasn't started walking again, but I continue licking my way up his neck. Nuzzling my way to his ear, I pull his lobe into my mouth and suck gently before sinking my teeth in.

"Oh, damn," he groans as his hand snaps out to the wall. Releasing his ear, I pull back. The cool air rushes between our chests at the loss of contact, and it feels intrusive. Ares's eyes meet mine, a sea of blackness staring back at me. Taking my hand out from under his shirt, I brush my thumb under his eye, caressing. I lean in and place a small kiss right on the tip of his nose. "What do you see?"

"You, I see all of you." Ares takes a few more steps and my back hits something solid, before he pushes his body against mine. My head falls back and my eyes close, rolling back in my head. "I can feel you," he breathes into my chest, his head lowered. Moving his hips back from mine, his hand slides between us and settles low on my stomach. "I can feel your desire." His fingers slide lower, just shy of placing his hand between my legs. I don't know if I'm scared, or excited. Both I think.

Something low clenches when his hand travels in the opposite direction, under my shirt. His flattened palm moves to my side, his fingers on my back with his thumb bumping up my ribs. He stops his upward ascent when his thumb grazes the underside of my breast. My nipples tingle inside my bra. I can already imagine his hands there, his mouth. "Laura." His voice is thick, his words almost a mumble. "May I touch you?" When I only squirm, his hand leaves me. I feel the immediate loss of heat.

I wrap my arm around his neck again and, placing my mouth at his ear, I whisper, "Please, Ares."

His body undulates into mine. "Say it," he demands, as both of his hands lift to the wall above my head. My hips are locked against his and every inch of my body is aware of his.

"Touch me, please." Ares makes a sound of pure satisfaction as I gasp the words. His hands go to my waist and he lifts me off his body, setting my feet back on the ground. My legs are unsteady, I didn't feel the strain of staying wrapped around him before, but I do now.

His hands, still around my waist, inch up and take my shirt with them. I feel the cold air on my exposed stomach. With his eyes locked on mine he drops to his knees in front of me.

Without a wasted second, he kisses just below my navel. Every muscle in my body tightens at the feeling of his warm tongue sliding under the waistband of my jeans. His hands are braced on my waist as he tugs my body closer to his mouth. My head falls back, and I gaze up, but I'm not really even seeing. I'm too lost in the feeling of Ares kissing his way up my body until he reaches my bra. The only things holding me up are my shoulders against the wall and his hands. My heart is beating so fast, I know he can hear it and possibly feel it against his tongue.

He pushes my shirt all the way up over my breasts. I look down at him, then search the surrounding area. We're in a hallway, I know we're on the first floor still, but that's about all. This area is unfamiliar to me. My hands cover my breasts; I don't know who else is here. Anyone could walk up on us. Ares makes a low noise in his throat, and I'd feel threatened if I had any sense, but instead I admonish him. "Ares, what if someone walks in?" Removing my hands, I shimmy, my shirt falling over his hands still on my ribs as I cover myself. Defiantly, he wraps both of his hands over my bra-covered breasts. I suck in a breath, my nipples hardening even more with his touch.

Darkness closes in, like night is rapidly falling. "No one would see us unless I allowed it," he murmurs, his voice low. Using his teeth, he lifts the hem of my shirt as he moves up from the floor. He stoops over me before releasing my shirt to the same position it was in. I'm again exposed to him, only now he's standing above me, his eyes impossibly dark as his gaze remains fixed on my body.

Ares brings his hand up to his mouth, and he licks the side of his thumb before running his tongue over his top lip. My lips part as I get that deep clenching feeling low in my belly. Tilting his head, he brings the same thumb to my mouth and places it right in the center of my bottom lip. Angling his hand, I feel the tip of his thumb touch my tongue. I close my mouth, rolling my tongue over his finger. Ares's other hand goes up to my neck, and his fingers tighten, causing me to arch and release him.

When I open my eyes again, Ares is watching his hands as he pulls the cups of my bra down. The damp thumb that was just in my mouth goes right to my pebbled nipple. I jerk, the new sensation almost more than I can bear. Ares stands back, his hand going to his mouth. "Take that off." His head nods in my direction. I'm not sure if he means the bra or shirt, but I reach around my back to unhook the bra, I'm not taking my shirt off in the hallway. Reaching my hands in the sleeves of my shirt, I pull the strap of my bra down one arm, and then the other. Ares grabs the center of my bra and pulls it away the moment my hands are free. He dips his chin in my direction, and now I know he wants the shirt off, too, but I shake my head in denial.

He groans, widening his legs as he narrows his eyes on me. "Fine," he mutters, his body slamming into mine. The air in my lungs escapes on a whoosh as he melds our bodies together. "Sorry," Ares apologizes, then bites the side of my neck roughly.

Placing my hands on his waist, I let my fingers inch up under the fabric of his shirt. Ares kisses his way back to my lips, giving me small nips as he goes. When his mouth reaches mine, he takes my top lip between his teeth. "I could devour you." His voice is a soft whisper. What does it say about me that I want him to?

Bringing his hands up over my hips, he continues until he reaches my chest. I lean forward, pushing myself into his hands. He makes a low sound of approval, his thumbs finding my nipples easily. Even over top of my shirt his hands feel amazing. A heavy pant falls from my lips when he gives me a light pinch, followed by his fingers circling my nipple. My hips rock forward to meet his. Taking my hands from his back, I tangle them in his hair, my arms over his shoulders. My skin begins to tingle as I drag in a breath. The thought of having all of him hits me. I want to be surrounded by him, filled with him. Closing my eyes, I drag my fingers down his back, and when he arches into me, I feel a pulling sensation in my chest. Tugging on the imaginary cord, I wrap it around me, encasing myself in Ares's shadows. His body sags into mine, his forehead hitting the wall behind me. My mind opens, and a rush of energy hits my nerves like an electric shock. I jerk, my nails scoring his back as I cling to him tighter. Gritting my teeth, I push back the feeling, shoving the invading powers back into Ares.

His back arches and his mouth opens, but no sound escapes. Even though we're standing within his created shadow, I can see perfectly when his eyes snap open, and instead of the pitch black, they now have a constellation of starry white dots. Looking into his eyes is like seeing into the far reaches of space.

"Ares!" A panic-filled shout erupts from me as I place my hand on his cheek. What did I just do to him? Head still tilted back, his eyes close slowly and his head bobs as he takes in deep breaths. "Are you okay?" My voice is barely a whisper now, and I use my other hand to lift the back of his head. "Should I get someone—Dante? I don't know what to do." My voice breaks.

"Okay…" Ares finally stammers, "I'm okay." He takes one step back and stumbles, ending up on the ground as he drops like his legs wouldn't support him.

"Oh, God," I fall to my knees, tugging my shirt back down. "Dante, Dante!" I scream. The house is too big. He probably won't hear me. "Tell me what's wrong. What can I do?" I plead, my hands running over his chest and face.

"Just need a second," Ares mumbles, his large body sprawled across the floor in the hallway.

"I'm so sorry, I'm sorry." Tears blur my vision. "Dante," I call out again, my voice strangled with emotion.

"What's going on?" Mia's voice is on the edge of hysteria. She drops beside Ares's head, her hands shoving mine away. "What did you do to him?" she accuses.

I stand up, backing away, tears falling down my face faster than I could catch them if I tried. "I don't know. We… I." I can't find words. "Help him," I plead, backing farther away. Ares's head lolls to the side in my direction, his eyes slitted open. When I don't move, his hand reaches out toward me. I shake my head. I can't go near him, and I don't understand what I did to him, or if I could hurt him more.

"Go," Ares demands, closing his eyes. He tugs his hand from Mia, who has wrapped her fingers around his. Rolling my lips in, I glance at him. I can't leave him, even if he wants me to. I can't. "Laura," he calls, sitting forward, his chest and shoulders sagging with the exertion.

I inch closer, unable to stay away, and I fall on my knees again as I place my hand on his back, steadying him. He leans into me as soon as I'm close enough that he won't fall over again, sighing.

Mia stands and she's the one who backs away now, her face contorted in confusion. "I don't know what you're doing to him, but I will not let you hurt him." I look up at her, feeling helpless. Ares's head is in my lap now, his body surrounding mine like I'm the one needing protection. His fingers dig into my back and leg, his face burrowing deeper into my stomach.

"Go, Mia." Ares's words are stronger than just a few moments ago. I look down, peeling my chest away from him so I can see his face. His eyes are open, and I can see the tawny brown irises. There are no white sparks in sight. I sag and wrap my arms over his head. Tears of relief fall as I sob into his hair. Several minutes pass, neither of us willing, or able, to stand while Ares regains his strength.

A throat clears from a few feet away. "Mia told me you needed me?" Dante sounds dubious as he takes in our positions crumpled on the floor.

"I could have used you, like, five minutes ago. This house needs an intercom."

Dante's head jerks back like I've shocked him. "Okaaay," he adds a few extra syllables to the word. "What did you need?"

"I broke Ares," I spout, still uncertain of what exactly happened.

"She did not break me." Ares huffs as he lifts his head from my lap. "Really?" he asks, sounding more like himself. With a sigh and more effort than it should take, he leans away from me and comes into a sitting position. Dante walks over offering his hand, which Ares accepts before rising to his full height. I watch him like a hawk, expecting him to collapse any second again. Ares rolls his head around on his shoulders and arches his back a few times; once he's done, he walks over to me with a purpose. Reaching down, he gathers me from the floor with his hands under my arms.

I'm too shocked to do much other than allow my feet to bear my weight. "I'm not broken." Turning to his brother he announces again, "She didn't break me." I nod my head and point toward the floor where we were moments ago.

"He couldn't even stand up. We... I... and then... his eyes. I'm not sure what I did to him," I stammer, still freaked out.

Dante walks over and places his arm around my shoulder. "What about his eyes?" Dante coaxes, his voice encouraging her.

I look over at Ares. "You know how they get all dark?"

Dante's brows pinch together. He looks between me and Ares. "Ah, yeah. Did it scare you?"

"No." I wave my hand dismissively. "They changed, but they looked like, like... I don't know. Different."

Ares walks over, stopping in front of me. He bends his knees so that we're eye level. "How did they change?" I look down, afraid again, he's not mad now, but he might be when he realizes I did something to him. His finger slips under my chin and forces me to look at him. "Tell me."

"They were all dark," Ares nods, wordlessly telling me to continue, "but there were these sparks of white, like stars. I thought I really hurt you. Are you sure you're okay?"

Ares places his other hand on my cheek and, leaning forward, he whispers, "May I?"

"Always," I answer, even with Dante's arm wrapped around my shoulders. Ares places a feather-light kiss against my lips.

When he pulls back, he looks up at Dante as he fights a small grin. Watching the two of them, I feel a sense of satisfaction that I have no reference for. I don't have any reason to feel satisfied at all.

"What?" Dante asks, looking around like he might see what has the smile trying to break free on Ares's lips.

"See," I lean over, whispering, "Something is wrong with him." I keep my eyes on Ares, expecting something to happen any moment.

"What exactly happened?" Dante questions me, peeking at Ares from the corner of his eye.

"I don't know, one second we were... kissing, and the next

his eyes go all starry night, and he falls over. He could barely speak."

"Kissing?" Dante looks over at his brother, his eyes now narrowed. "Ares, have anything to add?" His arm falls down around my waist, and he pulls me tighter to his side.

Ares makes a scoffing sound. "I didn't just fall over. I tripped." He brushes at the sleeve of his shirt, not meeting anyone's eyes.

"On what, your ego? Because there wasn't anything else to trip over." I'm a little perturbed he's downplaying the whole thing. What would have happened if we weren't at home? My mind starts spinning. What if it happens every time we kiss—I mean *really* kiss? I turn to face Dante, and confess, "It was more than kissing; we were making out." It's only then I realize I don't have my bra on anymore and have no idea where it even is.

Dante's eyebrows shoot up. Facing off with his brother, his voice holding an edge, he demands, "Did you claim her?"

Ares raises his hands in surrender. "Absolutely not." He pauses, his eyes move over to mine. "She claimed me."

CHAPTER 10

My mind goes completely blank for a brief moment. Then Ares's words filter back in. *I claimed him*—what does that even mean? "I did what?" I gasp, feeling like I can't catch my breath. My heart is pounding against my chest, flooding my ears with the heavy thud.

Ares comes back to stand in front of me, his eyes locked on mine. "Laura, breathe." What is he talking about? I am breathing. "Here, like this, in," Ares takes a deep breath through his mouth, "and out. That's it, Laura, just follow me, in and out, in and out." I nod mimicking his breaths.

My thoughts begin to clear. "Did you say I claimed you? As in, I did something to you that you didn't have a choice in?" I wrap my fingers around Ares's wrist. His hands are on my shoulders, and Dante's arm is still wrapped around my waist. Completely shocking me, Ares throws his head back and laughs, he laughs so long, I start to think he's come unglued.

"Laura, sweetheart, you couldn't have claimed me if I weren't willing, it doesn't work like that."

"Why are you laughing at me?" I shuffle my feet, remembering there is still so much I need to learn about their world.

Ares's face sobers. "I'm not laughing at you." I narrow my eyes at him. "Well, that's not how I meant it," he amends. Placing a kiss on the tip of my nose he adds, "I'm sorry."

"Milo and Ollie will be home soon, why don't we head to the room? I'm sure they'll want to know what happened, too." I can't read Dante's voice; is he mad? I peer up at him, but he's making a point of not looking at me.

I take one quick look behind me, expecting to see my black bra lying on the floor, but it's nowhere in sight. There's no way I'm asking Ares what he did with it in front of Dante. I need some of my dignity.

As soon as we reach Ares's bedroom, I excuse myself to the bathroom. I have more questions than I know how to ask, and I'm not sure I'm ready to hear the answers. Facing the mirror, I look at my reflection. My lips are still a little puffy from Ares's kisses and I have a few purple love bites on my neck. I have no idea how I'll hide hickeys at work tomorrow, or at school on Monday, for that matter. Placing my hands on the counter near the sink, I lower my head. There are so many things I need to be focused on—my mom, finishing school—

yet my love life with four guys is the only thing I can't seem to get off my mind.

There's a light tapping on the door. "Coming," I call out, taking a deep breath. I need to find out exactly what I did tonight, and what it means for our future. I cannot do that hiding in the bathroom.

Pushing out the door, I see Ollie standing there waiting for me, his legs crossed at the ankle and his arms folded over his chest as he leans against the wall. His shirt is a little wrinkly around the waist, evidence of wearing an apron, but his eyes are smiling at me. No judgment, no expectations, no demands to explain what happened—just Ollie. I peer around, noting that we're alone.

I walk right into his arms, face-planting into his chest. He grunts and then chuckles, wrapping his arms around my back. "That bad?" he asks after giving me a few moments. I toss my head back and forth, but don't come out from the safety of his embrace.

"Are they mad at me?" Ollie's always been the most level headed. I haven't seen his emotions get the better of him since the first night he showed me his gift, even then he was madder at himself than anything else.

Rocking me back and forth from left to right, he asks, "Why would they be?" His tone is incredulous.

I chance peeking up at him, and he pauses as his eyes meet mine. "Ares said I claimed him," I whisper.

Ollie rolls his eyes. "The bastard—he'll never stop gloating. We'll have to listen to him tell the story a hundred and twenty-seven times."

I sag. "Ollie, I'm being serious."

"You think I'm not? He's a smug bastard, and you just handed him the keys to the kingdom." Ollie teases, his tone light. I know he loves Ares and he's trying to make me feel better.

"It was scary, I don't think I ever want to do that again," I mutter, nuzzling my face against Ollie's soft shirt.

He pushes me back, holding me at arm's length. "Now, don't go saying that, you'll break all our hearts and make Ares's head bigger than it already is." Ollie pulls me back into his chest and places his chin on top of my head. "That's the goal, you know, for all of us."

"But—" I splutter.

"There are no buts, Laura," Ollie interrupts. "We didn't tell you before about the bonding because you already have so much going on, but I'm happy you know now. You think you hurt Ares, but you're wrong. He wasn't prepared, but I can promise that what you did, didn't hurt him any more than it hurt you. It just took his body a few seconds to recover." Ollie intertwines our fingers together and raises our joined hands, flapping them at our sides.

Leave it to him to take a serious conversation and make me feel silly. "You really want that? I feel like he didn't have a choice, like I took something from him without asking."

Releasing one of my hands, he tows me to the bed with the other, and drops down with a huff. "Yes, the simple answers is *yes,* Laura. I want to be claimed, bound, whatever you want to call it, to you and to the others. It's what I've wanted since the moment I met you."

I bite the corner of my lip, taking the seat next to him. "What does it change?"

Ollie tilts his head to the side as his eyes go unfocused. "Well, let's see. So, just for starters, it will make it easier on both of you to be apart."

"Huh?" I say, and that's about all I can muster in my confused state.

Ollie knocks his shoulder into mine. "How do I explain this? Now that you've claimed him, it's like you have a piece of him with you, and it's the same for him, I guess." His lips and nose twist up. "It's not nearly as creepy as it sounds."

I place our joined hands in my lap, running my finger down each of his. "Okay, I can see how that would be good. What else?"

"You'll have more access to your connection to him, be able to harness your abilities better. Think of the connections like a filter—no—like a surge protector. We'll be able to divert any excess energy." Ollie nods like he's happy with his assessment, then looks down at me with a wry grin. "I'm probably the worst person to explain this to you."

I swat his chest with our hands and lean my shoulder onto him. "Why didn't you guys tell me sooner? It might have made things easier, and don't give me that bull about having too much to deal with."

He sighs. "That really is part of it, but... but we were a

little," Ollie pinches the fingers of his free hand together, "worried we would scare you away in the beginning. You've done a pretty good... okay, a fantastic job at handling everything we've thrown at you," he amends when I give him a pointed look.

"I guess I can't blame you guys too much, but I think it would be best for everybody if you guys filled me in on any other big surprises that might happen. I really thought I hurt him. What if we had been driving or something when it happened, and he would have crashed?" I can't get the image of Ares lying on the floor, completely helpless, from my head.

"I don't think he'd be driving while doing that." Ollie smirks, adding quickly, "But, Laura, Ares's reaction to the bond is a direct indicator of the strength of the bond. It could be completely different with each one of us."

"I don't understand. Does that mean it's not a strong bond because it weakened him?"

"No, not at all. I'm saying the bond is so strong, he took a few minutes to process the power loop, and Ares is one of the strongest of our kind." Ollie's eyebrow rises like he's just given me a big piece of information.

"So, it's a good thing then?" I ask tentatively.

"A fantastic thing." I look over and find Ares leaning against the doorframe, his ankles crossed, and he looks utterly relaxed. My cheeks go hot just seeing him. How did he sneak up on us without me hearing him?

"So, the eye thing?" I wave my hand near my face.

"Might have just been part of the process, or it could be a

physical manifestation of our combined abilities." Ares runs his eyes over me, stopping at the side of my neck. I almost raise my hand to cover the bruise he left behind. "I'm more than happy to test out a few theories." His voice goes husky. At least I know he's feeling better.

Ollie wraps his arm around my neck and mock whispers in my ear, "See. He's impossible—a total gloater."

I hide my smile by pinching my bottom lip between my teeth at Ares's expression. He looks both smug and irritated at the same time. Ollie chuckles, lying back on the bed, dragging me with him. I curl on my side, my head pillowed on his shoulder, it's been a long day. "Should I do everybody?" Ollie stiffens, his head lifting off the bed to look down at me.

"Say again?" he asks.

Now Ares chuckles, his sounding much darker. "Yeah, what was that?"

"Bond with everyone, or do I wait? How does it work? I'm not even sure what I did with Ares."

Ollie's head slams back down onto the bed. "I'm gonna die," he mutters under his breath. "Why don't you tell me about what you guys were doing, and I think we'll figure it out." Ollie offers. I feel a breeze as Ollie lets out a low grunt, laughing the next second. Ares is standing at the end of the bed, the evidence of the pillow he hurled at Ollie falling off the side.

Sitting forward, I cover my face with my hands. "Wait, just wait a second. It was because we were…" I can't bring myself to say making out, it seems way too juvenile, but I don't know what else to call it. "Kissing and stuff," I finish.

Ollie sits up next to me, all traces of laughter gone from his voice as he says, "It's more than that, you have to have a true desire to connect, to bond, but yes, part of the process is physical."

I peek through my fingers looking at Ares when he asks, "Do you regret it?" He looks down, his eyes going back and forth like he's seeing something I can't. He sounds hurt.

I drop my hands, letting him see my face. "Ares, I did something to you without even understanding what it was. I was terrified that I hurt you and that you would hate me. I don't regret it—couldn't if I tried. But I'd be lying if I said I wasn't still a little scared."

Ares comes over and crawls into bed. "I can deal with that."

When Dante and Milo come in a few minutes later, they pause at the doorway. Milo's eyes jump around, avoiding the bed. It almost feels like we walked in on them in the middle of a conversation. "Hey," I call out, hoping to ease the tension.

Dante walks into the room, a big bowl of buttery popcorn in his hands. "Movie?" he offers, and I nod, grateful for the normalcy.

Milo shuffles his feet like he doesn't know what to do. "Thank you for helping cover my shift, Milo." He looks up at me then, his blue eyes watching me.

After a long second, he nods. "No problem, it was nice to

see Gran and Gus." He's here and talking, but something feels off.

"Oh, good." I fold my arms over my stomach and look away from him. Maybe he's mad at me for the Ares situation. There's a distance between us, and remembering this morning in the car, I turn to face Ares.

"Gloria knew about us." It's not a question.

"Yeah," Ares answers anyway.

"Well, if she knows, and Maggie knows, why can't we tell Milo's parents?" My eyes move over to Milo who has finally made his way into the room. His steps halt, and he turns to look at me with an expression of downright shock on his face.

Ares's head follows my line of sight. "I guess we could tell all our parents." Ares holds up his hand when Ollie makes a whooping sound. "But we need to make sure they understand that this isn't something we can celebrate." My neck snaps in his direction. Ares sighs and corrects, "I didn't mean it like that. I meant that they need to keep the information to themselves... for now."

Milo's face is split into a wide grin when I turn to face him again. His eyes bouncing around between all of us. "Do you want to call your parents?" I question, happy that Milo's spirits seem to have lifted, but nervous about what it might mean.

"They're picking me up tomorrow, we can tell them then." Butterflies assault my stomach. Dante rubs his hand over my thigh, and I wonder if he knows how freaked out I am. "We can all go to Columbia tomorrow. I only have two extra tickets for the banquet, but we can hang out before and after," Milo continues, his voice laced with excitement.

I plaster a smile on my face, but on the inside my thoughts are spiraling out of control. I have to meet his parents tomorrow, and eventually I'll have to meet Ollie's parents, as well as Dante and Ares's. What if they don't like me? What if they think I'm not good enough? Clearly, we don't have the same backgrounds—I didn't even know about the existence of Infinities until I met them.

I slide my butt lower on the bed and fall backwards. How the hell am I going to make it through this? What will they think about there being five of us? Dante told me that there aren't any other pairings that have as many as we do. Using my inner elbow, I cover my eyes as I fight off the headache that is settling over the bridge of my nose.

The guys all continue talking about the weekend. Ares easily agrees to go, even saying it would probably be best to get away for a few days, especially after everything that happened with Mia tonight.

I block them out soon after. There isn't anything to be done about meeting their families. It's something I knew would happen eventually, I just hadn't realized how comfortable I'd gotten with the idea of pushing the prospect off to a much later date.

Dante cuddles up to my side soon after, his face wiggling under my arm so he's nuzzling his face next to mine. I let out a weighty sigh, and my fingers brush along his hair, reminding me of the tiger he turned into just yesterday. I stroke behind his ear, and he arches into my touch. "What does it feel like when you change?" My voice is soft.

Dante pauses his movements. "I still feel like me, but just a more basic me. My thoughts are simpler, but they're still my thoughts." I nod, that sounds good. About right now, I'd love to be able to let my insecurities go.

"Does it hurt when you change?" I know my questions might be intrusive, but I can't seem to help myself either.

Dante doesn't seem to mind as he settles in closer to me. Turning on his side so his mouth is near my ear, he wraps his arm around my waist. It feels like we're having an intimate conversation even though we aren't alone. "No, it doesn't hurt. When I'm about to change, I get this restlessness, like I can feel the fur under my skin."

I turn to face him, our noses inches from each other. "Do you know, once when you touched me, before all this, I thought I felt fur? We were in art class," I pause, my eyes going to the thick leather strap he wears around his wrist. My fingers go to the little bit of uncovered darkness I can see. I peer back up at him. "I remember seeing this. I wanted to know what was under here so badly that I almost couldn't stop myself from touching you."

Dante's eyes close, and when they reopen, the amber of his eyes has gotten brighter. I let my fingers dance along his arm, but I can't stay away for long from the mark we all share. My fingers itch to explore it. The bed shifts as the others move about, getting comfortable. I don't take my eyes off Dante. "Why do you hide this?"

Dante shrugs. "I don't know, I guess it's because everyone else's marks are covered. It feels private, like it's not for everyone."

"What about me?" My question is bold, but I can't take it back. "Is it for me?" I pull the closure of the band, loosening it before he even answers.

Dante swallows and his eyes are wide. "Yes, yours." His voice is gravelly. I strip away the thick band as I keep my eyes locked on his. My palm covers his mark. Dante's eyes fall closed again before he snaps them open and his lips part. A heady sense of power fills me. It's not the power of Dante sharing his abilities with me, it's more like I have a power over him, like he would never tell me no, not to anything.

Bringing his wrist up, I kiss his mark, and Dante gasps, his eyes blown wide. I place his hand down right between us and inch closer to him, so he's tucked into my body. Wrapping my arm over his back, I cuddle him close and let my eyes fall closed. It's barely ten o'clock on a Friday, but I'm exhausted. I don't have the energy left to worry about tomorrow and what new challenges it might bring.

CHAPTER 11

"Can you grab me more eggs?" I peer over my shoulder, Dante and Milo are both in the kitchen with me. Ares and Ollie were still sleeping when I got up, but Milo was already awake and showered. My stirring woke Dante, so I decided to make us all breakfast. I'm not great in the kitchen, I've never had the seemingly limitless supplies that come along with the Costa house, but making the basics is easy enough.

Milo shuffles over with a new carton of eggs in hand. Stepping up close, he looks over my shoulder as I crack a few more eggs into the large mixing bowl. After a dash of pepper and a big pinch of salt, I push the bowl aside. "What time are we meeting your parents?" Dante asks, his tone light, and why shouldn't it be? He doesn't have any reason to be freaking out, it's not like he'll be the one meeting them for the first time today.

The spatula slips from my fingers, clanging on the counter. "Sorry," I mutter, mostly to myself, before nabbing it back up to turn over the round sausage patties in the skillet on the stove.

"They'll be here around noon," Milo answers as he walks back over to the island and takes a seat next to Dante.

My eyes leap to the digital clock on the microwave—that's only in a few hours. I still need to shower and figure out what to wear. I take a calming breath, blowing it out unnecessarily slow. I clear my throat, hoping all my doubts and insecurities won't be obvious. "Are we coming back tonight?"

"That was the plan, but I'm not sure now. What do you think?" I expect to hear Dante answer, but he doesn't. I turn to face Milo, realizing that his question is directed at me.

"Uh…" I puff out my cheeks. "Should we ask the guys?" I don't know the right answer. I know Milo probably wants to see his family, but would we all be able to stay together like we have been? The thought of spending the night alone in a strange hotel room has me wringing my hands. Dante tilts his head, his eyes running over me.

"We'll ask them when they get up," Milo confirms. I turn back to face the pans on the stove. The rest of the sausage is just about ready, so I pour the eggs into the skillet and begin slowly stirring them with the silicone spatula.

It's like the smell of food wakes the others. Ollie comes shuffling into the kitchen, his hair hanging around his shoulders and low-slung, flannel pajama pants hanging off his hips. Long, lean lines of muscles rope up his torso. He doesn't have the slab of abdominals that Ares has, but his chest and stomach are no less appealing because of it. His eyes are a little puffy with sleep, like he didn't even really wake up before coming out. He looks positively adorable.

Ares steps up behind him, his dark hair made darker because it's still wet. He's dressed in a fitted black button-down shirt with the sleeves rolled up, exposing his tanned forearms. His tawny brown eyes search the room until they land on mine. Heat rises in my cheeks for no other reason than he looked at me. I focus my gaze back on breakfast, stirring the eggs slowly as they begin to congeal.

"You're making food?" Ollie comes over and he places his chin on my shoulder, his hands going to either side of my waist. I nod, biting my lip. The air is suddenly thicker; all four of them are here, and I'm a little overwhelmed.

We haven't had much time to be all alone together. In the evening, after work, when we're all in the room it's different. It's like I've come to know what to expect, but this is some-what new. There's a new dynamic happening, one where we don't always have to hide, and the guys are starting to change. I can feel it in the way they look at me. Ollie has always been free with his affections, and since yesterday I've felt a close-ness to Dante that wasn't there before. And I can't even think about Ares without flames licking my insides.

I swat Ollie's hand with my spatula as he reaches for a sausage patty on a paper towel lined dish. "Hey!" He smirks and brings the corner of his knuckle to his lips with a grin. He sucks the side of his finger into his mouth and pouts. I can't pull my gaze away. Ollie drags his knuckle over his mouth, tugging his lip down as he does. Boys' lips have no right being that full and pouty, and my teeth sink into my lower lip as I force myself to pay attention to the hardening eggs in the pan.

"Can someone grab plates?" My voice comes out raspier than usual. I let my eyes close, pretending I didn't just sound like I was trying out for a phone sex operator position. Ollie steps away from me, his hands lingering as he does so.

As soon as he's gone, Ares invades my space. I don't know how he can make himself so much more intrusive than Ollie, but he manages it with ease. He slinks up behind me, and his solid frame hovers just millimeters from mine. Ares's hands are much more possessive, and he wraps them over my shoulders, coming around to the front of my neck. When his thumb brushes along a tender spot, I remember the love bites he left me last night. He hasn't spoken yet, but my body sinks into his. All thoughts of the others seeing us falls away. A feeling of contentment I didn't know I was missing settles over me. "Mornin'," he breathes, running his hand up the column of my throat, causing my head to fall back against his chest. Ares kisses my temple, and then the corner my mouth. I hum my response.

The sound of plates hitting the granite counter jolts me, and I open my eyes, unaware I'd even closed them. I slide the pan over to a burner that isn't hot to stop the cooking process.

I know the moment I turn around my whole face will be beet red, even my ears are hot.

Taking a step away from Ares, I busy myself getting the rest of the sausage from the pan. Thankfully, the oven beeps moments later, and I bend down to retrieve the cookie sheet filled with canned biscuits. I had planned to make a quick white gravy, but I'm way too flustered, and my hands are shaking as I place the pan on top of the wooden trivet.

Taking a few steps back, I look over the simple breakfast, and a sense of accomplishment settles over me. I did this, not because I had to, but because I could, and I wanted to. I spin on my heel, my lip pinched between my teeth. "Food's ready," I announce a little shyly.

Unsurprisingly, Dante is the first to grab a plate and get in the line that is forming. He only adds two pieces of sausage and one biscuit, and I frown when he scoops up a small portion of the eggs. Does he not like breakfast food? There's not much Dante turns down, but I haven't really seen him eat much in the morning. We're all usually rushing out the door for school.

Walking over he extends the plate to me, his eyes a little wide. I take the dish as my mouth falls open—he made this for me? He doesn't say anything, just grins down at me before turning back to grab another plate.

They scrape the egg pan empty, and not a morsel of sausage remains. I should have made double. I'm not used to cooking for so many, especially since my mom barely ate enough to stay alive. The kitchen remains fairly quiet as we eat, and Mia's presence in the doorway a few minutes into the meal forces some light conversation.

After she arrives, I keep my eyes on my plate for the most part, still unsure how I should feel about her. My head tells me I should feel sorry for her, I know she has feelings for Ares—hell, maybe even for all of them—but the other part of me, it may be my heart or something else, tells me to keep her away from what's mine.

I all but growl when she leans her elbow on the island next to Dante. Everyone at the island looks over at me, and I can't even pretend it wasn't me. Dante, for his part, gets a small satisfied grin on his lips, and he looks down at his plate then back up at me. Mia looks around like she can't believe no one is going to say anything, her pretty face in a deep frown.

I lower my head. I don't know what it is about Dante that makes me so crazy. I don't think I would have acted the same if she were next to Milo, or even Ares for that matter. There's something about him that brings out a different side of me, and I'm not sure I understand yet. "Sorry," I mouth the words to him so no one else will hear. He shrugs his shoulder while still sporting the grin.

Milo leans over, looking past Mia and Dante, to me and Ares on my other side. "Are we staying in Columbia tonight, or coming back here?"

"It's up to you," Ares answers without looking up, taking on the role of the leader.

"Do you want to stay?" I ask Milo, he turns to Ollie on his other side.

"We could, but it's up to you," Ollie offers. I stand up from my stool, taking mine and Ares's plates since they're already empty to the sink. A quick rinse and I shelf them in the dishwasher, and then I place my rump on the front of the sink, crossing my arms over my middle.

I'm trying very hard to ignore the fact that Mia is here, listening to our conversation, when she asks, "You guys are going to Columbia?"

Ollie slaps a hand on Milo's back. "This guy has some fancy ass football banquet tonight. We're just tagging along."

My nerves are frayed, and I look over at the clock, noting the time. I really need to get into the shower, and I also need to know what to wear and whether I need to pack. I tip my chin down and look at the floor, waiting until I have an answer, or for Mia to leave so I can ask. Pursing my lips, I peek over at Ares. He's already dressed for the day, but he's not much help. He usually always wears slacks and a button-down—the only exception is when he's at home relaxing.

"I'm going to grab a shower," I say over the guys' conversation, still debating if we're going to come back home tonight. Ares stands immediately with his eyes on mine. He opens his mouth but looks over at Mia, whose eyes are glued to him. His brow furrows as he brings his hand up over his mouth.

"I need to grab a few things, I'll come with," Milo states, surprising me, before taking his plate to the sink and setting it down.

Ares's eyes narrow on Milo's back before he glances at his brother and Ollie. His mouth pops open and he mumbles, "Let me know what you guys decide so I can make arrangements." Then he strides out the door before any of us can beat him to it.

Mia stares in his direction long after he's gone, her brows pinched together as she bites the corner of her nail. Focusing on Milo, she tilts her head before she gives a doe-eyed expression. "I love Columbia. Mind if I tag along, too?"

Dante chokes on the bite he just shoveled into his mouth. I round the bar and pat his back as he coughs. "Oh, um, I'm not even sure we're staying yet, and we're meeting up with my family," Milo stammers.

Mia's face twists into a wry grin. "Oh, that'd be perfect. You guys don't mind, do you?" Her voice comes out almost like a whine. I roll my eyes, ready for this show to be over. Ares is the smart one; he got out of Dodge.

"I'm going," I deadpan before anyone can form a response. Milo's eyes go wide, like he can't believe I'm leaving him to handle this. I shake my head at him, he can handle it, he a big boy.

Ares is leaning against the headboard when I open the door. His legs are crossed at the ankle, shoes off, and his fingers are laced behind his head. Coming to a complete stop, I accuse, "You play dirty."

Without an ounce of regret, Ares shrugs his shoulders. "You have no idea." The *yet* hangs unspoken between us.

Planting my hands on my hips I tell him, "She already invited herself along."

Ares rolls his eyes, looking more his age than I've ever seen. "She's not coming."

"Oh no? Then why didn't you stick around to tell her that?" My voice is airy, but the challenge is clear.

"I have other things I'd rather be doing than wasting my time on her." Ares's pupils start to bleed past his irises. My heart rate quickens. He's only across the room, but it feels like he's so far away. Ollie told me it would be easier to be apart, but he didn't mention how hard it would be when we're together. My hand goes up to my neck, my fingers dancing over the base of my throat, as I fight the pull I feel to touch him.

Ares licks his lips. "Come here." His chin dips down as he peers at me from under his lashes. My feet take me closer without thought, and I stop at the edge of the bed. "Closer," he beckons, his eyes closing as he takes a long blink. Planting my knee on the bed next to him, he doesn't move. I brace my hand on his wide shoulder, bringing my other knee up to the bed.

"I need to get in the shower," I remind both of us in a voice barely louder than a whisper.

"We have a little time," Ares promises, his hand wrapping around my waist. As I settle my rump down on my heels, his eyes search mine, and the darkness in his expands even farther. "Are you okay?" I swallow, not expecting him to ask that question. When I don't answer right away, his hand reaches up to brush my hair over my shoulder. "I know there's a lot going on, but are you okay with what happened between us?"

My mouth goes a little dry and my tongue feels thick. I jerk my head up and down a few times. "It feels different," I confess, dropping my hands in my lap. Ready to have some answers and information, but a little unnerved to be about talking about it.

"I know, *Cara*," Ares tells me. "I'm sorry I didn't tell you about it sooner."

I look down at the buttons on his shirt, not sure I can meet his eyes as I ask, "Does it feel different to you, too? The connection?"

I chance a peek up at him and see that he's relaxed back against the headboard with one hand on the side of my thigh, and the other palm up on the bed beside us. He gives me a look that says I'm crazy for not already knowing it's different for him, too. But it's not condescending; it's more like *how could you not know*. "Yes, it does," he answers anyway. Reaching for my shoulder, he pulls me against him, and I settle into his side with my head on his chest as I rearrange my legs. I know I need to get ready, but I can't tear myself away from him.

Ares's head knocks back against the wall. "Don't tell the guys, but I really would rather just stay here," he admits as his fingers trace over the skin on my inner forearm.

"I'm nervous," I divulge, since it feels safe to say it, alone with him. He wraps his arms around my shoulders holding me tight to his side.

"You have nothing to be nervous about, but I understand why you are." He settles himself back, keeping his arms locked around me. "I think meeting them will help you understand a little bit more about our situation."

The door opens without a knock, and I look up without moving from my position. Mia stops in the doorway. Her face blanching as she gazes at us on the bed, her eyes leave us long enough to take in the rest of the room. Her brows draw together before looking back at us.

"Mia?"

"I looked for you in the office," she answers Ares before he can question why she's here. This will get really old, really fast. Mia's eyes track the movement of my hand as I push myself against Ares's thigh, preparing to get up. His arm, however, tightens against my side, locking me in place.

"I'm not working today," he tells her gently. Mia licks her lips and shifts her weight.

"I need to talk to you." Her eyes dart to me. I know she means alone.

Ignoring her silent plea, Ares says, "All right, what did you need?"

Mia shifts again, her hip jutting out to the side as her chin lifts an inch. "It's private."

"Mia…" Ares says her name with a patience I didn't know he possessed.

"I'll leave you alone, but first I just need a few minutes. You can spare a moment," she rushes out.

I'm torn. I don't want her here, especially in what I've

come to accept as our space, but I also don't want to be dealing with her every five minutes. And I have a feeling Mia is prepared to do whatever it takes until she feels like she's been heard.

I glance up at Ares, and his mouth is a thin slash. There's no way I'd want that look pointed at me. Mia folds her arms under her chest looking like she isn't at all intimidated in the least. I pat Ares's thigh. It's strange looking at this woman who I know has a history with him. I was uncertain, insecure even, last night at dinner. "It won't work," I tell her, feeling remarkably calm considering I growled at her twenty minutes ago.

Mia ignores me. "Ares, a minute. Please."

"You don't understand. And I'm not saying that to be mean or spiteful, I didn't even understand myself." I try again.

"Don't act like you know me," Mia seethes, her cheeks going red. "You can't possibly pretend to know him or me."

I let out a sigh, shaking my head. "See, that's what I mean. If you truly understood, you'd know how wrong you are. You thought you knew him." Leaning back, I tilt my head to look at Ares, his face is soft, and the edge I'd always thought he carried is absent. He gives me a slow blink, one that, even in this moment, I find terribly alluring. I sigh again, but for a different reason.

"I know him, you think a few weeks could outweigh years?" Mia blusters.

"Seconds." My eyes are still on Ares as I tell her, "Seconds was all it took, one look into those fathomless eyes, and I knew him on a level you'll never be able to understand." Ares drops a kiss to my forehead, his hand circling around the back of my neck.

"Bullshit," Mia curses, her voice on the verge of shouting.

Ares squeezes my shoulder once before he shifts so he can stand from the bed. "Mia, I never meant to hurt you." There's that patient tone again, but I can hear the frustration in his voice.

"Well, you did," Mia snaps back.

"I'm getting that." Ares squeezes his temples between his thumb and fingers.

"You can't expect me to just give up, to let go without you even knowing everything I feel, everything I've done to be with you."

"It doesn't matter, Mia, none of it matters." Ares pauses for a brief second before saying, "*Cara*, go get in the shower." His tone is completely different when he addresses me.

I trail my hand over his back as I walk past, not at all concerned that I'm leaving him alone with her. The bond between us gives me more reassurance than any words could.

CHAPTER 12

$\mathcal{I}$ run my hands over my jeans several times. I went casual, just like the guys, except for Ares, of course. My shirt is new, made out of a super soft sweater material in black with oversized sleeves. The hem hits right at my waist, just shy of exposing my belly. It's one of the most comfortable things I've ever worn, but I still feel kinda cute. I need to be careful lifting my arms though. I think I gave Ollie a shot of my bra when I was pulling my hair up into a high ponytail.

I've looked at the clock so many times, I don't think the hands are actually moving anymore. Ollie comes over and grabs my hands, lowering himself so he's hunched down in front of me, with a sly smirk tipping one side of his face. "So, how's it going?" he questions, like he's an underpaid school counselor. I roll my eyes and try to pry my hands free from his. Ollie chuckles, completely unrepentant. "I don't know how many times we can tell you to relax, sweetie. I promise they'll love you."

I narrow my eyes at him for teasing me, but I'm grateful for the reassurance. "I've never done this before," I whisper, letting my nerves get the better of me.

Ollie's eyes soften. "You really don't have anything to worry about, I promise."

"But... there are four of you," I stammer, as I lean in close so only he can hear me. I have seen little of Milo since breakfast, he seems almost as nervous as I am. Dante is sitting on the couch watching TV, while Ares is still at the island where he's been diligently working on a laptop for the past hour. Ollie looks at me in confusion. "And there's only one of me." I raise my brows, hoping he understands what I'm trying to say.

"Milo has three dads, one mom," Ares says from the island.

Ollie's head jerks back a fraction of an inch. "That's what you're worried about?" His tone implies it's the most ridiculous thing he's ever heard.

I grab the sleeve of his shirt, tugging him closer. "That's all I can think about. This is… this isn't something I…" I roll my lips together. I don't know how to explain what I'm feeling. I never in a million years thought I'd be in a relationship with two guys, let alone four. I can't kick the feeling that people will think badly of me, like I'm not loyal.

Ollie gives me a second to get my thoughts together. He

rises from the floor and takes the seat next to me, keeping hold of one of my hands as he does. Dante's head swivels in my direction, his eyes roaming over Ollie and me on the couch opposite him. I bite my bottom lip, deciding I need to just get it out there. "What if they think I'm a whore?" The doorbell rings as soon as the words leave my mouth.

Ares is now looking at me, too, and heat spreads from my neck over my cheeks. Dante is off the couch and next to me in a blink. "No one will think that," Dante grimaces. "No one who matters will think that," he amends, taking my face between his palms.

The bell rings again, and Ollie stands, dropping his hand onto my shoulder. "Listen to him, Laura. I'll get the door." He jogs off as I wring my hands together.

"I know what people say about girls that have, you know… have lots of boyfriends." I thought it was impossible for my cheeks to get any redder, I was wrong. The screech of Ares's chair moving draws my attention. He beckons me to him with a crook of his bent finger.

I stand, reluctant to leave Dante's side but unable to deny Ares. As I approach, his arms open and he welcomes me into his embrace without an ounce of reservation. "I'm not going to pretend it won't ever happen. People won't always understand us, but," with a finger under my chin he directs my attention up to his face, "I can promise you that will not happen here today, not with any of our families."

I swallow, my back straightens, and I pull myself away from his hold. I feel like I'm being dramatic, but all of this is so new to me. "Okay." I nod my head several times, telling myself I can do this. Ares doesn't release my arms and his eyes are scanning my face.

"Hey, guys," Ollie's cheery voice fills the room. Ares is blocking my view of the doorway, but I know when he moves Milo's parents will be there. My throat goes dry, I can't even swallow.

Dante bounces up next to me. "Hey," he calls back with a smile on his lips. He seems excited, and now that I take a second out of my own head I realize Milo, Dante, and Ollie all appear pretty excited. Ares turns, but I pull his arm close to my body so when he does, I'm still clinging to his bicep. Dante closes the distance between us and sandwiches me between them.

Ollie saunters over, going around me and taking up residence right behind me. I feel his hand snake around my waist as he lines himself up with my back. I notice a woman in the doorway, and when she sees us, her eyebrows pinch as her mouth slowly opens. No words come out before she closes them again, her head tilting to the side.

She's pretty, with medium brown hair that has hints of red and gold as the light glints off of it. She has it pulled back in a swooping low side bun and a few tendrils escape, framing her pretty face. She's not wearing a ton of makeup, but I can see hints of sooty lashes and rosy cheeks. She is long and lean, taller than my five-foot-six-inch frame, but she's also wearing heels. She takes one step in our direction.

"Mom." Her heads snaps to the right. "Dads." Milo nods at

the three men I haven't even glanced at yet. He passes them and heads right for his mother. Her face morphs the seconds she sees him. The confusion melts away to a beautiful smile that reaches all the way to her pretty light blue eyes.

"Milo," she responds with an unabashed joy as he makes his way over and wraps her in a tight hug. He's a few inches taller than she, so not by much, but he dwarfs her in size. When he pulls back, she doesn't let go. Watching him from arm's length, she grins at him.

I glance away from them long enough to see the three men openly staring at me. It takes everything in me not to slide behind Ares's wide back and pull Dante with me. Two of the men are big—not Ares big, but close. The third man is shorter, maybe an inch or so shorter than Milo. I know immediately which one is Milo's biological father. It's the eyes—he has the same navy-blue eyes as his son.

Is that hard on them, or does it even bother them? I glance at him now. He's in jeans and a fitted, button-down shirt, just like Milo's other dads. All of them look fit, and I would never guess that any of them were old enough to have a child Milo's age.

I inch my hand over to Dante's chest, barring it across him like I'm somehow protecting him, but I don't sense any threat. I think I'm just really nervous. The man furthest to the left tilts his head, his eyes watching my every move. "Milo, is there something you want to tell us?"

I hear a throat clearing as Milo turns to face our group, an easy smile on his face as he raises his hand, gesturing over to us. My fingers itch to pull him over. I feel beads of sweat dotting my upper lip. When did it get so hot? Is Ollie doing this to me?

"Laura, I'd like you to meet my parents. Linda," he wraps his arm around his mom's tiny waist, "Matt, Phil, and Stephen." He points to Matt first, the one with the same striking eye color as Milo. Phil turns to look at Milo, then back at me. Stephen lifts his fingers up to rub the stubble on his jaw.

"No shit," Matt curses, his eyes going between me and back to Milo at a rapid pace. Linda reaches around Milo and swats his arm, and it looks to be more of a habit than an actual reprimand.

She takes a step forward, her eyes only on me. "You're..." She clears her throat and tries again, "Are you?" Her shoulders fall the tiniest bit, and she looks over at Milo, a helpless little expression on her face.

"Yeah, she's ours," Milo confirms, releasing his mom and heading over to us. Ares takes a step away, making room for Milo at my side as I make a distressed noise—totally unintentional, but there all the same. So, instead, he moves behind me, and Ollie scoots over so I'm more in the middle of them.

If they think my behavior is strange, no one acknowledges it. Phil goes over to Linda's other side, not quite touching, but close enough too. Stephen just grins, he tries to hide it behind a big hand, but gives up rather quickly. "Laura, huh? When did you find this rag-tag group?" Matt's eyes twinkle, and if I didn't know any better, I'd think he was Ollie's dad.

Trying to find my voice, I croak, "A few weeks ago."

I hear a gasp. "Milo Andrews," Linda says in that mom voice every kid knows. His back goes rigid.

"Oh, boy." Phil rolls his eyes. "You've done it now," he mutters, bracing his arms over his chest.

"I cannot believe you hid this from me!" Linda's voice goes from angry to weepy in a matter of seconds. I can't see any tears, but the emotion is clear in her tone.

"Mom," Milo's voice is whinier than I've ever heard it, "it's not like that. I didn't want to keep it from you." He looks behind me at Ares, his nostrils flaring as he widens his eyes in an *are-you-going-to-help-me-out-at-all* expression.

"It was my fault." I raise my hand like I'm volunteering for the punishment. Milo snaps his neck to look at me. "I… you see, I didn't know about…" I circle my finger around our group, stuttering.

Linda wrings her hands together. There's no anger on her face, but her lips are twisted down. Matt reaches over and drops a hand on her shoulder. Phil steps closer so his arm brushes hers, and the next thing I know, she bursts into tears. I jump back, my mouth falling open as I stare at her. Matt pulls her in, putting her head on his shoulder as Phil rubs her back and shoulders, making soft reassuring sounds.

Stephen rolls his eyes on a sigh, and Linda reaches up and swats him again, still not looking up from Matt's chest. He chuckles. Within a few seconds, Phil pats her back, *sorry* he mouths to us with a wry grin.

Milo starts to squirm next to me, and I can tell he's struggling. Only a few seconds more and Linda is straightening her back, wiping her cheeks with a delicate finger under each eye. Her cheeks are flushed, but not nearly as bad as I look when I cry. She even cries prettily. Matt looks down at her and nods like he's proud. He kisses the top of her head in a gentle gesture and looks over at us.

Linda waves her hand, her voice still a little breathy as she says, "That was… I'm so sorry." Her nose crinkles up in embarrassment.

"That's okay." I find myself saying to ease her obvious discomfort.

Linda stomps one heeled foot and widens her arms before rushing over to our group. I back up, and my body slams into Ollie and Milo behind me. I hear a sudden chuckle as her arms wrap around whoever she can reach, and she's crying again.

I stand there, frozen, as she shakes against me, her face buried in my hair. My eyes must be big as saucers as they meet the men in front of me. Phil mouths *sorry* again, actually rolling his eyes this time, while Matt lifts his hands, pantomiming an embrace. He's saying that I should hug her? I pull one arm free and wrap it under her arm, around her back. I'm still stiff, but I give all the effort I can into hugging a complete stranger. Stephen grins and gives me two thumbs up.

"Laura, I'm so sorry. I'm not usually a basket case." Linda tells me for the third time.

"It's okay," I reply, which is the same thing I've repeated every time she's told me. They seat her and me at the island, her with a cup of coffee Matt made her, and me with a glass of water. Milo is to my left chatting like nothing strange just happened a few minutes ago. Phil seems to be in deep conversation with Dante, while Ares is again working on his laptop. He's on the opposite side of the counter, and his eyes dart up to me occasionally.

I fiddle with the glass in my hands, spinning it a little just to have something to do. I'm not good at the small talk stuff, I never really had to practice it much. As a waitress, there are only a few things people want to know from me: what food is good, where the bathroom is, and if I can bring them more ranch. This is different, I don't know where to start.

"So," Linda begins, her eyes going over my face again, "tell me why we're just hearing about you." Ares looks up then, giving me his full attention.

Taking in a deep breath, I return her gaze, and answer, "I didn't know anything about being a Synergist, or about any of this really." My shoulders shrug. "It took the guys a little while to convince me they weren't crazy."

Linda frowns, her eyes going over my shoulder. "But—"

"Mom, we should probably head out. We can talk about it in the car," Milo interrupts, saving me from explaining what I'm not sure I understand myself.

CHAPTER 13

"I'm sorry, Milo. It's an emergency, or I wouldn't go," Stephen tells him after returning to the room following a brief phone call.

"What's going on?" I whisper to Dante, watching Milo reach up to give the man a hug.

"Stephen is a surgeon. He must have been called into work," Dante answers.

"Well, at least I got the call before we left." Stephen heads over in my direction with Linda wrapped under his arm. He gives Linda a soft squeeze with a disappointed frown on his face. "I'm really sorry I can't stick around longer, Laura. I can't tell you how much I'm looking forward to getting to know you."

Milo comes to my side. "It's okay Dad, really," he answers for both of us.

Stephen quickly hustles out the door thereafter, leaving the rest of us to figure out the driving situation.

After a short debate about riding in two vehicles, we finally settle on all riding together in a black suburban. Phil and Matt are in the front. Ares, Linda, and I are in the middle row, which leaves Dante, Milo, and Ollie crammed into the very back. Good thing Columbia is only a forty-minute ride. I offered several times to trade places with Dante—he's the tallest of those in the very back—but he refused, not meeting my eyes. At one point it was on the tip of my tongue to demand he change seats with me, but I bite my lip to keep the words in. I narrow my eyes on him; I don't like it when he ignores me, that feeling of wanting to punish him wells up inside me.

I turn to face Ares, pleading with my eyes for a distraction. Everything feels so raw, like one little thing will push me over the edge and I'll lose my shit, it won't be nearly as pretty as Linda and her crying episode either.

Ares lifts his arm and tucks me into his side, I close my eyes, absorbing the calm he's exuding. "Ready?" Phil questions everyone in the car, looking in the rearview mirror briefly before pulling onto the long driveway.

"I got another room at the hotel. We'll be there while you're all at the banquet this afternoon. I have a few things I need to finish up with work. What are the plans for this evening?" Ares breaks the silence in the car a few minutes into our trip.

"We should celebrate." Linda claps her hands together once, like she's been waiting to say something for a while.

Ares, ever bossy, apparently even with Milo's parents, shuts her down immediately. "Not this time." He at least softens his words when he tells her. Linda turns to face him, her eyes narrowed like she might argue. Before she can, he continues, "We have bigger issues than having to convince Laura what she is to us." Ares looks down at me, his lips tip up in an infinitesimal smile. He returns his gaze to Linda and any evidence of his face softening is gone. "Laura's mom disappeared not long after they moved here." I feel a hand on my shoulder from one of the guys in the back. "The circumstances are suspicious." He drops the information in a matter-of-fact fashion, sounding completely unaffected. I try not to let it bother me, since I've noticed Ares's demeanor can change depending on who's around.

"Oh, honey, that's terrible." Linda grabs my hand, petting over my fingers. Her concern seems genuine, and I don't really know how to process it. Directing her attention back to Ares she asks, "What are you doing about it?" I wince at her tone, she sounds like she's accusing him of failing me somehow.

Completely unbothered by her question he answers without hesitating. "I'm still gathering information at this point. That's why we haven't announced ourselves to the community. There's more to this than we can cover in a short car ride." I wrap my hand over his thigh, leaning on him a little more. I don't like the way he's taking on all the responsibility.

Linda seems to take the hint that Ares has told as much as he's going to right now. She stays quiet for a few minutes with her gaze focused out the window. With a heavy sigh. she pats my leg. Her touch is different from the guys, but I don't feel as uncomfortable as I thought I might. Taking her hand from my leg she reaches over her shoulder and Milo places his hand in hers immediately. "I really am so happy for you guys." I can tell she's close to getting weepy again. That makes me uncomfortable.

"We're happy, too, Mom," Milo interjects before she can say much more.

"How about dinner?" Phil offers from the front seat. "I can see if the hotel has a private room available, or we could just find a nice, small place to grab a bite later this evening."

"We can have dinner at home where we can all be comfortable," Ares chimes in. He turns so he can see Milo in the backseat. "Or we can stay in Columbia, it's up to you." I'm pressed so close to him, I feel the muscles in his torso shift as he turns his body.

"I'm okay with going back home, but I feel bad that everyone came all the way out here just for this," Milo answers.

"Milo, this is important. We want to be here," I tell him before thinking about it, and I glance over at his mom, feeling a little self-conscious for speaking up.

Linda's lips are tipped up in a smile. "She's right dear, we all want to be here."

"I know," Milo mumbles from the back seat.

THE DRIVE to Columbia goes pretty fast considering the seating arrangements. We pull up to a fancy hotel with valet parking. I notice a young guy coming over to the driver's side window, and his eyes go wide as we all pile out of the SUV. Dante and Milo are shaking out their limbs and stretching the moment they crawl out of the back.

Reaching for Dante first, I rub my hands over his shoulders and back trying to help alleviate the soreness. Dante rolls into my hands, reminding me of the big cat he is. After his quick rub down, I head toward Milo; he's twisting his neck from left to right while his shoulders bounce from him rolling them. He's a few inches shorter than the other guys, so I'm able to reach his neck and shoulders a little more easily. I give him a few quick squeezes before rubbing my hands down his back. "I'm getting in the back on the way home," I demand.

Another valet comes over with a wheeled brass cart to help retrieve the bags from the back. "We don't have any bags," Ares speaks up as he extends his hand to the man, and when the valet pulls his hand back, I see a flash of light green. He tipped him just for walking over.

Ollie lumbers over, the long lines of his body seemingly unaffected by the car ride. He drops his arm over my shoulders and leans some of his weight onto me. My feet stumble before I recover, and he laughs before adding more weight. I grit my teeth but bear the weight, taking a step with him hanging off of me. "Give me a piggyback ride?" Ollie jokes, lifting his leg like he might try to jump on my back. I giggle and bend my knees ready for the challenge.

"Your ass would drag on the ground," Milo teases. Ares waves to us from the entrance of the hotel lobby. There's a wide spinning door, but he holds open the regular glass door and waits. Glancing at Ollie, I know he's going for the circle door, and I grin because so am I.

Like little kids, we go through the full circle once before he lets us out in the lobby. He came into my slot, so our steps were stunted as we passed through together. I peer up at the high ceiling and an appreciative whistle leaves my lips. "Holy wow."

Ares is already at the counter talking to a woman in a crisp suit behind the desk. Linda and Matt are a few steps over with another young woman. Dante sidles up next to me, brushing his body against mine. Ollie, Dante, and I head over to Ares as he signs a sheet of paper. The girl helping him check in has a flush on her cheeks as she looks at him, and a bright smile on her face displaying perfect straight teeth.

"Thank you," she beams, pulling out a pamphlet from the desk. She slides the flat keycard into center of the paper. "Your room number is eleven forty-nine." She points to where the number is written, going over information on how to call the front desk or get room service and finishing with an, "Enjoy your stay. If there's anything you need, don't hesitate to call."

Ares nods, barely glancing in her direction. He takes the pamphlet with the key and hands it over to Ollie's waiting hands. Ares's palm goes to my lower back as we follow Ollie to the bank of elevators.

"First, I'm going to see what room my parents are in, so I'll be over in a few minutes," Milo tells us, making his way over to Phil as his mom and Matt finish up at the front desk.

Dante reaches for my hand as we enter the elevator, and I glance around to see if anyone noticed. He was holding my hand while Ares had his hand on my back. The girl at the front desk is looking in our direction, but her eyes are glued to Ares, so I don't think she even noticed me. As the door closes, Ollie punches every number on the panel, Dante leans against the wall shaking his head while Ares groans.

The ascent is slow as we make a stop on every floor, and by the time we hit the eighth floor, I'm ready to smack Ollie myself. It doesn't help that two girls around our age got in our car on the third floor. I'm pretty sure they were heading down and only got on because they saw Ollie standing by the doors.

The coy glances only lasted a floor or two, before they ask, "You guys from around here?" Dante folds his arms over his chest and continues looking straight ahead. I try to hide my smile by biting my lip.

Ollie, my ever-friendly guy, answers for them. "Not too far, how about you guys?"

"Visiting family." The dark-haired girl sighs. "We were

hoping to find a good club to go to tonight, or something fun to do. You guys know any places?" She looks up at Dante and bites her full bottom lip.

My head tilts to the side and I'm about two seconds from grabbing Dante. He glances at me out of the side of his eye, not moving as the girl encroaches on his space.

"Nah, we're only in town for a few hours," Ollie offers, his tone friendly but not overly so.

"You guys want to hang, find something to do?" Ares wraps his arm around my neck from behind. The lighter-haired girl watches the movement but says nothing. The door sweeps open again, only to close moments later. The dark-haired girl giggles. "Did some kid hit all the buttons and jump out or what?"

Ollie grins, it's cute and boyish. "It was me, I confess." He chuckles. "I don't know why I do it."

"What floor are you?" Dark-hair reaches for Dante's forearm and I grab the back of his shirt, tugging him to me before her hand makes contact. Dante's arms fly out to balance himself. Her eyes go wide, and she makes a snorting sound like she's shocked. She eyes her friend with a smirk. The door slides open again.

Ollie's easy smile falls when he sees my face. He leans back against the wall waiting for our floor to come. The two girls huddle closer together, peeking over at me and letting out a few giggles.

Finally, on the eleventh floor the door opens, and I rush out, upset with myself for my behavior. "We're in three twenty-six." The dark-haired girl leans out, holding the door open as she tells the guys their room number. "Freak," she mutters as she releases the door before stepping back and laughing with her friend. That last part was directed only at me.

Ollie uses the key and opens the door without saying anything. I push into the room as soon as it beeps. Taking a second to glance around, I look for what I think would be the bathroom. I feel fingertips on my inner elbow, but I pull away, heading for a closed door across the living room. It's not just a hotel room, but a suite bigger than any room I could have imagined.

When I open the door, it reveals the bedroom I expected to see, with a wide bed, wooden nightstands on either side, and a TV positioned on a low dresser. I close the door behind me for privacy. I didn't really need the bathroom, but I did need a few minutes to myself.

Three short taps land on the door within five minutes. I heard the outer door open a few minutes ago, and I'm assuming Milo has finished up with his parents, but I don't have the nerve to go out there and face them yet. I acted like a jealous idiot.

The knocks come again, more insistent this time. "Laura." Of course, it's Ollie.

"Yeah?" I try to force lightness into my tone.

"May I come in?" he asks.

"I guess," I say on a sigh. I could go hide in the real bathroom, but there isn't really any point. The door opens slowly, and Ollie peeks his head around the frame looking for me. He steps through the crack before closing it behind himself. He drops his back against the door, not approaching me. I don't know what to say. I expected him to come in his usual self, to smooth things over. But he isn't even talking. I pick at the fabric of the bedspread. "I'm sorry." I settle on apologizing, hoping they aren't too mad at me.

"For what?" His voice sounds off. I look up and find Ollie staring straight ahead, not looking at me at all.

He's going to make me say it. I swallow, not liking the way he's acting. "For the elevator, for acting like... like." I look down at my hands unable to finish.

"Like a jealous girlfriend?" Ollie adds when I can't find the right words, and his eyes finally meet mine. But he doesn't have his usual easy grin. Instead, his lips are a thin slash and I can see a tic in his jaw every few seconds, telling me he's grinding his teeth.

I don't know what to say. I don't know why he's the one in here and not Dante. Are they all mad at me because I can't control this shit I have going on involving him? Blowing out a deep breath I say, "I don't know what comes over me, ever since he told me about Delaney and the kiss, I just get... I get this feeling..." I wave my hand in front of my chest.

"What kiss?" Ollie interrupts.

"At school on Friday, Delaney kissed him, and he told me he kinda kissed her back." I can't keep the hurt from my voice.

Ollie uses his shoulders to push himself off the door and

he walks over to the edge of the bed where I'm sitting. "Yes-terday?" He drops himself next to me, his shoulders falling in a sag as he hangs his hands between his legs.

I curl my knee up and nod. If he doesn't know about the kiss, he probably doesn't know what happened at my camper either. "It's all really confusing," I confess, my hands in my lap. "Ares says I don't have to share you guys, but you have to share me." I can't even look at him when I say it. It's so fucking embarrassing. "How can I ask that of you guys? It's not fair. And the jealousy, I don't know how to deal with it."

"You're not asking us, we're asking you."

"That's not how I feel. I feel like you guys don't have any other choice."

Ollie bumps his shoulder with mine. "You're right about it not being a choice." He holds up his hands when I flash my eyes to him and open my mouth. "But not for the reasons you think. I could walk away Laura, so could Milo." I rub my fist over my chest, trying to ease the pain his words cause. Ollie pulls my hand down, holding it in his own. "When we realized what you were to us, we could have all walked away and never even spoke to you. It would have been hard, but it's possible."

"You didn't, though."

"No, we didn't. Honestly, it never even crossed my mind. I knew from the very first time I laid eyes on you that you were our future." A little piece of me melts with his words. Ollie is being serious, not his normal joking self. His words are carrying weight.

"But you're mad at me about the elevator?" I peek up at him from under my lashes.

He sighs, looking at the door in front of the bed. "Not so much mad as a little hurt."

I squeeze his hand, which is still wrapped around mine. "What, why?"

"You didn't drag me away from them." He tries to force a lightness into his tone, but it fails.

"Because I've never doubted you."

Ollie's eyes jump to mine, his lips parted on an inhale. "What do you mean?" he whispers.

I wince. "Well, that's not really true. When we first hung out, I was a little jealous about you and Milo. But I was crushing heavily on all three of you. Once I got to know you a little better, I kinda," I shrug my shoulder, "well, it just didn't bother me so much anymore."

Ollie goes rigid beside me, his hand pulling away from under mine. "So, you growl if someone gets close to Dante, but you don't care if you think I'm with someone else?" His jaw is pulsing again and his head shakes before he lets out a dark chuckle.

Realization dawns, he's upset because he thinks I care more about Dante. "Ollie." When he doesn't look at me, I stand up in front of him and sink to the floor on my knees, my hands on his thighs so he doesn't have any choice but to see me. "Ollie, I didn't drag you away from those girls because I didn't think I needed to. I trust you." His chin tips up stubbornly but his eyes dip down to me. I walk a little closer on my knees, pushing myself against his. "I'm not jealous because I know you care about me, not because I don't care about you, which I do."

Ollie looks down at me then, he bites his bottom lip, but he can't hide the little grin pulling at his mouth. Reaching forward he snags me under my arms and lifts me up, tossing me on the bed. "Stop being so dramatic," he accuses, mock indignation in his tone.

"Oliver," I snap as I push up on my elbows with my eyes narrowed on him. He chuckles unrepentantly and flips over so he's crawling toward me. When he's above me I let my head fall back to the bed. His eyes roam over my face, lingering on my lips. I think he's going to kiss me, and my stomach tightens in anticipation.

Ollie lowers his body to the bed, bringing his face closer to mine. With a slowness designed to make me comfortable, he brushes his lips against mine then pulls back to look at me. I lick my lips, hoping he's not done. His eyes fall closed as he leans back in, and this time he doesn't pull away after one peck. He tilts his head to the side so he can push his pillow soft lips against mine with more pressure. I sigh, my lips joining his as he lets his mouth open more. Ollie kisses like he behaves, all teasing and sweetness. Every time I think he's going to take the kiss a little further he pulls back, making me chase him.

The tip of his tongue finally touches my lip and I let out an embarrassing moan of appreciation. His traces my bottom lip then flicks up to the top. I reach out grabbing his shirt at the side of his waist. Ollie never seals his mouth to mine, but his tongue dips inside, coaxing my tongue out to meet his. His breathing grows heavy.

I feel his hand land on my lower stomach, his palm not moving but putting a tiny bit of pressure right under my belly button. I curl my legs up, and it takes everything in me not to lift my hips off the bed so his hand would slide one way or the other.

"Hey, you guys almost ready?" Milo's muffled voice floats through the door.

"Coming," Ollie singsongs then snickers, not stopping the kiss.

"I have to be downstairs in twenty minutes," Milo adds. I let my head fall back to the bed. Ollie bangs his forehead on the mattress beside me a few times before he reaches down and shifts his lower body, a slightly pained expression on his face. Lifting back up, I watch his hand leave his groin. My eyes dart up to the ceiling, pretending I didn't see him.

"I gotta go, I promised I'd go with him when he got the tickets."

"I don't mind, Ollie, I'm glad you'll be with him. We'll be here when you get back," I assure him.

He stands up, making a big ordeal out of it, groaning and grumping like an old man. With his hand extended to me he helps me from the bed, smoothing his hands over the back of my hair with a twinkle in his eye. "I can't wait to give you a full pillow perm." He sighs wistfully.

"A what?" I swat his hand away.

"A pillow perm. You know, get you all hot and sweaty so your hair goes all crazy and wild. A pillow perm." I groan, rolling my eyes. He just laughs while towing me to the door.

Ares glances up from the laptop on his knees, his eyes taking in my hand tucked into Ollie's, and the boyish grin on his face. Without a word he focuses back on his computer.

Dante isn't anywhere in sight. Milo is facing a large mirror near the main door, wiggling a maroon tie around his neck. His white button-down shirt is tucked into a very fitted black pair of pants. I gape a little at his bubble butt. Half the time he's in gym shorts or loose sweats, and they don't do his backside a bit of justice, because holy hell he's got an ass.

Ollie's finger wipes at the corner of my mouth, alerting me that I've been caught staring. I make a face and push his hand away, wiping under my lip just in case. Milo turns and he has a scowl on his face. He looks so handsome; his hair is styled away from his face, showing off his killer jaw and his navy eyes. Either ignoring or unaware of my gawking, he shoves his thumb into the waistband of his pants while bending his knees. "I can barely fucking breathe." He yanks his dress shirt out of his pants. As soon as it's all the way out, he undoes the buttons and loosens the tie at his neck, keeping it tied while slipping it over his head. The shirt and tie get tossed to the back of the couch, leaving him in the sinful pants and a skintight white undershirt. Milo's arms are corded with thick ropy muscles and veins. His wide shoulders bunch up as he pulls off his last shirt. My eyes travel down his chest to a thin line of hair just below his belly button. His stomach is ripped, his abs standing out, and I finally get the term six pack.

As my gaze continues down, I see a definite bulge in the front of his pants—they're that tight. I look away then, feeling like I've violated him somehow. "Please tell me someone has slacks I can wear," Milo's voice is gruff. Ares sets his laptop on the coffee table and stands as he notices Milo's state of undress. "I wore these fucking things three weeks ago." Milo makes the statement into an accusation. His eyes shoot to Ollie like he thinks this is part of some prank.

Ollie lifts his hands, one still joined with mine, in surrender. "I didn't take your pants." He doesn't hide the laughter in his voice. Milo's eyes narrow.

"You can try mine, but they'll probably be too big," Ares offers, already pulling open his belt. My mouth goes dry, they're going to strip, standing right here.

"Anything is better than these nut huggers," Milo mumbles acerbically. He's not wearing a belt, so he sucks in his rock-hard stomach, going almost to his tiptoes to unbutton his pants. His face is red by the time he lets out a huge breath of relief when he opens them.

My fingers cover my lips, but a giggle escapes. Milo tries pushing his pants down his hips, but they get stuck at his thighs, the open fly showcasing his privates indecently. I release Ollie's hand and cover my eyes as I spin around so I'll stop ogling him. And hopefully he won't notice my shoulders shaking, because I can't stop the laughter from bubbling up. I hear a loud, long ripping sound seconds later, coming full circle. I look back at Milo holding his black pants high in the air with a satisfied sneer on his lips. He tore them off.

"Dude, you've been working out." Ollie grins.

That comment has Milo's lips thinning. He drops the pants on the floor, straightening to his full height. I let my eyes travel from his black socks and up. My eyes get stuck on his thighs—how could I not have known what Milo was hiding under all those baggy clothes? I've been staring so long I missed Ares taking his pants off. He leans over, kinda tossing Milo his pants. My eyes are volleying back and forth between the two of them now. Ares's shirt is just a little shorter than his boxers. He's not as cut as Milo, but everything is thicker, no less powerful. I don't even know where to look.

Milo steps into Ares's pants, and he has to stick his leg straight out so his foot comes out of the bottom. When he places his foot back on the ground the fabric pools over his foot a bit. Widening his legs so the pants won't fall, he tucks his undershirt over his boxers. "Thanks man," Milo mutters shaking out his shirt and sliding his arms in the sleeves. Ares crosses his arms over his chest, completely fine standing there in his shirt and underwear.

"Shit, fuck." Milo pinches the side of the waist after tucking in his shirt and buttoning the pants to hold them up. They aren't clown big, but they're definitely oversized. "Can I get your belt?" His eyes are wide, his movements rushed.

Ares hands him his belt without a word. Milo slides it on, cinching it at his waist to hold the pants in place. His arms drop to the side and he shakes his head. "This shit blows."

I walk over to him, feeling more confident now that he's dressed. Placing my hand on his forearm I look up at him. "You look really beautif… handsome," I correct myself at the last second. Milo's eyes soften as his shoulder sag.

"Thank you." His voice is pitched low and his cheeks are a little pink. Did I embarrass him? "You coming?" Milo asks Ollie over my head.

"Yep, ready when you are."

I step back as Milo makes his way over to the sofa to put his shoes on. When he rises, he shakes out his leg, letting the pants fall. The shoes keep them from hitting the floor and he sighs. "Thanks again, Coach would have chewed me out if I had to wear jeans." Ares nods before sitting back down on the couch. I hadn't realized he wouldn't have anything to put on.

Ollie walks over and gives me a gentle peck on my lips before meeting Milo at the door. He's distracted, not even looking back in my direction. "Bye." I wave. "Have fun, and congratulations," I call quickly as Milo opens the door.

I get a short, "Thanks," as he exits.

CHAPTER 14

"Where's Dante?"

Ares lifts his head from his computer. "Not sure. He said he was going for a walk." He shrugs, like it's no big deal. My thoughts immediately go to the girls on the third floor, but I shake the idea away, he wouldn't do that. I hope.

"I thought you weren't working today?" I take a seat on the couch with him, but not too close.

"I'm not."

"You've been on the computer every spare second since this morning. If you're not working, what are you doing?" I lean over, peeking at the screen.

Ares raises a single brow. "Feeling neglected?"

I roll my eyes; if he'd asked me that a few days ago, I might have gotten self-conscious, but I hear the teasing tone in his voice. Ares pushes his laptop back on the table and relaxes into the corner of the sofa, his arm going over the back. I take in his bare thighs. "Do you want me to go grab your bag from the truck?" We all packed a change of clothes, it hadn't been decided when we left if we were staying overnight or not.

"One of the guys will later. What did you and Oliver talk about?" The quick topic change jars me. I raise my fingers up to my lips, wondering if he knows the conversation ended in kisses. When I don't offer an immediate answer, he prompts, "He seemed pretty upset when he went in there."

"How much do we tell each other?" Ares tilts his head to the side at my question. "I mean is *everything* open between all of us?"

He pinches his lip, his eyes going unfocused. "I don't keep things from them, but I don't tell them everything either," he answers cryptically. That doesn't give me very much information. Ares lifts and scoots closer to me on the couch, his eyes going hooded. "Is there something you want to tell me?" His voice is gravelly, changing the atmosphere.

He doesn't even need to come any closer, yet I already feel his pull, the pull to crawl onto his lap, to touch him. My hand goes to the cushion between us, inching nearer. "I'm just trying to figure out how much we share?" Where did that husky tone come from? Certainly not me.

Ares licks his lips, his chin dipping down so he's looking at me from under his inky lashes. "My time with you, *Cara*, when we are alone, is only ours." He trails his fingers over my arm, inching higher until his fingertips are dancing over my collarbones. This conversation is taking a different turn. I swallow, my mouth feeling dry. I look away from his lips, because if I don't, I won't be able to concentrate long enough to talk to him.

"What about other stuff?" My cheeks heat under his gaze. "Like, if I talk to you about something, should I assume everyone would know?"

Ares's fingers continue with feather-light touches over my chest, making their way up my neck, and stopping when the tip of his index finger strokes my bottom lip. His eyes meet mine. "That depends on what it is. If I think it's something they need to know, something they should know, I wouldn't keep it from them." I nod, incapable of speech as his finger traces over my lips.

Ares leans in then and, sliding his palm around to the back of my neck, he angles my face up, his lips hovering over mine. "You said 'always,' that I could always kiss you." I don't answer, instead I lean across the cushion between us and steal the kiss he was keeping from me. He makes a clicking noise with his tongue, admonishing me. Ares jerks the arm I was leaning on out from under me, and my side hits the cushion, causing my breath to whoosh out of my lungs. I look up at him, my eyes wide with surprise.

He leans down, his nose near my chin, and kisses my lips softly. The stubble on his chin tickles my nose as he continues to plant open-mouth kisses on me. The tip of his tongue slides past my lips, and I shiver when I feel the smoothness of the underside of his tongue tease mine. He retreats, but I snap my hands to the back of his neck, keeping him there while I twist my tongue around his.

I feel the seat shift as Ares moves to stand, his mouth locked against mine as he turns so our noses brush. Kneeling next to the couch, Ares presses his chest against mine, pushing me into the cushions. I pant out a heavy breath when his lips leave mine to trail little nips and kisses across my jaw. I push him away when he moves down to my neck. "Makeup." I can't imagine the concealer I used on my hickeys would taste good.

He growls, moving up right behind my ear and sucks hard enough that I know I'll have another spot to cover. My back arches off the couch, spurring him on. Ares's hand skims up my side, his thumb going for my breast. He finds my hardened peak even through my bra. Making a circle around my nipple, he mimics the same movement with his tongue in my mouth. Something low in my stomach clenches when he pinches my nipple between his fingers and sucks on the tip of my tongue.

My heartbeat thrums against my chest, skipping a beat every now and then. I lift my hand to Ares's chest to see if I can feel his, and as soon as my palm lands over his heart, I feel it racing almost as fast as my own. "Goddamn," he mumbles against my lips. I have no idea why he's cursing, but I really don't care either. Breaking way from his kiss, my breath comes in choppy pants near his ear. Needing air, but not wanting to stop, I take his lobe into my mouth and bite down. Ares makes a deep sound in the back of his throat, and his hands pull me in tighter against his body. Heat flushes across my skin as I get the same tugging sensation I felt with Ares when we bonded. Opening my eyes, I see him leaning over me with his jaw clenched tight. Reaching up I stroke my finger just under his eye, all traces of white obscured with blackness. "What do you see?"

He inhales deeply, his nostrils flaring. "Right now, I see the heat rising off your skin." His hand grazes over my body, stopping at the apex of my thighs. "I can see the thrum of your pulse fluttering here." His hand moves back up, caressing the hollow at the base of my throat. "The way your pupils blow wide when you're looking at me, the way your lips tremble when I get close." Ares leans in again, stopping just before our lips touch. His eyes close on a slow blink. "But that's nothing compared to what I can feel."

A quick set of raps against the door has me shooting upright. I straighten my sweater and run my hand over my hair in an attempt to smooth it. Ares drops his forehead to my thigh, rocking back and forth. "If this is anyone but Dante, I'm going to kill them."

Heaving himself off the floor, Ares stalks to the door of the hotel room. I can't help but admire the way he moves. Snapping the door open, he looms in the threshold for a long second before finally stepping back to let Dante enter.

Dante looks around, his eyes a little narrowed until they fall on me. He shoves both hands down deep in his pockets, and his shoulders round down as he lingers a few feet away.

Aggravation curls my lip. I'm disappointed with him, but mostly I'm frustrated with myself for my behavior. Ares lets the door fall closed and makes his way over to the side of the room. He opens a small wooden cabinet, and I see several rows of mini bottles of alcohol, a few bottles of water, and assorted nuts and juices. Ares nabs two tiny bottles. Not bothering with any of the glasses, he twists off the cap and downs the first bottle's contents.

"Milo and Oliver already down at the banquet?" Dante questions. The answer is obvious.

"Where have you been?" I don't mean to sound accusatory, but that's the way it comes out.

Dante lowers his eyes to the floor. "Just walking around." I can't tell if he's lying or not. The way he's avoiding eye contact makes me think he might be. I tuck my hair behind my ear, watching him. When I don't ask any other questions, Dante comes over to the sofa, sitting on the other end away from me. The silence that falls is heavy and awkward. I don't know what to say. Should I apologize for the way I acted in the elevator, or expect him to for not getting himself out of the situation?

Ares returns and he takes a seat on the arm of the sofa right next to me. The differences between them are so glaringly obvious. Dante has always been a little out of reach, while Ares has inserted himself into my life from the first moment we met. Even when I think I'm finally beginning to understand him, something happens that threatens that idea. I fidget, my hands and legs restless as the silence grows between us.

"How long is this thing supposed to last?" Ares asks, leaning his elbow on the back of the couch.

Dante shrugs. "A few hours I think."

"If we're going back to the house tonight, I need to make a few calls to get dinner squared away. I was thinking since Linda and the guys know, it won't be long before our parents and Oliver's know. We should get ahead of the ball on this one and make sure we're the ones to tell them. I know Mom will have a stroke if she finds out from someone else," Ares says sounding resigned.

"You know she'll be on the next flight out as soon as we tell her."

"I know she'll want to." Ares looks down at me, biting his bottom lip. "If we do a video call, she might not chew me out too bad if you're there." His eyes plead with me.

"Now?" I gasp. I had to meet Milo's parents today, now theirs?

"It's just a video, and it won't be as awkward. She can't even attack you," Ares offers, his voice sweet.

"Attack me?" I seem to be incapable of more than questions at this point.

"Not like that—don't be crazy. I mean she won't be able to assault you with hugs and tackle you with her excitement." Ares actually rolls his eyes. I, however, am not really as mollified with his explanation as he seems to think I should be.

Before I can muster a response, Ares sits up straight. "All settled. Let me get the food situation arranged for tonight, and we can call her. You guys get this weird tension you have going on sorted out, because Mom will spot it a mile away, and then there won't be any stopping her from coming." Under his breath Ares adds, "Not like it'll help." He stands, dropping a tender kiss at my temple, and strides into the bedroom area. The door closes as I sit there reeling. Not only do I have to meet their parents, but I also have to deal with Dante.

While I'm staring straight ahead, still in shock, Dante rumbles next to me, "You're mad at me." It's definitely not a question.

Taking a deep breath and squaring my shoulders, I turn to face him. He's in the opposite corner of the couch, his large frame somehow looking smaller with the way he's tucked into himself. It doesn't diminish his appeal in any way, though. Peering at me with those gorgeous amber eyes and a slightly nervous expression, his chin tilts down.

I look away, I won't be able to get the words out if I have to look at him. "I'm really confused," I confess, dropping my hands into my lap. "I thought it was just Delaney making me feel so... so jealous, but it's not just her. It's you."

The cushion between us shifts as Dante rearranges. "I promised that nothing like what happened with Delaney would ever happen again," he says, like I only need his word to erase his actions.

"Yet when we were in the elevator, you didn't do anything to stop that girl from getting close to you, trying to touch you. What if she would have kissed you? Would you have even stopped her? And I was standing right there."

"Of course I would have stopped her, but I wanted you to."

I snap my neck in his direction, my mouth probably hanging open. Finally, I manage a very confused, "What?"

"I wanted you to claim me as yours, let them know I was with you," Dante tells me with such certainty that I can't help but believe him.

At a loss for words, I circle my fingers over my temples. Deciding to give him a bit more information since he's divulging his own, I tell him, "There's something about you that makes me crazy... territorial." I settle on that word when I can't find another to fit. Glancing at him from the side of my eye, I see his lips lift in a barely there smile before it's wiped off his face like it never existed.

The couch shifts again as Dante inches closer. "I think that has something to do with my abilities," he confides, but I have no clue what he means. "My animal," he amends.

Licking over my lips, I give his idea some thought. Could it be? But why would I react differently to him, considering he's the animal and not me? "I'm not sure that makes any sense, Dante."

"I don't let many people in. I've always been a bit of a loner, but I've also always had this feeling," Dante's hand waves over his torso, "of dominance I can't always control. I don't like being told what to do, where to go. Hell, that's how I ended up living in the apartment above the garage, because I knew Ares didn't want that." Dante runs his hands up and down his thighs, no longer looking at me.

"Once my ability manifested, it was easier to understand

why I'd always been this way, but..." He lets the sentence dangle, not finishing his words.

Getting antsy I prompt, "But?"

Dante's fists clench over his legs. "But it's completely opposite with you; that part of me, my tiger, turns into a total pussy cat with you," he winces at his words, "and craves your attention and affection."

I swallow the lump in my throat. "So, do you think me feeling like this, has something to do with us sharing your ability? That I'm feeling extra," heat flashes across my face, "bossy and needy with you because of your animal?"

Dante scoots closer again until he's right next to me with his arm behind me on the back of the sofa. "It could be, or maybe you're just more dominant than me," he says with an easy acceptance.

I drop my head into my hands. "Uh, I'm going to go with no on that." My voice is a little muffled coming out through my hands.

Dante leans in even closer, his nose nuzzling my cheek near my ear. I stiffen, I knew he was close, but not that close.

Dante's lips part and I feel the press of an open mouth kiss on my jaw. His nose runs across my cheek until his lips are at the corner of my mine. "So, you okay with this?" I'm not sure what *this* means, but Dante bobs his head up and down in a jerking motion. "I was kinda mad at you, but more at myself, because I was acting like a spoiled brat with a new toy."

He makes a grumbling noise that rolls up his chest. His voice is even deeper as he says, "I'm totally okay with that."

A small burst of a laughter erupts from me and Dante locks his lips on mine, stealing the sound and my breath. Without a thought I bite his bottom lip. He jerks back, his tongue smoothing over my nip, and my eyes widen in shock when I see a dot of blood welling up.

"Oh my God, I'm so sorry," I blurt, grabbing his jaw with my hands, and Dante gives me a shy smile while looking down with a small shrug.

"I was asking for it."

"No, you weren't, Dante, that's not okay. I never want to hurt you. That was wrong. If you did that to me, I would me upset and feel more hurt than just physically." Dante wraps his hand around my wrist while still cradling his face. "People shouldn't hurt each other, Dante especially if they lo—" I stop before saying the entire word, "—care about each other; it shouldn't ever be like that."

"That was just a little nip, Laura, I don't want you to hold yourself back from me. I know what that's like. So please, don't do that with me." I look in his eyes, and he seems earnest, not upset in the least.

I resolve to make sure that doesn't happen again. There's a huge difference between the bites and nips Ares gives me in the heat of the moment and what just happened. I may not have intended to hurt Dante, but I was trying to punish him a little bit. I place a gentle kiss on his lips.

He grins at me, happy that I've dropped it. Leaning back in slowly so his intentions are clear, he keeps his eyes open and kisses my lips softly. I run my palms over the barely visible stubble on his jaw and delve into his thick dark hair. Dante's eyes fall closed, the weight of his head dropping into my hands as he exposes his throat to me. He completely trusts me, even after what I just did, he doesn't have any reservations. I place an open mouth kiss on his Adam's apple, then tilt his face back to me.

Dante's mouth parts on a sigh as I brush my lips across his. My heart is still heavy from what I did, so I keep the kisses slow and sweet, not taking anything more than what he's giving me. Heat invades my senses, making me think I might be about to spark up, but the burn is low compared to what I feel when Ollie touches me, so I let the worry go and allow the heat to continue to build inside of me.

Dante makes a deep sound, almost like a growl, as the heat rises, and I shiver as goose flesh pebbles over my skin. With my thoughts solely on Dante, and the intention of never hurting him again, I release some of the heat building inside me.

The effect is immediate, Dante's back bows, and his eyes fly open. Not a sound escapes his parted lips. But before I can ask him what's wrong, I feel a shifting in my body, almost like my insides are rearranging. It only last seconds, but when the feeling is gone, I can't help feeling like something just changed.

Dante sucks in a few deep breaths, his eyes still wide on mine. "Holy shit," he mutters, his voice half growl.

He doesn't need to say more, I already know what I've just done. I bonded him to me.

CHAPTER 15

"*W*ell, I'd say as far as make ups go, that one was pretty damned successful." Ares lays the sarcasm on thick.

I narrow my eyes at him, pissed that he's making light of the fact I bonded another person to me without their consent. Dante, for his part, seems completely content—happy even—about the development.

He didn't almost pass out the way Ares did, but he collapsed back into the couch, his eyelids drooping low. I made sure he was okay—brushing his hair way from his face and holding his hand—and thankfully I didn't scream for help the way I did for his brother. I don't think the hotel would appreciate me screaming bloody murder for all their guests to hear.

Ares gets a gleam in his eye, and I'm pretty sure that

gleam doesn't mean anything good for me as he rubs his hand over his lips, trying to hide his grin. "This is going to be easier than I thought."

"What is?" I question, still running my hand over Dante's thigh, because it seemed to help Ares recover when I was touching him. That's the reason I don't want to take my hands off him, it has nothing to do with the fact that it feels like another piece of my soul just slid into place.

"Convincing my mother to stay in Italy," Ares answers cryptically.

"Wishful thinking," Dante chimes in, his body languid as he relaxes back into the sofa and pulls me with him to lie across his chest. I don't bristle at all. In fact, I curl into him, inhaling his scent into my lungs.

My eyes grow heavy. The adrenaline kick I got after bonding with Ares seems to have been a one and done kinda thing. It might have had more to do with the fact that I thought I'd killed him than the actual bonding.

Ares takes the seat I was mostly in moments ago and opens his laptop. Good. He's giving us a few minutes before calling. With his thigh almost under my butt and Dante's heart under my head, I absorb a feeling of wholeness I didn't know I was missing. If it's like this bonded to two of them, what will it be like once it happens with all four?

Ares is typing on his computer when I hear a woman's husky voice call out "*Ciao!*" My eyes pop open to see a beautiful, dark-haired woman waving vigorously from the open laptop. A man's face pops up next to her, and she leans over to make room. I bolt upright, worried they could see me draped over Dante.

"Hey, son!" the man calls. "A call on Saturday afternoon? We haven't had one of those in ages." All lightness in his tone disappears when he asks, "What's wrong?"

"Why would you assume something is wrong just because I'm calling my dear parents?" The man scoffs, Ares's charm completely ignored. "William, your son is in trouble." His face disappears from the screen, but not before the woman tsks him.

Her thickly accented voice admonishing him as she scolds, "Stop it. My boy isn't in any trouble are you, *Tesoro*?"

"No, Mamma." His accent elongates the word. If I hadn't heard it myself, I would have accused anyone who repeated Ares's words of being a liar.

She clucks her tongue again, not looking at the camera. Another man bends to view the screen and his eyes narrowed much like I've seen Ares's do. This must be William.

"You always assume the worst," Ares doesn't hide his grin, "and even though that's usually the case, it isn't today."

The other man returns, both of their faces looming next to Ares's mother. "Where's Dante?" I see her search the screen, but Ares is zoomed in close and his shoulders fill the space.

"He's here." Ares jerks his head over in our direction. I wipe my face off, and pat down my hair, he could have given me a little more warning.

"Hi, Mamma," Dante calls, and that's just adorable. Dante's accent is not nearly as pronounced, but I'm going to tease both of them mercilessly about it. Ares sets the laptop on the table and leans back, so all three of our faces are visible.

She sees Dante first, her face splits into a huge grin. "Dante—" She barely gets his name out before her pretty mouth falls open. "*Dimmi?*" she demands, her voice just above a whisper.

"*Certo,*" Ares answers her question, and I don't even understand.

The woman stands, and then falls back to her seat as the camera goes a little pixilated. "Truly, *Tesoro*. Tell me this is her?" Her voice holds an edge of pleading.

Instead of answering, Ares says, "Mamma, this is our Laura. Laura, I'd like you to meet our mother, Rosa." I lock my eyes on the screen awaiting her reaction.

Rosa's voice is dead calm when she demands, "Malcolm we need a plane."

"And our fathers," Dante cuts her off, "Malcolm and William."

"William," Rosa calls out, like he's not standing right next to her.

Grabbing hold of his sleeve, she stares up at him. "I need a plane." Rosa looks back into the camera. "No, Ares, you come get me. *Velocemente.*"

Ares shakes his head. "Mamma, I can't shadow walk you here from Italy." He tells her like he just told a child Santa isn't real, all delicate and sweet.

"You must. I need to be there. See, I told you we should have stayed." Rosa switches over to Italian, and her words are rushed. William runs his hand over her shoulder and shrugs at us through the screen in a *what-can-you-do* gesture.

"Mamma," Dante calls. "Mamma!" he tries again. Rosa looks at him, her face pinched into a frown. "Mamma, would you like to say hello?"

Rosa slides him a glare, and if I thought she was talking fast before, her words are a blur now. Dante winces and sits back to let his mom ream him out. I keep my mouth firmly closed, there is no way I want to be on the bad side of this fiery woman.

Reaching over, I grab Dante's hand, and as her eyes track the movement, her words stall. Her gaze finally lands directly on mine. Rosa sucks in a deep breath. "Amanda?" I startle hearing my mother's name from a woman I've never met. Ares leans forward, his face filling the screen again, and all traces of lightness are gone from his tone. "You know her mother?" He sounds accusatory.

I watch Rosa's head bob around the screen as she tries to get a better look at me. "Is she Amanda's daughter? But that cannot be. Ares, let me see her." Ares leans back, and he wraps his arm around the back of my neck, his fingers touching his brother's shoulder. Dante squeezes my hand, reminding me he's here as well.

"Dio, you look just like her," Rosa mutters, her eyes eating up my face. "How can it be?"

"Mamma, do you know something about Laura, about her mother?" Ares's voice isn't as harsh, and he almost sounds like he can't believe what's happening.

"I had no idea." Rosa's fingers lift to cover her mouth, and a look of absolute horror covers her face as her eyes grow glassy.

"Mamma," Ares snaps, "do you know what's going on, or where her mother is?"

"No, *Tesoro*, I haven't seen Amanda in," Rosa's eyes lift to the ceiling, "almost eighteen years when I helped her escape Leon."

Her words hit like a lead weight. She helped my mother escape who? And eighteen years ago? That would have been right before I was born. It's Ares who finally speaks. "I need you to tell me everything you know."

"Not like this." Rosa looks around, like someone might be listening. Both of her men are standing by her side and she reaches up, grabbing their hands. "I'll be there soon; do not let her out of your sight." With that ominous warning, the screen goes black. The only problem is I don't know if she was warning them *about* me or warning them *for* me.

Ares slams the lid of the laptop down and springs up from the couch. I can sense his frustration. Now that he knows someone has information, he's going to go crazy until he knows everything. He spins on me. "Did your mom ever mention a Leon?"

I shake my head no on instinct, but I'm trying to think back, did she? "Not that I can remember."

Dante pulls me in close, and Ares is stomping around the hotel room like the floor personally offended him. He stalks over to the sofa and I sink into Dante. I'm unfamiliar with this side of Ares, he's angry and maybe even a little volatile. The lights in the room dim, casting long shadows on the carpet.

Ares drops back onto the couch and opens the laptop. The left corner is a mess of black spider webs when the welcome screen pops up. "Shit," he curses, and it looks like someone dripped paint behind the glass, but most of the screen is still visible. He enters his password quickly. Moving his fingers on the trackpad, he highlights one of the lower icons.

It pulls up another login screen. He pounds the keyboard harder than necessary. Once his information is accepted, he hits a pull-down menu with a tiny magnifying glass. He types the name Leon into the search bar before hitting enter.

Several items pop up, all with the name Leon, and he scrolls down quickly, only glancing at the information beside each name. "This is ridiculous; there are one hundred seventy-two Leons. It will take me days to run these down. By that time, they'll be here."

Taking a chance, I reach out and place my hand on his shoulder. Ares flinches, but relaxes under my touch. His head falls forward into his hands. "Now we have something to go on, it sounds like your mom might give us some answers." I hope he sees that as a good thing.

Ares turns his head, looking at me. "It also means my mom might have something to do with why you've been living out of a fucking RV your entire life." He says the words like they taste bad in his mouth, like he couldn't think of a worse fate than that. I take my hand back, feeling hurt for some reason.

If Ares sees the hurt splash across my face, he ignores it, instead choosing to pace again. Even without any pants, he's still intimidating. Coming to an abrupt halt, Ares digs his phone out of his front pocket. Putting it to his ear after hitting one button he says, "Hey, doll, I need your help." He looks at me, but quickly averts his gaze. "Yeah, I need you to perform your magic." I listen to the one-sided conversation, growing angrier by the second. There's not a hint of anger or frustration in his tone. In fact, he sounds flirty. I would bet my last hundred dollars that I know who's on the other line.

"I want you to log in to the Infinity database—yeah, you know all my information. I'm looking for someone specific, but I can't remember his last name." Dante tangles his fingers with mine.

"Right, so the name is Leon." He pauses and listens. "Yeah, I know there's a lot of them, but that's why I'm asking you. You're the best at getting me what I need." I bristle, because he doesn't even have the decency to leave the room. I know exactly what he's doing: he's using her to get what he wants. But it still infuriates me to hear him talk to someone like that, to use that teasing voice.

"You can rule out anyone under thirty—no, make that twenty-five. Give me any information that's listed on their pairs, whether they have them and their names." Ares turns his back to me, he lets out a low chuckle and adds, "You're the best... anytime."

I dig my nails into my palm, well past angry and into the furious zone. Dante drops his head to my shoulder, his hand still in mine, but he's no longer trying to distract me. He knows Ares went too far. We all do.

Ares puts his phone back in his pocket, and he still hasn't turned to face me, but I don't think I even want him to. He'll look at me with those dark pleading eyes, and I'll feel like I'm overreacting—that what he did wasn't so bad and that I should just let it go.

"We'll see if anything comes up in the next few hours." I don't say a word to acknowledge Ares. After a few more seconds of him stalling, he eventually turns around. It's not like there's much else for him to do, we're stuck in this room that I thought was huge a little while ago, only to discover it is truly small.

Ares doesn't take the seat next to me, he doesn't sit at all, but instead he busies himself by looking over the laptop, like it's even a concern. He could probably buy two a day. "Are you going to pretend that didn't happen?" I question him when I can't hold it in any longer.

"What?" His tone is already defensive.

"So, I see you are."

"I needed something done, she's my employee. I asked her to do it." Ares crosses his arms over his chest looking down at me. I, however, don't feel the slightest bit intimidated by him.

"You call all your employees 'doll'?" I tilt my head to the side like it's a real question. Ares opens his mouth like he might respond, but I cut him off. "You realize that's sexual harassment, right?"

Ares's face darkens. "We've been working together for years, she wouldn't claim sexual harassment," he scoffs.

"Oh, is that how you always address her? Or is it just when you're using her for something you need?" I make finger quotations around the word need. "And what a list I'm sure she's accumulated over the years."

"Are you actually pissed about this?"

"Oh, I'm more than pissed about it. You think it's okay to treat people like that, especially someone you act like you care about? That's a bunch of shit. If it's something she's paid to do, you ask her professionally. Not like that." I wave my hand, getting madder and madder.

He opens his mouth again, but I keep going. "You're using her, there isn't anything about it that is okay." I stand up, pushing into his space. There's no way I'm backing down. If he's willing to talk to her like that with me standing right here, what else is he willing to do to get what he wants?

Ares throws his hands up in the air. "You're right. I knew exactly what I was doing, and exactly what to say to get her to do what I wanted. I will not apologize for it, because it would be a lie. If using her helps me protect us, then I'll do it every time."

"Where do you draw the line, and at what point will it be too much?" I'm yelling now, leaning closer to Ares.

"Never." He tips his chin up. "Think about that, Laura. I'm not some superhero, nor do I have any illusion I'm the white knight. I'm the one who does the dirty work. The one who will always put our family first. If it takes me hurting someone else to do it," Ares shrugs, both his jaw and eyes hard, "then so be it."

I take a step back. "At what cost, Ares? We could have sat here all afternoon and gotten that information. She doesn't have magic powers that make her better with a computer—not that I'm aware of, anyway," I scoff.

"Laura," I look down at Dante, his eyes are still a little droopy. "He knows where to draw the line, Ares would never do anything to risk you, and what you mean to us." How could he know what I'm thinking? I thought I had every confidence in Ares after we bonded, but apparently that's not true because hearing him talk to Mia like that brought back a wave of insecurities.

"Says the guy who kissed another girl a few days ago," I snap. I'm being defensive, and I know it. Dante lowers his head, my razor tongue succeeded in shaming him into silence.

I spin on my heels, heading over to the windows across the room, feeling horrible for lashing out at Dante, but too embarrassed to apologize like I should.

Peering through the gauzy curtains, I see the busy street below. People are coming and going from several hotels and loading into waiting cars parked on the street. Some have wide smiles as they chat with friends. How many of them are actually happy, not just plastering on a smile because that's what's expected?

I've been pretending myself, pretending that not knowing what happened to my mom isn't killing me a little bit every day. Pretending I don't feel guilty when she isn't my first and last thought.

The guys have been taking up a lot of my time and energy, which is both good and bad. Good, because I can't dwell on the fact that my mom is missing, and bad, because I feel guilty for going on with my life. Cradling my forehead in my hands, I take a deep breath. I should be relieved, feeling a push of excitement, determination—anything—with this new information. Instead, I'm too worried to get my hopes up, because I think it's going to be another let down. Frankly, I'm scared it may lead to answers I'm not ready for.

Ares and Dante give me space, and neither of them tries to fill my head with false hope or promises that everything will be okay, for which I'm grateful. The quiet grows oppressive within minutes. I want to apologize to both Ares and Dante, but I don't really know the protocol. Mom and I never really argued, and I've had little experience with friends. I glance over my shoulder and see Dante sprawled out on the couch, his large frame taking up the entire sofa. Ares isn't in sight, but the door to the bedroom area is open, so I'm assuming he's in there.

Making up my mind, I walk over to Dante and take a seat near his hip on the edge of the couch. His eyes open slowly, and he gives me a half smile. That's all the permission I need to tell him, "I'm sorry I snapped at you."

He doesn't tell me it's okay, instead he says, "It happens."

"Are you feeling okay?" I run my hand through his hair and Dante sighs.

"Very okay." He snuggles back into the sofa, his arms reaching out to pull me onto his chest. I lay there with him for several minutes—half on the couch and half off—until his breathing has evened out, and his body has gone slack with sleep.

That was the easy one. Dante was probably a lot more forgiving considering we just bonded. Ares, on the other hand, is going to require a lot more finesse. I'm still mad at him and think he should be the one to apologize, but I can be the bigger person and admit I was wrong, too.

I tap on the open door lightly, not wanting to wake up Dante. I know Ares won't be sleeping. He never sleeps during the day. "You don't need to knock," he rumbles.

Rounding the door, I close it so it's just barely cracked. I spy Ares leaning against the headboard, his knee kicked out to the side as he looks at the laptop on the bed in front of him. He glances up at me, his eyes scanning my face.

"Sorry," we both blurt at the same time.

I sag a bit, relieved that this won't be some big fight or an awkward apology where I'm the only one who admits I did something wrong.

Ares stands up from the bed and walks closer to me and there are still several feet between us when he stops. He places his palm behind his neck and squeezes. "I, uh…" He stammers, before admitting, "That probably wasn't necessary." Ares looks down at the ground then back up at me. "Asking Mia like that." He winces like he hates admitting it.

"I could have tried talking to you about it, instead of being so sarcastic." I study my striped socks against the carpet.

Ares steps closer and he bends his knees, so I can see his face. I peer at him from under my lashes. He moves fast and wraps his hand around the back of my neck, pulling me into his chest. I curl into the embrace, wrapping my arms around his waist.

"Was that our first fight?" My voice comes out a little muffled from his chest.

Ares chuckles. "I don't really think that qualifies as a fight, sweetheart."

"Then let's never fight," I decree, like it's possible for people to never argue.

"Okay," he sighs, like he feels exactly the same way.

CHAPTER 16

ilo enters the room first, and he's all smiles, holding a large wooden plaque in his hands. I readjust my legs so my feet hit the floor. I've been curled up with Dante on the sofa for the past half hour. He's been asleep, but he wrapped his arm over my waist when I lay down next to him.

Ares is sitting on a desk chair near the window; he's been working on creating his own list of Leons since we literally kissed and made up an hour ago. It's getting harder to pull myself away from him every time he touches me. Knowing it was just he and I in the room, with Dante asleep on the sofa a few feet away, helped cool me down. I know I'm not ready for the next step, but I'm so very close.

Ollie piles in after Milo, wrapping his arm around his

friend's neck and squeezing their faces together. "We got an MVP in the house!" Ollie hollers and makes some barking noises.

Milo's cheeks flare pink, but his grin is wide. "Knock it off." He shoves Ollie away, setting his plaque on the table near the entrance. His parents aren't far behind, and Linda comes in, rubbing his shoulder as she passes.

"Did you guys decide what we're doing this evening?" Matt asks, stepping up behind Linda. She leans back into him and reaches her hand out to grab Phil's, like it's the most natural thing in the world. I scan my eyes over them, checking for signs of jealousy or any indication that one of them isn't happy, but I can't find any evidence that they're bothered by the arrangement. Will that be us one day? I look over at Milo and Ollie still near the door, completely comfortable with each other, and at Ares who has turned to see the room. Dante's eyes are now open, and he's watching Ollie tease Milo with a little grin.

I realize—for the first time—that it might be possible. Watching Milo's parents together has made me understand that this isn't just some fantasy, we could have what they do. My eyes meet Ares's gaze, he's been watching me. In that moment I understand what he meant when he said he would do anything to protect us. I would, too. He tips his chin down and gives me a lazy wink; it's like he knows exactly what I was thinking.

Dante sits up behind me, stretching out his long body, and

he groans on a long exhale. "How did it go?" His voice is low and raspy from not being used in a while. There are several things I like about Dante, but his voice has to top the list. I shiver but play it off like I was just repositioning myself.

"It was fine, same as usual, a bunch of jocks stuffing our faces while the coaches take all the credit for our hard work." Milo walks over to the small dinette set near the mini fridge and plops down.

"They harassed Milo about school again." Ollie rolls his eyes, choosing to head to the sofa. He plants a kiss right on my lips then throws himself on the couch, dislodging Dante and me.

After righting myself I look over at Milo's parents, wondering what they'll think about the PDA. Either they didn't see or don't care, since no one is looking at me like I shouldn't have let him kiss me.

"I took care of dinner, we can just give them a call when we head home so they'll know when to deliver it. Oliver, I figured you might want to call your parents, we talked to ours while you guys were gone."

Ollie groans from behind me, but peeking at him, I see the easy grin on his face. "I'm going to get hell for not telling them sooner. Just so you know, Ares, I plan on telling my mom it was all your idea." It sounds vaguely like a threat.

"I assumed," Ares answers dryly.

We spend another hour or so in the room. I don't think anyone is in a hurry to stuff ourselves back into the car for the ride home. Ollie tells us little stories about all the athletes and their families to keep us entertained, while Ares continues to work on his laptop. Milo's parents took up seats with him at the table not long after coming in. It's been so much easier than I could have ever imagined meeting his family. I can only hope meeting the others will be just as pain free.

Ollie called his dad from the room and told his family Ares was throwing together a little congratulations dinner for Milo and wanted them to be there. I hope they like surprises, 'cause they're sure in for one.

EVENTUALLY WE DO pile in the Suburban. Ollie, Dante, and I are in the back, with Milo, his mom, and Ares in the middle, and Phil and Matt up front again. I keep my legs tucked in close to give the guys as much room as possible, but I'm actually more comfortable back here than I was in the middle row. I think it has more to do with me being next to Ollie and Dante, and not sitting next to Linda, than the ride itself. Lowering my head to Dante's shoulder I let the low conversations and the smooth ride lull me until I'm almost asleep.

I EXCUSE myself to Ares's room not long after getting home. Being around all these people for any length of time is exhausting, and half of them aren't even here yet. Mia greeted

Milo's parents like old friends. There are no awkward, stunted conversations or behavior with her—she fits in with them like she was meant to be. That might actually be more about me being petty than the truth, but that's how it feels seeing her ingratiate herself with them all so easily.

I know I won't have much time before someone comes looking for me. Ares said dinner should be here soon, but even a few minutes alone is better than sitting there feeling like an intruder among these people who have known each other forever.

"Hey, bae." Ollie enters the room without knocking. I lift my head off the bed, staring him down. "Yeah, I didn't think that one would fit," he says without an ounce of regret.

"That has to be the stupidest pet name I've ever heard, *bae*," I scoff, dropping my head back to the bed melodramatically.

"Uh oh, someone is cranky," Ollie singsongs. He grabs hold of my foot and slides his thumb up my instep and I squirm. It doesn't really tickle, but it feels funny.

"I'm not cranky." My voice sounds like a pout, even to myself.

Ollie chuckles with my foot still held captive. "It's okay, I'd get crabby, too, if someone deprived me of my awesomeness all day."

Peering up at his cheekiness, I can't help but grin. "You got me," I confess. His hands warm up as he circles the bottom of my foot with his thumbs. Ollie bites the corner of his lip, the silly banter evaporating as the atmosphere shifts.

"If this is too much, tell us."

I look away, feeling guilty about leaving them. "I'm just not used to being around so many people, well, people who are focused on me, anyway. I'm used to blending in, disappearing."

Ollie's hands begin to move higher up my foot until he's circling my ankle. "Honey, I don't think you ever disappeared. You might have wanted to, but people always notice you, even if you don't realize it."

Ignoring his comment, I fold my arm over my eyes and sigh, letting his magic hands and fingers knead away my worries. Ollie lifts my leg higher, and I feel the bed dip as he kneels on the end. My calf lands on his shoulder as he continues his heated massage up my leg. If I were sitting up, my mouth would be hanging open and I would be drooling—it feels that good.

When he squeezes just above my knee, I moan. I hadn't realized holding my thighs together in the car could make me sore. "Feel good?" Ollie asks, his voice low.

"God, yes," I answer, before realizing how dirty it sounds. Ollie flattens his palm on the back of my leg and slides it down to the mattress. He digs his fingers in a little and slides them back up behind my knee. When his palm shifts a little, going to the inside of my thigh, I open my eyes slowly and pull my arm away so I can see him. His lips are parted as he watches his hand move over my leg. He stops again, right before his fingers touch me, and I think the little sound I let out is disappointment.

Ollie's eyes jump to mine, and this time his eyes remain locked with mine as his hand moves down again. Instead of pulling back when he almost reaches the apex of my legs, his hand stills there, all warm and filled with so many possibilities. I feel the pressure of his palm lighten as one finger traces up the center seam of my jeans.

The door bursts open and Milo is standing there, his eyes jumping from my leg up on Ollie's shoulder to his hand, which is now back to massaging right above my knee. He swallows thickly. "Hey, guys, Ares sent me. Dinner is here, and so are your parents." For a second, I lie there frozen, unsure of what Milo is thinking.

Ollie gives my leg one last pat. "All right, princess, time to put your game face on."

I sit up straight, reaching back to swat him across his stomach. "Don't call me princess, either."

"Okay, swoppsies."

I groan out a long-suffering sigh, although I appreciate Ollie trying to lighten the situation. Chancing a look over at Milo, I find him giving Ollie a little elbow jab in a playful sort of way. My relief is swift.

"Are we really doing this whole pet name thing? 'Cause I can live without it," I tell Ollie as I rise from Ares's low bed.

Ollie wraps one arm over Milo's head and comes to me with an open arm. I fall in beside him while he walks between us. "Of course, I need a special name for you, dumpling, you're my little pooh bear."

Milo actually groans at that one. "Jesus, let's go." I wrap

my hand around Ollie's waist but grab onto Milo's shirt at his side. He looks over at me, like it might have been an accident, and his face flushes pink when I don't let go. I could really get to like this.

NOT TOO SURPRISINGLY, meeting Ollie's parents turned out being relatively easy. When they noticed Milo, Ollie, and I walk into the dining room, none of them batted an eye at our group. One of his dads, Adam, sent a wink in our direction while Scott gave Ollie a hug, with me and Milo still at his side. None of them questioned what I was doing with the group, and from the look on Ollie's mom's face when he told her that I was their Synergist, I don't think it even crossed her mind I could be more than a casual girlfriend or acquaintance.

It took a bit of convincing for her to believe I was, in fact, who he'd said. "Oliver, if you're lying about this..." His mother, Carolyn, warned. I don't think she even knew what to threaten him with; he doesn't even live at home at this point.

"Seriously, Mom, do you really think I would lie about this?" Ollie drops into the chair shaking his head. "I mean, this," he waves his hand around, encompassing the entire room, "is kind of a big deal."

"It's not like it would be the first time. Remember Hawaii?" Carolyn crosses her arms over her chest and looks down at Ollie.

His cheeks flush bright pink. "I didn't tell you I found our

Synergist. I just told you I thought I would find her if we moved to Hawaii. Did you ever live in Hawaii, Laura?"

I can't hide my grin. "No, can't say I have."

"Well, look at that, your motherly wisdom was right all along," Ollie deflects, sucking up to his mother at the same time.

"It's really nice to meet you, Laura." I turn to see one of Ollie's fathers behind me. "Scott," he introduces himself, while Ollie and his mom share a little banter. I glance between Scott and Adam; there's no way for me to know which one is his biological father.

"Hello." Crossing one arm over my stomach, I wrap my fingers over my elbow. I don't know if I should shake his hand or what. At least with Milo's mom, Linda, all the guesswork was taken away, but it seems like Ollie's family might be better at giving me some space to adjust.

"I'm assuming there's a reason we've never met before, and how it's possible that you seem to be the same age as the boys, yet I've seen nothing about you in the directory?" Scott's keen eyes assess me. There's nothing but curiosity there, no mistrust. But he's looking at me like I'm a puzzle he has to figure out.

"I think Ares and the guys could explain it better than I could. I didn't even know about any of this until I met them at school."

Scott's head tilts. "How peculiar." Straightening, a smile stretches over his face as he adds, "I can't wait to get to know you."

Adam drops his arm over Scott's shoulder. "Hey there, short stack."

I've never really thought of myself as short, I'm pretty average at five foot six. Ollie's mom comes over before I have a chance to respond. Her eyes scan my body, lingering on my face. She squints briefly, but then her lips lift into a kind smile. Now I see why I can't find much resemblance to his dads, Ollie looks just like his mom.

Without an ounce of reservation, Carolyn leans in and wraps her arms around me. She doesn't squeeze me too much, and she releases before I have to decide if I should hug her back. "Welcome to the family, Laura." And it's that simple.

Being in a group this large, I'm able to mostly sit back and observe. Linda and Carolyn are obviously friends, since they sit next to each other and chat easily. There are too many conversations going on to make out what they're talking about, but I thought I heard Carolyn mention work.

"Are we eating or what?" Milo questions, his hand over his stomach like he's starving.

"Go ahead," Linda waves dismissively at a long table against the wall filled with several silver chafing dishes of food. Needing no further direction, Dante and Milo each grab a plate and lift the lids off the containers. A spicy scent hits the air, and my mouth waters. They reveal small bites of seasoned chicken and ground beef, followed by pans of Mexican rice and two types of beans. Once all the lids are off, I'm near drooling. It looks like they had an entire Mexican restaurant menu delivered, and I'm not complaining.

Ares pushes a plate in my hand and ushers me behind Dante. I fill my plate with so much yummy goodness, I need both hands to hold it as I walk over to my seat. I take the open spot between Milo and Ollie, my eyes eating up the food before I even have a chance to taste it.

"Mia," Carolyn calls out. I look up to find the two women embracing for a long second. Mia doesn't have any problem returning her affection.

Linda's eyes meet mine; I secure a mask of indifference over my face. I'm pretty good at pretending not to care, so I don't think she questions my act at all.

"Did you come to celebrate with us?" Carolyn asks, her smile wide.

"Oh, I don't want to intrude. I just wanted say hello," Mia replies coyly.

"Nonsense, sit. Have you met the lovely Laura?" Carolyn waves a hand in my direction. "We're just so lucky the guys found her."

"We've met." Mia's voice is tight, but her acting skills are even better than mine because her smile doesn't waver. "I haven't been back here very much since we moved to the city." Mia glances at Ares. "Tell me what you guys have been up to?"

I ignore her and their conversation as Mia takes a seat. Carolyn moves over so Mia is between herself and Linda— and directly across from me.

Dante's hand lands high up on my thigh. He squeezes but continues eating. Once everyone begins eating, the room conversation quiets down. Little topics pop up about the food, and Linda asks Milo about school, but it's all pretty light.

Pushing my plate away, I rub my stomach, already regretting the second helping. "Have you heard from Rosa, or do you know when they'll be in?" Linda wipes the corner of her mouth with a cream, linen napkin.

"I would assume they'll be on the first available flight, knowing her. But no, I don't have any specifics," Ares tells them.

Scott steeples his fingers, his elbows resting on the table. "I don't know about you guys, but I'm dying to know how this happened. Laura, you said you didn't know about Infinities?"

Glancing around, I find almost everyone's attention is on me. Squirming in my seat I look over at Ares, hoping he understands that I'd rather one of them explain. His chin dips enough so I know he gets it. "It would be easier if everyone were here, but it could be a few days before my parents arrive, and we don't have that kind of time." Ares leans back from the table, doing a quick survey. "Mia." She jolts like a little lapdog excited for her owner's attention. "I'm sorry, would you mind giving us a few moments?"

Her face falls, but she's quick to recover. "Of course. Linda, Carolyn, it was great to see you. We should catch up soon." After a brief hug for both of the women, she's out the door, her head held high as she goes.

Ares looks over at Milo's parents. "We already talked a little bit about Laura's situation, so I'm sorry if this is redundant." Focusing now on Ollie's parents, he explains how

Dante first met me at school and that I knew nothing about the Infinities.

Once he broaches the subject of my missing mom, Carolyn's face falls into a heavy frown. "How long has she been gone?" she questions, directing it at me.

"Several weeks now."

Carolyn makes a sound of censure. "Ares, you should have come to us sooner."

"You may be right. When I spoke to my mother, she seemed to think she recognized Laura; she called her 'Amanda'. Is that name familiar to any of you?" he asks them all, but focuses on Linda and Carolyn.

"Amanda, you say?" Linda looks over at me, her eyes narrowing like she's thinking back. "I don't think so—nothing that rings a bell." Her shoulders bunch up like she's sorry she can't be more help.

"She also mentioned a Leon." Ares considers the men a little more closely.

Adam's face twists up in a sneer. "Only one Leon I know of, and he was bad news."

Ares perks up a bit at his declaration. "I get the feeling they may be one and the same. Who is he and what is his name? Where can I find him?"

"You can't. I'd say he's been dead for sixteen years." Adam tilts his head and nods. "About that anyway." Adam looks around and sees he has everyone's attention. "You all know the story. I can't believe you guys aren't remembering this."

"What story?" Dante rumbles, his voice thick from not having used it much over the last hour.

Adam rolls his eyes. "You know, the cautionary old tale of not eliminating the competition."

"You mean the guy who killed his pair and tried to take his powers?" Ollie asks sounding stunned.

"You guys really don't know about this? Huh, I thought all parents told it to their kids." Adam rubs his fingers over his mouth.

"Can you just tell us?" Ares's tone is too demanding to be an actual question.

"I did, it's that simple. A guy found out about his pair, decided he didn't want to share his Synergist, and killed him trying to absorb his abilities somehow. No one really knows what he did, or if they do no one talks about it, but I know whatever he did almost killed him and the female."

"But you said that guy is dead, right?" Milo looks between Ares and Adam.

"Yeah, pretty sure it had to do with what he had done, and we're not really designed to handle more than one ability."

I open my mouth ready to ask what he means—I already have several—but with one look from Ares, I snap my lips closed.

"He was actually erased from the directory," Scott adds. "I didn't think it was a good idea at the time, but every-one wanted to forget what he had done, make like it had never happened."

"What about the female? What happened to her?" Dante

wraps his arm around the back of my chair, his fingers rubbing my shoulder.

Adam looks over at Scott. "I don't know. I don't think anyone ever really talked about it." Scott shakes his head like he doesn't have a clue either.

"Do you think she was my mom?"

CHAPTER 17

*I*t's the only conclusion I can come to, well, that makes any sense anyway. If that guy really did something like that, and it involved my mom, it could explain some of her behavior. If she didn't know he was dead, she had good reason to always be hiding and moving us around.

Hell, she probably thought she was protecting me all these years. I mean, I knew she thought she was, but I never really believed there was an actual threat. It would also explain why she never told me about being in an Infinity. She didn't want me to go through what she did.

"I'm not sure, *Cara*, but we'll figure it out." The conversation dies down quickly. No one here has any real answers, and we need to wait until we talk to Ares and Dante's parents to really know anything. Even then it'll only be an assumption.

Without my mom to confirm the information, it's still just a guessing game.

But there's something else that's bothering me. After we've all said our goodbyes for the evening—some awkward in my case—I ask the question that has been making me doubt everything I think we've learned. "Ares." He hums a response, distracted. "If Leon is dead, and we think my mom didn't leave on her own…" I let the subject sit for a moment.

"Then who took her?" he finishes my question for me. Apparently, I'm not the only one unconvinced.

"Yeah. Who took her, and why?"

I'm up early Sunday morning. I've lain in this bed for as long as I'm physically able, and I need to get up. All the guys are still sleeping, so sneaking out of bed shouldn't be an issue, especially since Ares sleeps like a log. Inching out of the covers, I lift my leg over him and crawl away. He doesn't even stir.

The closet door slides open soundlessly as I grab a pair of jeans and a long-sleeve t-shirt. The guys said Maggie had my shift covered yesterday, but there's no way I'm leaving her hanging for a third day. I hope one of them is up in time to drive me to work, I would hate to have to wake them. It's been such a crazy few days.

Leaving the lights dimmed low, I start the shower and do my morning business while the water heats. Stepping under the spray I let out a heavy sigh. It wasn't long ago when just taking a shower would have been a big ordeal. The luxury of having indoor plumbing is something I will never take for granted. I wash my hair first, wanting to let the conditioner sit while I wash and rinse my body.

I linger under the spray much longer than needed, just letting the hot water cascade over my back and neck. When I finally step out my fingers are a little pruned, but I feel more relaxed than I have in a few days. My bond with Ares and Dante is complete. I haven't had very much time to get comfortable with what that means, but it's almost like I don't need to. They're now part of me, and I'm part of them, but it doesn't feel strange. It finally feels like I'm headed in the direction I was always meant to go.

With a fluffy black towel wrapped around my chest, I wipe the fog and condensation from the mirror. I'm probably leaving streaks behind, but I don't really care. When the glass clears enough and I can see my blurry reflection, I expect to see some physical change, some evidence that I'm not the same girl I was just a few weeks ago, but I don't. My hair is a little darker, but it's still dripping wet so that's no surprise. My cheeks might be the slightest bit fuller, which also makes sense because I've been eating three meals a day, if not more. But those aren't the changes I was looking for. I'd expect that something as profound as finding your pairs and bonding to them would change something deep within you, and it has. I can feel it, it's just not visible.

As I'm heading over to grab my clothes, I hear a light

tapping on the door. "Yeah?" I call out quietly. Instead of an answer, the door pushes in. Dante is standing there all scruffy and sweet looking, with his hair all mussed up and his eyes hooded with sleep.

"Gotta go," he mumbles, shuffling right past me to the little alcove with the toilet. I turn around to give him privacy, but it doesn't seem like he needs it. Seconds later I hear him relieving himself. A little giggle escapes. I've been peeing next to strangers my entire life, but nothing has ever felt this intimate. The toilet flushes and I pretend like I haven't been standing here in a daze since he walked in.

I feel Dante's heat as he nears me from behind, and his big hands run down my sides to the end of the towel. "You're supposed to wash your hands, you know." I'm not really bothered. I know he was touching himself to go to the bathroom, but it's not like he peed on his hands. Dante makes a low growling noise, and his heat is gone as he moves away to wash his hands under the faucet. He doesn't even bother drying them before coming back and dropping his sopping-wet, freezing-cold hands onto my shoulders. I suck in a deep breath and try to squirm away. "I was just kidding," I plead.

"Too late." Dante leans in and runs his nose along my shoulder; his lips trace the water droplets he left behind while his hands go to my waist. "Why are you up so early?" I let my eyes close, between his kisses and that deep voice of his, I'm a total goner.

"Getting ready for work."

"Anything else?" Dante continues over to the crest of my

shoulder, moving around to stand in front of me, and his hooded eyes meet mine.

"I went to bed kinda early," I hedge

Dante cups my shoulders. "I want to make sure you're okay."

I look over his shoulder to glance at his reflection in the mirror. He's wearing a thin blue shirt and boxer briefs. It would be easier to distract us both, maybe make out a little bit before anyone else wakes up, but I know I need to deal with all the crap happening. If I don't, I'm bound to lose my shit at the worst possible time. "I'm confused," I admit, not really sure what else to say.

"About what?" Dante grabs my hand and tugs me over to a bench seat that I thought was more for decoration than actual sitting. Dante lowers himself into a sprawl, his legs stretched out far in front of him, and his back curved against the wall.

Tucking my towel tighter against my chest, I sit next to him. "I don't know, it just seems like there's so much going on. All that stuff with Leon might actually explain why my mom did a lot of the things she has, but not everything. We don't even know any of that stuff for sure yet. I keep asking myself why she would come back here." I pause and look over at Dante. "If your mom really helped her escape that Leon guy, why would she come back here? That's the part that doesn't make any sense. She's been hiding us for years, only to bring us right back to the place she ran from, and before she disappeared, she told me she thought this was where we belonged, like we could actually live here and not have to move."

Dante wraps his arm around my back, and he lets out a heavy sigh. "I'm not sure. Maybe she found out that Leon was dead and thought it would be safe to come home, if this really was her home."

Dropping my head in my hands I let out a frustrated groan. "See? I need answers, but I just keep coming up with more questions."

Smoothing his palm over my back, Dante pulls me a little closer. "We'll figure it out, Laura, we need a little more time."

We fall quiet for a few moments until I shiver from only being wrapped in a towel. Dante stands and pulls me with him, grabbing both of my hands. "Why don't you get dressed, and I'll see if I can scour some breakfast for us." He drops a tender kiss on my lips that I'm sure he wasn't expecting to go any further, but I reach for him when he begins to pull away.

Wrapping my fingers around the back of his neck, I hold him in place. Dante stills under my hands. I love that I have that effect on him. Leaning up on my toes I deepen the kiss, pushing my lips against his roughly. He returns the kiss with just as much fervor. His hands go to my waist and he lifts me, my toes are barely grazing the floor as he walks us over to the wall.

Once I feel the coldness on my shoulders, he sets my feet back on the ground, and then spins me around so I'm facing away from him. I gasp, the quick movement catching me off guard, but he leans his body into mine, trapping me between his hard body and the unyielding wall.

Dante lifts my hands and spreads them out to our sides, and his knuckles fold over mine. His knee goes between my legs securing me even more. "Laura," he rumbles my name against my ear. I push my hips back against his as my answer. I have no idea what I'm asking for, but my body seems to know exactly what it needs.

Dante rolls his hips against me, and I feel his hardness on the back of my leg. He kisses the back of my neck and shoulders so slowly I think I might go insane with want. Every time his lips linger, my heart rate goes faster until I'm breathing in short little pants.

The pressure of Dante's knee between my legs disappears, and I feel his hips rock against me again, but this time I can feel his erection between my legs as he pushes against me. Arching my back more, the towel rides up. There's not much between us, only his boxers and my towel, which will not be in place much longer if his hips keep swiveling like they were made to undress me.

My heart skips a beat when he releases my hand and his goes immediately to my hip. Dante's fingers bite into me as he squeezes me tightly. I use my free hand as leverage to push back against him even harder. He makes a low sound in his throat, something between a purr and a growl, and he licks my back from the top of the towel to behind my ear. As he rises, he pushes his hips up into me.

We're fused together as tightly as possible without actually being joined. Now, just his hips move as he holds me in place. I feel something building inside me, my muscles coiling tighter as I reach for the one movement that will bring me over the edge.

"I've wanted to touch you since the first time I saw you," Dante whispers right behind my ear. I sigh, his voice taking me even closer to the edge. My skin begins to heat as a flush rushes over me. It feels like my body is covered in tingles, small tremors of delight coursing through my system until everything is centered right between my thighs. The feeling is almost too much as a wave of pleasure crashes over me. I cry out against the wall, my body loosening almost immediately as smaller waves of pleasure crest over me.

Dante makes a low groaning noise right behind my ear and, tangling his fist in my hair, he pulls, forcing me to arch more against him. His movements slow and his weight releases me from the wall. His hands move to my hips again, this time holding me up for a different reason. My legs feel like jelly, and I'm pretty sure if I stepped back the towel would hit the floor.

When my arms feel like they'll be able to move without trembling, I grab the edges of the towel, holding it so I can secure it. Dante smooths his hands over my back and hips, making sure the towel is straight. It seems silly after what we just shared, but I enjoy the feeling of him running his hands over me anyway.

"Let's go get back in bed." Dante's voice is a rasp as he

peppers my exposed skin with little kisses. I feel him use his tongue, flat and wide as he licks over my neck and shoulders.

"I can't, I have to work." My voice is husky, too.

"Call in," he demands, turning me to face him again. I scramble to fix the towel, but he leans down and kisses me with gentle strokes of his tongue until eventually he pulls back.

"I can't call in." He knows I can't.

Dante sighs. "I guess I should get you some breakfast then."

"Thank you," I whisper, and not just for the offer of food.

Dante gives me a quick peck and slinks out the bathroom door. I stand there frozen for a few moments thinking about what just happened before grabbing my clothes to get dressed.

Ares, Ollie, and Milo are still asleep when I exit the room, or I thought they were anyway. As I pass by the side of the bed, Ares reaches out, cuffing his hand around my ankle. When I peer down at him his eyes are dark, not fully black, but close to it. "Mornin', *Cara*." His hand glides up the inside of my leg. How long has he been awake?

"Why are you up so early?" I drop to the bed at his hip keeping my voice in a low whisper.

Ares crooks his finger at me, motioning for me to move closer. I lean down, my chest against his side. "I heard this noise." Ares makes a deliciously low sound. "That sound would wake me from a coma, *Cara*. I want to feel it." Ares skates his fingers up the column of my neck until they wrap around my throat. That sated feeling I had evaporates as Ares continues to whisper, "Want to hear you call out my name while you make that sound." I squirm next to him, not sure what to do about the lusty feelings he's provoking.

Ares's hand goes under the blanket to the center of his body, my mouth goes dry as I track the movement. Could he be touching himself? My eyes leap up to his, then over a few feet to where Milo and Ollie are sleeping.

Ares chuckles. "Just making adjustments." Swallowing thickly, I bite my lower lip. My heart is beating like a hammer against my chest. Ares's pupils expand even farther as his head tilts to the side. "Oh, sweetheart, what I wouldn't give for a few hours alone with you right now."

"Hours?"

Another low groan sounds from Ares as he closes his eyes. "Dante said he was driving you to work, I'll be there to pick you up this afternoon."

"Uh, okay." The change of topic throws me for a brief moment.

"We're going to need to talk to Maggie about you not working so much."

I bristle. "I need to work, and I'm not just going to bail on her."

"Laura, I'm not asking you to bail on her, but we have a lot going on. It would be better to cut your schedule down now than to leave her hanging when we need you here." Ares runs his hand over my leg soothingly. "My parents should be here today or tomorrow. Who knows what we might learn, what other stuff we might be dealing with?" Ares licks his bottom lip. "We also need to work on your abilities; we need to make sure you can control them."

I hate that he's making sense. I've been working for years, and I don't know what I'll do if I don't have something other than my mom to focus on. "I'll talk to her," I admit, sounding defeated.

"I don't want it to upset you." Ares tucks a long strand of hair behind my ear; it's still a little damp, since I was trying to let it dry a bit before braiding it.

My shoulders droop. "I don't mean to be pouty about it. It's just jobs aren't always easy to come by when you don't have a home address or telephone."

"I can't believe I haven't thought to get you a phone," he states absently. "You have a home address now, and I'll get you a phone today. Getting, or even having a job now isn't an issue."

"But I didn't have those things, not when Maggie took a chance on me, and I don't want her to think I don't appreciate that." In a more serious tone I add, "If I want a phone, I can buy one, I have some money." I've been taking care of myself for a long time.

Ares actually rolls his eyes at me. "I don't even need to buy one, I didn't turn in my last phone after an upgrade."

Milo stirs, so I lower my voice again. "I have to go."

"Don't leave right away, I want to talk to Dante. I'll meet you in the kitchen." Ares pulls me down to plant a hot kiss on my lips. I barely have time to return his affection before he's pushing me away and getting up from the bed with me still lingering where he was lying just moments ago.

"You start that, and you won't be going into work today." Ares saunters into the bathroom, leaving me to stare after him.

I FIND Dante in the kitchen leaning over the stove. "Hey," I call to announce myself. "Ares said he wanted to talk to you before we leave." Glancing at the microwave, I note the time.

"Okay, I made us some eggs." Dante tilts the pan, pushing some scrambled eggs onto two plates already waiting on the counter. Taking a seat at the island, Dante puts one plate in front of me.

"Oh my." The words pop out before I can stop them. The eggs are still runny, not even what some restaurants would call soft.

"What's wrong?"

"I think these need just a few more minutes in the pan." I grab his plate before he gives himself salmonella. Dumping both plates back into the pan I turn the burner on low.

"I was trying to hurry," Dante tells me, a little dejected.

"It's okay, Dante, just a few more minutes and they'll be all good. Did you already put salt and pepper in them?"

"No, I don't really cook much," he admits shyly.

"Well, thank you for trying." I make sure to meet his eyes, so he knows I'm not being sarcastic, or flippant. I really do appreciate his effort. Dante lowers his head, but it doesn't hide the flush on his cheeks "Do you like ketchup on your eggs?" I add, changing the subject.

"Sure, I'll grab it." Dante pops up from the stool and heads toward the fridge. Ares steps through the doorway already dressed in a black thermal shirt and grey sweat pants. Seeing him like this—all dressed down and comfy—makes me feel special. I don't think Ares allows many people to see this side of him, he's always so untouchable in his slacks and vests. I have to admit, though: I love his tailored wardrobe just as much.

"Did you make enough for me?" I focus back on the stove pushing the eggs around the pan. He's so damn distracting. Grabbing three clean plates from the cupboard, I divide the eggs between us.

"Dante made them; I was just finishing them for him." I bump my shoulder into Dante, sitting in the middle between them.

I eat quickly, keeping track of the time while doing so. "Laura said you wanted to talk?" Dante finishes up his eggs even quicker than me.

"Just wanted to get on the same page. Laura and I spoke about her talking to Maggie, lightening her schedule."

Dante peers at me from the side, like he's wary of my reaction. "And you agreed?"

I huff. "Yes. I get we have a lot going on, but I feel guilty about it. She just hired me."

Dante crinkles his brow. "Laura, you do realize Maggie

has been running that diner forever, and she didn't even really need to hire you when she did."

Placing my plate in the dishwasher, I pause. "Say what?"

"That was why Milo and I were so confused when we saw you there the first time. She hired you because she wanted to, not because she needed to."

My guilt morphs into something else. Did she pity me? Maggie never acted like she was giving me a handout. I worked for everything I earned, and the diner definitely seemed busy enough to need me. I lean my butt against the counter, my eyes going up to the ceiling as I think.

"Don't overthink it, Laura. You needed a job, Maggie gave you one. That's that," Ares states, like he knows exactly what I'm thinking.

I narrow my eyes on him, "And we're sure you can't read minds?"

"I don't need to read your mind, *Cara*. It's written all over your face."

Dante chimes in, "Yeah, an open book." He swirls his hand over his own face but means mine. I roll my eyes and pull a face. Let's see if they can read that one. Dante lets out a burst of laughter.

"What's so funny?" Ollie asks, stumbling into the kitchen. "You guys already eat?" His nose lifts into the air.

"Just some eggs, good morning." I push off the counter. "We need to head out."

"Good morning, sugar tits."

Ares chokes on the bite of eggs in his mouth, spluttering

all over his plate. It would almost be worth it to let Ollie call me that just so I could see this reaction.

"Oliver," I chastise with no real heat.

"What? That one fits amazingly well," he scoffs, like I'm the one being ridiculous.

"Good bye, *boys*," I call over my shoulder as I head to the mudroom for my sneakers.

CHAPTER 18

*M*y shift at the diner drags on. We haven't been as busy as usual. Even so, I wait until my shift is almost over before asking Maggie if we could talk. Closing the door behind her, she guides me into her small office right off of the kitchen. "Maggie, first I wanted to tell you thank you for giving me a chance here, I know it's difficult to hire a girl with no real contact information," I blurt before I lose my nerve.

"You looked like the trustworthy type." Maggie leans herself back against her desk, relaxing a bit.

"Well, it really means a lot to me. I wanted to let you know." I fidget with my hands, now comes the hard part. After being here all day, I still can't wrap my head around her only hiring me because she knew I needed a job. I think she really needed the help, and I feel terrible asking her to shorten my hours. "I also wanted to tell you, that… that I might not be able to work as many hours going forward." Not looking at her, I rush on, "There's just a lot going on right now. I'm not sure I can keep up with everything. And now I basically live with the guys, I don't need the money as badly. I only have a few more months left of school. I don't want to drop out now. I'd rather be working here than going there, but I just can't quit. I'm sorry."

She doesn't respond right away. Lifting my gaze from my shoes, I find Maggie watching me with a curious smile on her face that looks like it's made of acceptance more than anything else. "Are you quitting altogether?"

"Not if you'll let me stay."

Maggie lets out a weighty sigh. "Good. I've gotten used to having you and the boys around."

That's it? I don't know what I expected her to do or say, but it wasn't this easy agreement. "So, you'll let me stay on one or two days a week? I mean, I can cover until you find a replacement, of course." I straighten my back, half expecting her to fire me on the spot.

Maggie's lips twist and she plants her hands behind her on the desk. "A few days a week sounds fine. Why don't we say Friday, and Saturday?" She doesn't seem angry at all; maybe the guys warned her.

I nod, probably too eagerly. "That would be good."

Maggie pushes herself away from the desk, and she comes to stand in front of me. Both of her hands reach out, and she cups my shoulders. "I always knew you wouldn't work here long." She looks over my shoulder, her eyes focused on something behind me. "You guys are on the right track," her eyes start to glaze over as a fog covers them, "but watch out for the one who knows." Her voice takes on a monotone edge.

"Knows what?" My question comes out a little high-pitched. I don't know why her eyes frighten me so badly, but they do.

"You guys back there?" Ares's voice jolts Maggie, and she steps back shaking her head.

"Right here." Maggie releases me, all evidence of her episode gone from her face. I open my mouth to ask her what she meant again, but Ares opens the door and pokes his head into the office. He looks from Maggie to me, then back to Maggie.

"We were just getting Laura's new schedule straightened out," Maggie tells him before he has an opportunity to ask anything. To me she says, "Don't worry about us, we'll be fine. I'll see you after school on Friday." I open my mouth to ask her about what she said, but Maggie tilts her head, widening her eyes a fraction.

Instead I mumble, "Yeah, okay. That works." Still feeling a bit off kilter, I look away from Maggie. It's obvious she doesn't want to talk about the warning she just gave me. Ares pushes the door open, stepping fully into the room. He's eying both of us with what I'd assume is suspicion, but he waits us out, crossing his arms over his wide chest like he's expecting his presence alone is enough to have us squirming.

"Thanks again, Maggie. If you ever need me to cover a shift, all you have to do is ask, anytime."

"Good to know." Moving in she opens her arms, leaning in for a hug. Awkwardly I lean in with my feet rooted to the floor so only our upper bodies touch. In my ear she breathes, "He's not ready to know." Then she releases me in the same moment. Rolling my lips together I lean back, brushing my hands down my shirt and apron.

"Go on now, I'll see you Friday."

Without looking back at her I move closer to Ares, who's still in his *I-know-something-is-up* pose. I grab his bicep and give him a slight squeeze. He doesn't budge right away, and he continues staring Maggie down. "I'm starving, have you eaten yet?" It's only three o'clock, but I didn't take a lunch, so it's not a lie.

Ares's head turns to me and his eyes narrow. I gaze back up at him, hoping he can't read the secret on my face. His arms fall to his side, but he gives Maggie one last parting glance. "Linda and Carolyn both know. My parents should be here soon," he announces while opening the door again for us to exit.

"Good," is Maggie's only response.

ON THE RIDE home Ares keeps looking at me. I keep staring ahead like I'm not catching all his furtive glances. But after about five minutes I begin to fidget, rub the side of my face, and tuck my escaped hair behind my ear. I'm not good at this game. He however, is, and it's on the tip of my tongue to blurt out what she said, but I can't. Maggie said he wasn't ready to know, and I don't want to screw anything up.

"Are there any leftovers?" I finally crack, I can't keep up the silent broody thing he has going on.

Ares purses his lips, since that was not what he was hoping to hear. "You can have anything you'd like." He looks over at me waiting until I meet his eyes. "All you have to do is tell me." I bite my lip. He's making it seem like we're talking about food, but I know better.

"I really liked those chicken tacos. Are any of those left?" I avoid his innuendo.

Ares grunts and tightens his hands on the wheel. "We'll see."

I lean back in my seat as he slows to make the turn into the driveway, and even though it was hard telling Maggie I couldn't work as much right now, I do feel a hefty sense of relief. Knowing I'll have more time with the guys makes it a whole lot easier to appreciate the time off.

Ares brings the car to a slow stop, but he doesn't move to get out or even turn it off. "I will assume that whatever you're not telling me is because Maggie told you not to." Ares turns so his back is somewhat against the door and he can see me better.

I chew on my lip, warring with myself for not telling him. Ares sighs, squeezing his temples between his thumb and other fingers. "I will also assume she has her reasons, so I will *try*," he puts major inflection on the word, "to let this go."

Reaching over, I pull his hand from his face. "It's nothing bad, okay?" My hand is still on his wrist, and I offer the small bit of information, hoping it will ease him.

His mouth tightens, but he jerks his chin down once. The sun is still high in the sky shining down through the sunroof, and shadows dance over his features even as the light bathes him in a warm glow. "What are you looking at?" His question makes my cheeks flush, but I don't look away.

"You." I don't tell him how sometimes I wonder what I did to get so lucky to have him and the others in my life. Without their help I wouldn't have any idea what or who I was. I'd still be in that camper begging for my mom to come back, with no hope of ever finding her.

The corner of his lip curves up. "Do you like what you see?" His cheesy line makes me bark out a laugh, my head thrown back. It's something I would expect Ollie to say, not Ares. He's usually as smooth as silk.

I lower my chin, looking in Ares's direction when my peal of laughter subsides. He's leaning over the center console and his face is only a few inches from mine. Any lingering giggles die on my lips when he leans forward and seals his mouth to mine. Ares kisses me like he wants to steal my breath from my body with hungry little nips of his teeth, while stroking his tongue with mine.

My heart picks up to a steady gallop. The low console between us feels like an obstacle I want gone. It's keeping me from getting as close to him as I want, keeping him from getting as close to me as I need.

As if he knows exactly what I'm thinking, Ares slides his hand under my arm and lifts, pulling me over. Thankfully, the SUV interior is roomy, and with his help I crawl over. With the steering wheel at my back, I straddle Ares's thighs, never breaking the kiss.

Having him under me changes the dynamic of our kiss. I've never been the one to dominate a kiss with him before, he's always the one in control. With the roles reversed, I place my hands on his wide shoulders, and my hands trace over the thick muscles that lead up to his neck. Lowering myself onto his lap, Ares makes a low groaning noise. His hands tighten around my waist as he drags me even closer. My breath leaves in a heavy pant as our chests fuse together. There isn't an inch of space between us, and I wouldn't want it any other way.

My nose brushes against his as he tilts his head trying to deepen the kiss. I can already feel his hand traveling up my back, and I know right where it will land. Ares's palm settles on the back of my neck, his fingers tilting my head so he can hold me in place. Slitting my eyes open when Ares moves his lips down my neck, I see his inky lashes fanned over his cheeks and the tip of his tongue as he delivers a lazy lick up the side of my throat. I tilt my head back to give him better access, but I catch a glimpse of our surroundings.

We're sitting the driveway, a few steps from the side door where anyone could walk out at any moment. "Ares." My voice cuts through the fog and I curl myself against him. His hips lift from the seat as he grinds up against me. "Ares." His name is a breathy plea, but I'm not sure if I'm trying to get his attention or beg him to continue.

He hums a response, his mouth still on the side of my neck. He's not showing any sign he cares where we are or who might find us. "We should probably go in." I can't dampen the pout from my voice.

He groans again, but not the one I like—the sound that makes my toes curl. No, this one is born of disappointment. Ares's forehead hits my collarbone, and I run my hands through his hair, enjoying the feeling of him clinging to me.

"Give me a minute." His voice is gravelly as his hands go to my hips, and he squeezes me, halting my movements.

Scooting back a few inches, my lower back hits the steering wheel. "Sorry." I wince, because I told him we needed to stop, but my body had other ideas.

Ares peers up at me, the darkness receding from his eyes, shrinking back down to dilated pupils. "Why are you sorry?"

Pursing my lips, I widen my eyes then glance down at his groin where his erection is still obvious between us. "Um, I know that getting excited and not, um… uh… finishing can be painful?" It definitely comes out more like a question. I've heard more than my share of guys complaining about girls who are teases and the effects of blue balls.

Ares traces his thumb under my eye, and then over my cheek. "*Cara*, there aren't, nor will there ever be, any expectations between us. No matter how far we go, or have gone, you can always tell me to stop. There isn't a point where there's no turning back." Ares pauses; he's looking at me with an intensity I don't quite understand. "Do you understand what I'm saying?"

I lift my shoulders. "That you're okay making out?" Ares is older than the other guys, and I know he has experience with sex, everything about him oozes sensuality. If I'm being honest, it's part of the reason I'm more comfortable being with more than one of them at a time. There's a comfort knowing none of them will try anything with the others around.

Ares clears his throat. "Yes, I'm absolutely fine making out, but it's more than that. My reactions to you are my own; you're not responsible for sating me." I bite my bottom lip, this is the first time I've had any conversation about sex, and it's a little awkward.

Ares's eyes close slowly, and when he blinks them open, he exhales a heavy breath. "Let's head inside." Leaning around me he hits the button to turn off the car and then opens the door.

As easy as it was to climb on his lap, it's just about that awkward to climb out the driver's door backwards. My leg gets stuck over Ares's thigh, so I end up jumping on one foot until I can pull free. Finally, setting both feet on the ground, I straighten up and run my hand over my braid.

Ares reaches for my hand the moment he gracefully steps out of the SUV. I look around the drive, noting Mia's car is missing from her usual spot again, but that doesn't mean she's not here.

Ares notices my gaze and squeezes my hand.

"She here?" I ask.

"She was when I left to come pick you up."

"Where's her car?" Stepping up on the porch he pushes the door open, waiting for me to enter first.

"Don't know. I didn't even think to ask." Ares doesn't bother taking his loafers off, but he gives them a few extra wipes against the rug.

I kick my sneakers off and use my toe to line them up near the wall. "Finally! What took you guys so long?" I hear Ollie call from deeper in the house. Does he know how long we were sitting in the driveway? I peek back at Ares, and he gives me a slow wink.

Making my way to the kitchen, I find the guys all lounging in the living room area. Dante tracks my movements as I head toward the sink to wash my hands. I'm starving, so I waste no time rummaging through the fridge to find the leftovers I've been thinking about all day.

"Anybody hungry?" I call with my head still half in the fridge.

"Always," Dante answers from much closer than a few moments ago. Startling upright, I glance over my shoulder and see he's standing right behind me. "Hey," he rumbles, his eyes running over me like it's been days instead of hours since he last saw me.

"Hey, I'm going to warm this up, you want some?" I offer, lifting the silver tray filled with the small bites of chicken from last night.

"Sounds good, let me help." Dante takes the pan from my hand and sets it on the counter. With my hands free I have the urge to close the distance between us. Feeling braver since our bonding, I take a step in his direction. Dante looks at me, his brows raised. Wrapping my arms around his waist and completely invading his space, I lay my head against his chest.

Dante's arms come around me without hesitation. He dips his head to mine and inhales deeply. His body relaxes while squeezing me tighter. Before, I hadn't really realized the comfort a hug could provide—my mom was never big on affection—but it's quickly becoming addictive.

Leaning back without letting go I look up, and Dante gives me a sweet smile. "I'm glad you're home."

"Me, too, but I'm starving, so let's warm this up."

"I'll take a cuddle," Ollie interrupts, not even giving me a chance to release Dante as he pulls me from him and spins me around. "Hey, sweet cream." I roll my eyes but let myself be hauled against his chest. "Milo, come over here. Let's make a cookie." Ollie chuckles as Milo approaches me from behind. Hesitantly, he places his hands on my hips and leans his head near my shoulder. I thought Ollie's joke about making me a cookie sandwich was funny, but now that I'm in between the two of them, my humor evaporates. Heat rises up from my chest. "Switch," Ollie calls out the warning before he spins me in his arms so I'm facing a wide-eyed Milo. Ollie doesn't have an ounce of reservation as he smashes me against Milo's chest and seals himself to my back.

I think that it's only Milo's natural ability for strength that keeps us all upright. If Ollie put this much weight against me alone, I'd be a pancake on the ground. My breath leaves me on a whoosh as they crush me between them. "Can't breathe," I pant.

Ollie chuckles but steps back. I sag against Milo, not sure if I can hold myself up yet. With extremely gentle hands, Milo brushes his fingers over my cheek. "I didn't know he was going to do that. Are you okay?" Before I can tell him I'm fine, Ollie spins me around again. I'm getting dizzy.

"Oliver," I call out in warning.

"Oh, my God, I've got it!" Ollie exclaims.

Milo, still standing behind me, lets out a low moan before pulling me back to his chest—to protect me from Ollie, I assume. "What now?"

Ollie grabs hold of my cheeks, squishing them together. "You're my little Muenster," is all he says, like that's all the explanation we need.

"Dear God," Dante groans from the counter where he's dividing the chicken, rice, and beans onto two plates.

Unbothered with Dante's reaction, Ollie continues, "Don't you see? The best thing about a sandwich is the cheese, and the best cheese around for a sandwich is Muenster. You're my Muenster." He grins at me like he's waiting for my approval.

I shake my head, but Muenster is way better than a few of the others he's come up with. "I always thought you were cheesy." Ollie's mouth pops open like I've shocked him, but he throws his head back and laughs.

Milo and Dante chuckle along with him. "What's so funny?" Ares questions as he walks into the kitchen. He didn't follow me into the kitchen because he said he needed something from his office, so he missed the whole sandwich discussion.

"You really don't want to know," I tell him, giving Milo's forearm a squeeze before stepping away to help Dante with our food.

"MUENSTER?" It's not the first time Ares has questioned Ollie regarding his new love of the pet name he's bestowed upon me.

"What, and *Cara* is better?" Ollie defends. "So original."

"At least it doesn't sound like I'm calling her a monster," Ares bites back, clearly offended that Ollie is calling him out.

Ollie barks out a laugh. "Yeah, it sounds like you're calling her another woman's name."

Ares snaps his neck to look in my direction. My cheeks flare red. That's exactly what I thought the first time he called me *Cara*. "It means dear, beloved," Ares bristles. I frown, both of them are actually getting upset about this.

"Hey, it's fine, both of you can call me whatever you like." I look between the two of them. Ares's brows are pinched, but Ollie has a smug grin on his face, and he mouths to me *I win* when Ares isn't looking. I click my tongue at him, looking away.

"You guys want to watch something?" Milo pipes up from beside Ollie. We're all still in the kitchen, and I've been done eating for a while, but Dante is still snacking. We all just kind of ended up at the island.

"We could play a game?" Ollie offers.

"I don't want to play video games," Ares interjects.

"No one said it had to be a video game." Ollie looks up at the ceiling like he's thinking. "We could play charades, truth or dare, spin the bottle, seven minutes in heaven."

"Sounds like you just want to take turns kissing Laura." Ares snorts.

Ollie raises his hands in surrender. "Totally not was I was going for, but your house, your rules." He claps his hands together once, like it's been decided.

Ignoring him altogether, Dante asks, "Have you heard from Mom?"

Ares gets a pensive look on his face. "Yeah, Malcolm called. They couldn't get a flight until sometime today, so I'm guessing they won't be here until tomorrow."

Dante nods. "Do you think they'll stay?"

"For a while, probably," Ares responds.

"Should we tell Gloria and have her freshen up their rooms?" Dante's question perks me up. I noticed he said rooms, not room. Do they not all sleep together?

"They might get here before Gloria tomorrow morning. We should do it just in case," Ares answers.

"I can help," I offer, interested in what their rooms are like.

As a group we pass Dante's room and head down a hallway I haven't been to yet where there's a double door with a single handle. Ares pauses like he's gearing himself up to enter the room. My stomach twists with tension from how hesitant they all seem.

"This is weird." Ollie doesn't hide the fact that he's uncomfortable being in Ares and Dante's parents' room. They do, in fact, have more than one bedroom. Three to be precise. There's a large bathroom located off what I would call the master bedroom. The bed in there is almost as big as the one we made in Ares's room. On either side is a smaller room, each with a king-sized bed of its own. Before the bedrooms is a large sitting room with another smaller bathroom off to the side. Something like this would be nice for us, I catch myself thinking.

I'm not weirded out at all; maybe it's because I've never really met Ares and Dante's parents. Or maybe it's because I'm too curious about how they all live together to be weirded out.

"Just grab some clean sheets from the closet and be quiet," Dante orders, and I notice his gaze darting around quickly. I think he's reluctant to be here as well.

"Should we do the other rooms?" Milo's in the doorway; all of them seem hesitant to enter.

"Guys, it is just a bed. Here, I'll do it." I pull back the covers of the tightly tucked blanket and reveal crisp white sheets. "Are we just doing the sheets?" I don't want to throw the comforter on the floor if we're reusing it.

"I saw another set in the closet," Ollie offers before rushing away. I let the blankets and sheets fall to the ground, and Milo hands me the new, pale sheets before stepping back to the doorway right away. I roll my eyes.

Seeing me struggling with the huge bed, Ares finally comes in to help. After helping me tuck in the top sheet, he makes his escape. Dante brings me the folded comforter and matching blanket, his face twisted up.

Throwing my hands in the air I ask, "What is the big deal, were you guys not allowed in here as kids or something?"

"No, we were in here all the time. I slept in that room until I was, like, eight." Dante points to the right, meaning one of the adjacent rooms.

"Then why are you guys being so weird?" My hands land on my hips. I don't understand them. I slept next to my mom until I got too big to share our tiny bed with her.

"It's just different now." Dante shrugs, his face pinched.

"How? It's just a bed—a place to sleep, a place to… oh." I snag the blanket from his arms, tossing it over the sheets. No one says anything else as I finish making the bed.

I find the guys waiting for me in the sitting room area. They're all playing it cool, like they weren't just freaked out about their parents having sex. "Are we doing the others?" I motion to the two other rooms.

"No, they don't use those much." Ares winces with his statement. "Let's get out of here."

Instead of going back to the living room, we all migrate to Ares's room. I change into a soft pair of sleep shorts and a tank top before crawling into bed. It's still early—maybe around seven—but I know once I lie down, I'm not going to want to get up to change.

Ollie and Milo discuss what videogame they're going to play while Dante strips off his shirt and pants, leaving them on the floor—much to Ares's displeasure—and climbs in next to me. His tightly muscled stomach bunches as he leans down, and the feline grace I've noticed before makes more sense now that I've seen him in his shifted form.

"Did it hurt?" I wonder.

"Huh?" Unaware of my thoughts, Dante has no idea what I'm talking about.

"When you fell from heaven, did it hurt?" I roll my lips in, trying to keep a straight face. Ollie snaps his head around, which tells me he was listening.

Dante freezes, like, goes completely still with his hand still poised over the bed. I can't help it, I burst out laughing. Wiping the tears from the corners of my eyes, I laugh so hard it turns to just a breathy, hyena laugh.

"I'm so sorry, it just popped out. I couldn't resist." I tell them through my tears. Ollie lets out a few low chuckles before facing the TV again. "Don't be mad, I was just teasing." I trace my fingers over Dante's dark brows, smoothing them out. He's lying on his side, facing me. His features relax as I continue to run my hand over his face, moving to his hair.

Dante's hair is thick, but silky. His dark brown locks are a little unruly and fall into his light amber eyes. I scoot closer, so our noses are only about six inches apart, sighing as I watch him move into my touch.

"I was thinking how you make everything look so graceful, and that made me think of Dante kitty, and I was wondering if it hurt to make the shift?"

"Dante kitty?" His eyes close as he twists to bump my hand over his head.

"Well?" I ignore his query about my name for his tiger. What else would I call him?

"It doesn't hurt. The first shift did. It was like it broke all my bones and then put them back together, but only that first time." I suck a breath through my teeth. Damn, that sounds painful.

Dante opens his eyes lazily when my hand stills, my fingers still woven into his hair. "I want to kiss you," he breathes, and if I weren't so close to him there's no way I would have heard him, so I hope the others didn't. I still don't know how the PDA will go between all of us. I lick over my bottom lip at the mention of a kiss, and Dante's eyes track my tongue.

The bed behind me shifts as Ares finishes up in the bathroom and slides under the covers. My eyes go wide when Dante lifts his finger and traces it over my still damp lip. With his eyes locked on mine, he places the same finger against his lips, and his pink tongue darts out and curls around the tip.

My throat goes dry as I get a hollow pang in my lower stomach. With his lips still parted, he returns his finger to my mouth. Placing the tip on my bottom lip, he runs the pad over my parted mouth, pushing against the blunt tips of my bottom teeth. I close my lips around his finger, bringing my top teeth down just behind his nail. I curl my tongue around the tip of his finger, biting with my teeth, keeping him trapped. Dante inches forward and his eyes focused on my mouth.

I release him when I think he's going to lean in and replace his finger with his lips. His breaths are heavy and short as he looks down at his finger, my teeth marks clear near the knuckle behind his nail.

Looking back in my eyes, he traces the pad of his finger over his lips then sucks it into his mouth, his eyes closing like he's savoring my taste. I squeeze my thighs together as an ache forms that I can't do anything about, unless I want to go into the bathroom and take things into my own hands.

Ares curls around my back, his big body wrapping around mine. "Night, Ca... Laura." Ares plants a few kisses on my shoulder, his nose nuzzling behind my ear. I catch the fact he was going to call me *cara* and changed his mind.

"Sweet dreams, Ares." My voice comes out a little husky, but he settles in, holding me close.

Dante rolls onto his back, his arm folded over his eyes. I watch his parted lips and the rise and fall of his chest as he takes a moment. I could use a second to settle my body down, too, but with Ares pressed up against my back, I don't have any hope of calming my raging hormones. "Sweet dreams, Dante," I add closing my eyes. Their parents might be here tomorrow when we get up for school, so will Dante stay home? They didn't mention how long they've been gone, but I guess at least a year.

A knot of worry tightens my stomach. What if Rosa really knows something about my mom? I don't know if I should be more afraid of what I might learn or of not learning anything.

Pushing all thoughts of parents and school out of my mind, I let myself feel the weight of Ares's hand on my hip and his warm breath on my neck, grounding me to the here and now. There will be plenty of time to freak about what I learn once I actually know what it is.

Reaching over I lay my palm on Dante's arm. I feel his bicep bulge before he relaxes and his muscle is still firm under my hand, but not tensed. His hand covers mine and that's how I fall asleep. Dante and Ares beside me, with Milo's and Ollie's soft voices filling the room.

MY EYES POP OPEN. I have no idea how long I've been asleep, but the room is pitch black now, telling me everyone else is in bed, too. Something woke me up. I have a moment of déjà vu. Lifting my head from Dante's chest, I peer around the room. I can't see anything, so I close my eyes and think about what I felt when Ares shared his gift with me, the way the shadows danced over my arms, clinging to me. Opening my eyes, I can see the room in scales of grey, and it's still dark, but not the impenetrable darkness from before.

I scan the room wondering if Mia has returned, but the

room is empty. Ares's fingers flex on my hip as I settle back against the mattress. A noise just outside the door draws my attention, and my heart rate picks up although I'm not frightened. I know who's on the other side of that door; I just don't know if I'm ready to meet them while I'm tangled between their sons.

Dante chooses this moment to turn on his side and drop his forehead to my chest, his hot breath pushing right through the thin fabric of my tank top. He actually nuzzles his face against my breast, getting comfortable.

"Just a peek." I hear a feminine whisper as the door creaks open.

"Rosa," a deep male voice chastises, "they'll be up soon, it's Monday," he reasons, and the sliver of light pooling on the bed shrinks. I hold my breath, my eyes wide. Should I pretend to sleep if they come in? They can't fault me for what happens when we sleep, right?

I snap my eyes closed and try to even my breathing when the light flares again. "*Amor Mio,*" her voice pleads, "just a little peek, I won't wake them."

A heavy sigh and the light from the hall pierces the room. I don't move a muscle, and it's almost impossible to sit still when I know she's coming into the room. Remembering to breathe, I force myself to mimic Dante's breaths over my chest.

"What are you doing?" comes another masculine whisper from the hall. "You let her go in there?"

"Like either one of us could stop her—and be quiet! You

will wake them." The two men begin to argue in hushed whispers.

"She's here," Rosa announces like she's surprised I'm with them. Oh shit, should I have stayed in the yellow room? She strings together a rush of words in Italian ending in "*Grazie Dio.*" It's so hard keeping my eyes closed, I want to peek at her, but I'm afraid I'm going to get caught.

"Mamma?" Dante lifts his head from my chest.

"Shh, sleep, *tesoro*, I'm here," Rosa coos, and Dante drops his head back to my chest, not caring at all he's basically burying his face in my boobs.

"Rosa," one of the men calls again, and I sense her retreat. "You should leave them to sleep; you know how Ares struggles." The door closes gently before I hear another reply.

Dante molds his body to the front of mine, his face still level with my chest. My breath catches when his nose bumps my nipple. He freezes and, without moving a muscle besides his neck, he tilts his head back so I can see his face; his eyes are open as he looks up at me. Dante licks over his lips and swallows, his Adam's apple bobbing from the way his head is thrown back.

"You're awake," he rumbles. I nod, not sure of my voice. He reaches down, and his fingers trail up from the side of my knee and over my thigh. His hand stops at the bottom of my sleep shorts. They've ridden up, becoming more like a pair of panties while I was sleeping. His palm flattens, so his fingers wrap around the back of my thigh, right under the swell of my bottom.

Dante pulls my knee over himself, so it rests on top of his leg. His eyes close as he drags in a deep inhale. His nose finds my hardened nipple, and this time I know it isn't an accident. He moves his face back and forth a few times, brushing across my nipple, and the thin material of my shirt scrapes against me, adding to the sensation.

Opening his mouth, he huffs out a hot breath then blows out a cold little burst of air. I squirm and my knee goes higher on his hip. Leaning in, he touches my extended nipple with his tongue through the shirt, flicking back and forth quickly. I try to squeeze my legs together, but I end up rocking against him instead.

Dante is breathing through his nose hard, and I bite my lip, wondering if it'll be enough to wake up the others and praying it won't. Feeling my heart flutter in my chest, I can't tell if I'm excited or scared.

I wrap my arm over his shoulder, and my fingers delve into his silky hair. The fabric of my shirt is damp now from his tongue, and when he blows across me this time, I shiver. Dante's hand creeps up from my leg and he avoids Ares's hand still resting on my hip. His fingertips brush against the hollow of my throat, caressing down until he folds his fingers over the neckline of my tank top. Pulling down the material, it tightens over the back of my neck while he exposes more of my chest. The back of his knuckles brush against my nipple as he works the neckline lower.

My breath catches when his lips seal over my nipple the moment he exposes me. His mouth is hot, and oh so wet. My back arches, pushing my chest harder against him. Dante makes a low sound in the back of his throat, and I feel it rumble over my flesh. With one hand still holding my shirt down, his other hand moves from under his pillow, and he uses his thumb on my other nipple, mimicking his mouth. A tingle of awareness pools between my legs, it's almost like I can feel him there. Dante's lower half rocks against me, and I feel his hard length against my thigh. I want to scoot closer to him, to feel him where the ache is getting harder to ignore, but if I move, I'm afraid I'll wake Ares.

Releasing the shirt, his mouth stays attached to my breast, and the fabric springs back but can't cover me. Dante's hand travels over my stomach, his fingers pointed down as his palm lands over my center. With a hint of pressure right over my clit, and his lips still locked around my nipple, he sucks, and I know I can't last. Tugging my hand from his hair, I bite the fleshy part of my palm, my neck tipping back as I come undone.

Dante rocks his hand against me, making the sweet torture last far longer than I would have thought possible, and my hips jerk a few times when I get overly sensitive. He moves his hand from between my legs up and bringing it up to his face, he licks over his whole palm. Falling back onto the mattress he shudders.

Without an ounce of thought I follow him, clinging to his shoulder so I'm draped across his chest as he heaves for breath. I cock my knee over his waist, and he's still rock hard beneath me. When I shift my legs, he makes a deep, whining sound.

Brushing up against him, my body undulates against his. Dante's hand pushes my knee a little lower, and he lets out a little hiss, his eyes squeezed shut. Pulling back up so my leg drags against his length, his hips swivel.

Knowing what he needs, I continue the movement on my own. Trailing my mouth up over his chin to his parted lips, I kiss him with a passion I didn't know I was capable of, deeply hungry for him. Dante's neck lifts as his lower body goes rigid and he groans, but I seal my mouth over his, stealing the sound. After a few long seconds he grabs my leg tightly, stopping me from rocking against him.

He's still breathing hard, his chest heaving, but so am I. Closing my eyes, I relax against him. He's warm and solid, and I'm perfectly content being his living blanket.

It doesn't take long before Dante is back asleep, his hard body pliant beneath me. I lie there a few more minutes to make sure he's sleeping deeply before pulling myself away from him.

Now that the adrenaline has worn off, and my lust has been sated, all the what-ifs start filling my head. What if someone woke up while we were… I can't even come up with the right word. What if someone did wake up, and I was just too blissed out to know? How would they have reacted? How would I have reacted?

Shaking the thoughts away, I try to pretend like I didn't just hit second base with *one* of my boyfriends, while the other *three* were lying next to us. I decide to take my cues from the guys—it wasn't just me in this bed, Dante was right here with me the entire time. I will assume if he's willing to touch me like that with the others near us, then it's okay, fine. Not slutty, or bad. I'm not even going to let myself think about how it was also exciting and exhilarating, or the way my pulse was pounding against my ribcage. Nope, not thinking about that.

CHAPTER 19

"What do you mean, 'they're already here.' How do you know?" Ares tilts his damp head to the left. He isn't fully dressed yet. His dark trousers are still open at the fly, waiting for his tailored, white shirt to be donned and tucked in, which is still hanging over his little clothes butler. His mark is barely visible, peeking out over the top of his tight boxer briefs near his hip.

I bite my lip; what the hell is wrong with me? I can't seem to look away. Dante is still passed out in the bed, his big body all stretched out looking way too inviting. Ollie, not caring in the least that Milo is in the shower, stumbled into the bathroom a few minutes ago. Ares didn't bat an eye, so I assume it's normal for all of them.

The illusion of privacy only makes it harder not to watch Ares as he slides on a heavy-looking, metal watch—okay, who am I kidding? That thing is probably white gold, or platinum. It's not something he wears all the time, and he struggles with the latch, his lips pinched.

"Here, let me," I offer as I move to him. "Your mom came in the room last night," I answer, finally addressing his question. Flipping over his hand so I can see the underside of his wrist, I fold the latch over easily, and the band clicks into place. I don't release him though. I let my fingers trail over the thick veins roping up his arm. Ares has the sexiest arms on the planet. I think the fact that he's always so buttoned up in his long-sleeved shirt, only rolling them up at the end of the day, adds to the mystique.

"You were awake?" he questions softly, letting me explore.

"I woke up when she came in." The crisp hairs on his arm tickle my fingers.

"I'm sorry she woke you; she's never been patient." The last part comes out with a light chuckle.

"Your dads tried to stop her." My comment earns a snort.

"Like that could ever happen." I glance up at his face. He's clean-shaven and his jaw is smooth. I cradle his cheek as my thumb brushes under his bottom lip, causing Ares closes his eyes and lean into my touch. Tilting up on my toes I kiss his chin. Then I wrap my arms around his waist with my cheek against his bare skin while I let my hands run up and down his back. Without an ounce of hesitation, he winds his arms over mine, pulling me tight against him. Hugs are on the top of my new favorite-things list.

He doesn't jump away or even release me when Ollie comes out of the bathroom, looking a lot more alert than when he went in.

"Can we skip today?" I glance over at Ollie who's waiting for Ares to answer, but Ollie is looking at me with his clear green eyes wide, and his full lips turned down in a small pout. Pulling back from Ares's chest, I peek up at him.

"Don't look at me; he's asking you. I don't care if he goes to school. I just need him to graduate."

"But... I can't say if you go to school or not."

"Sure, you can. If you agree to stay home with us, we don't have to go to school." Ollie swipes his hands together like he's saying easy as pie.

Sagging, I feel like I'm totally letting him down when I say, "I have to go to school. I can't have the administration figuring out I don't have a real home number listed. Or noticing my address. I can't afford for someone to look too closely at my situation."

"Just call in sick," Ares tells me.

I look up at that. I've never really thought of calling the school to tell them I can't come in. "I could do that?"

"Yeah, you can, Muenster." Ollie throws himself on the bed, bouncing. Dante stirs, but doesn't open his eyes. "Skip day," he singsongs while shaking Dante's foot.

"Then shut the fuck up, and let me sleep," Dante growls.

Ollie's mouth falls open, but his eyes get a wicked twinkle. I lean my back against Ares's chest, and he drops his chin to the top of my head. "This is going to end badly," he whispers, but I can hear the smile in his voice.

Dante snuggles back into the blankets, his hands tucked under his cheek. Ollie scoots off the bed and stands near the bottom as he puts his hands on his hips. Ollie's bottom lip thins, and I see his tongue fold, hitting his top teeth. He sucks in a huge breath and lets out an ungodly loud whistle. I slap my hands over my ears, ducking my head on instinct.

Dante jumps up from the bed and takes a swing at Ollie without even seeing him. Ollie isn't quick enough to avoid the blow, but luckily Dante's punch lands on his upper shoulder. Ollie's whistle cuts off as he stumbles to the side. I jerk forwards, but Ares's arms wrap around me holding me in place.

"Why do you do that? You know it kills my ears!" Dante roars. Ollie starts out chuckling but then ends up groaning, his hand clutching over the spot Dante just punched. Dante steps off the bed, his face in a frown as he looks at Ollie, checking him over to see if he did any real damage.

Ollie finally answers his question. "Got you out of bed, didn't it?"

Dante tightens his jaw and shoves Ollie away again. "Asshole," he mutters darkly.

"You been eating your Wheaties? 'Cause damn, I feel like I got kicked by a mule." Dante snaps his neck, giving Ollie a dark stare. Ollie lets go of his injured shoulder and raises his hands with a slight wince, surrendering even though he's fighting a smile.

"My ears are still ringing you fucker." Dante hesitates and then asks, "I didn't really hurt you, did I?" His anger fades, leaving him looking a little sheepish with concern.

"He's fine," Ares answers, though I'm not sure Ollie is fine, he's still rubbing his shoulder. "Quit dicking around. Laura said Mom got in last night. If she knows we're awake, she'll be in here before you guys are even dressed."

Dante pushes his hair away from his face and, now that he and Ollie aren't messing around, I have a chance to take in his nearly naked state. Fitted dark blue boxers are doing little to hide his amazing physique. "Just give me a second to wake up," he mumbles. I turn away from him when I see his hand slide down the front of his body to adjust himself.

Ares brushes his finger over the top of my cheek with a small smirk tipping one side of his lips. Clicking my tongue at him, I head over to the closet to find something to wear for the day.

"Why are you so tired and grumpy anyway? Did you and Ares switch places last night?" Ollie sits near the head of the bed, and his back rests against the wall.

"How about I wake you up with a bucket of ice water and see how you like it?"

"Not in my bed! You guys want to start your prank shit, it won't be in my room," Ares tells them while tucking his shirt in.

"Speaking of *your room,* when are we going to get a more permanent situation set up?" Ollie asks.

"What are you thinking?" Ares tips his chin in Ollie's direction.

"I don't know, I just know it's something we need to talk about." Ollie looks around the room. "What about something like your parents have going on? A few extra rooms close together, and a chill spot where we can relax without someone always being around."

"You mean like Mia?" I poke my head out of the closet, interested in the conversation. I'm hoping my comment leads to Ares telling me when she might move out, but my question goes unanswered.

"Not to mention my parents. Now that they're back, who knows how long they'll stay," Dante adds.

"We could look, but it could take a while to find something we're all happy with. It might just be best to build. Plus, we have security to worry about." Ares is fully dressed when I step out of the closet. My own pair of fitted jeans and sweater are looking a little underwhelming compared to his slacks, shirt, and vest.

"Building would be awesome, but that would take months, maybe even a year before it would be ready. There has to be a better solution than just hanging out in this room until then," Ollie tells Ares, and he seems uncharacteristically serious about the whole thing.

"We'll figure it out. I'm actually pretty stunned Mia is still here anyway. I figured she would have moved, especially after dinner the other night."

I snort, and all three guys look in my direction. Luckily,

there's a gentle knock at the door, which saves me from having to explain my unladylike response.

"Better tell Milo to hurry up in there," Dante mutters as he heads into the bathroom.

I smooth the chunky fabric of my sweater down before taming my hair with my hands. Ares sends Ollie a pointed look, with one brow raised and his chin tipped down, warning him to *be good*. Ares takes one last look around the room sighing before opening the door.

"You're awake," Rosa announces, her voice more chipper than it should be, considering I know she hasn't had very much time to sleep in the last few hours. "Where is everyone?" I see her try to peek her head around Ares from either side.

"*Buongiorno, Mamma.*" Ares leans down and places a chaste kiss on his mother's cheek. A beautiful smile lifts her lips as she pats his back.

"*Saluto, figlio.*" When he leans back, she takes hold of his upper arms and gazes up at him. "*Finalmente*, you smile."

Stepping back from her, he holds out a hand in my direction. "We were coming out to meet you, but I know you've probably been making my fathers crazy trying to get in here."

Rosa swats Ares's arm with the back of her hand. Her eyes go straight to me, and I see a flare of recognition there. Butterflies fill my stomach, not just because I'm meeting her for the first time, but because of what I might learn from her. "You are Mandy's daughter," she says with absolute certainty.

"Mamma, this is Laura, Laura Fallen." He looks at his

mom, waiting for some confirmation about my name, but Rosa isn't paying him any attention.

"Did you know my mother well?" I finally find my voice.

"I thought I did, yes," Rosa replies. I think I'm the reason she used the past tense. She's probably questioning if she ever really knew my mother at all; I know I am.

Twisting my hands together, feeling very vulnerable, I sense more than hear Ollie coming to my side. Rosa and I are still staring at each other with so many things to say, but I definitely don't know where to begin.

"Milo and Dante should be out any minute. How about we head over to the kitchen? Gloria should be here soon. I'm hungry," Ares rambles, filling the silence.

That breaks the spell, and Rosa clicks her tongue, her lips pursed. "I can put something together. Tell your brothers to hurry." Rosa is out the door within seconds without looking back.

"Works every time," Ollie says and offers Ares a grin.

"What?" I ask, confused.

"Implying I'm hungry." Ares gives me a small shrug. "Getting us out of trouble is my specialty. I haven't always been the well-behaved sweetheart you see now." Ares runs his hand over the front of his vest. I know he's teasing, trying to lighten the situation.

Shaking my head and looking over at Ollie I say, "Has anyone ever accused him of being a sweetheart?" I hook my thumb in Ares's direction.

Ollie's eyes twinkle. "Maybe if you're comparing him to the devil."

"Who's the devil?" Milo comes out of the bathroom dressed in black joggers and a t-shirt that looks a little too tight.

"Ares," Ollie and I say at the exact same moment. Our eyes meet, and I can't hold in the giggles that erupt.

Milo gives a curious look but shakes his head. "Dante said we're skipping?" He ignores the whole devil comment.

"Say yes, say yes," Ollie pleads, the puppy dog look back on his face.

I let my grin slip, the gravity of what we'll be discussing today instead of being at school weighing on me. "If you think calling in will work, I guess we could skip today." My tone makes it clear I'm nowhere near as excited as Ollie, but he lets out a whoop and smacks a wet kiss on my cheek.

"Here, you can use this." Ares picks up his sleek phone from the top of the nightstand. As I go to take it from his hand, he pulls it back. "Don't let me forget to get you a phone after we have breakfast." I nod my head, but I don't have any intention of reminding him.

The screen lights up, revealing what looks like a picture of the cosmos, or an oil slick, with the time displayed across the front. "How do I unlock this?" I twist the phone around looking for buttons. Ares cradles my hand and places the phone in front of his face, when he turns it around and I can see the screen again, there are several icons, including a little white phone in a green box.

"It has facial ID, we can add yours in later." Ares is already walking away, gathering things from the room.

"Does anyone know the number?" Dante's out of the bathroom now too, and he's over by the closet getting dressed.

"Got it." Ollie grabs the phone from my hand, and he punches several buttons before handing it back. "Not the first time I've called in sick." He makes a pouty face, and I roll my eyes. He wasn't calling in because he was actually sick.

An automated voice directs me through several prompts before I'm leaving a message on the attendance line with my name, grade, and reason for my absence. I hit the red button to end the call, marveling at how easy it was. For my part, I added a little whine in my voice to make it sound good for whoever listens to it.

None of them seems to be in a hurry to leave the room, but I know it's my reluctance that is keeping us here. After another five minutes passes where the guys are all needlessly busying themselves, I muster up the courage to say, "All right, let's do this."

Dante wraps his arm around my side and pulls me in close. "Laura, we're here, and we aren't going anywhere." I sigh, clinging to his words and his body.

CHAPTER 20

$\mathcal{I}$ can smell the kitchen way before we get near it. The aroma of fresh-brewed coffee fills the air, but as we get closer, I can also smell something sweet and chocolatey.

"*Finalmente*. I made marocchino. Your Papas wanted eggs. Come eat." Rosa is bustling around the kitchen.

Ares and Dante's fathers are lined up at the island, each with a plate of scrambled eggs and sliced meats. They turn in our direction as we enter the room. "Morning, everyone sleep okay?" My face flames bright red because I wasn't expecting them to bring up our sleeping arrangements.

"Good, no thanks to Mamma." Ares's tone is light, making it clear he knows she was in the room, but also clear he's not upset.

"I knew you would wake them," William, the man who looks most like Ares and Dante, mutters as he returns his gaze to his unrepentant wife.

Rosa shrugs a delicate shoulder, her face impassive. She wipes the counter with a washcloth, pushing any stay crumbs into the sink and hanging it over the side after giving it a rinse. She's fairly tall, taller than me maybe at around five foot nine. Her dark hair falls over her shoulders in soft waves, and she's curvy—nowhere close to fat, but definitely thicker than what I would call thin. She turns, giving us her full attention. She has Dante's full expressive lips, but her eye color is all Ares's tawny brown.

"My boys," Rosa sighs, her arms stretched out wide as she waits for them. Dante heads over to her first. He wraps his arms around her back after she leans up to kiss his cheek, throwing her arms over his shoulders. The guys all leave me, forming a line so she can greet them, cooing in half Italian, half English. I stand awkwardly near the doorway.

Malcolm pushes back his stool and heads over in my direction. Ares's eyes track his movements, but he stays over with his mom. Malcolm reaches out his hand when he's standing in front of me. "Hello, Laura."

Accepting his hand, I return his gaze and shake. "Hello, sir."

His lip lifts at the corner, but he covers it quickly. "You can call me Mal," he offers. He doesn't look like someone you'd call Mal. Ares may get his dark hair from his mother, but he must get his fashion sense from his father. Malcolm, or Mal, is dressed much like his son, only he's wearing a tie, and he skipped the vest for an unbuttoned suit coat. It's barely nine o'clock in the morning. Now I really feel underdressed. "It's a lot to take in, huh?"

I swallow, because it is, more than he probably knows. I didn't even know what I was a few weeks ago. "Yes, you could say that."

"I remember meeting Rosa's parents, and William's." He leans in a little closer fighting a small smile. "I assure you, you're doing just fine."

I take a peek over at the others, wondering when they're coming back. "It's definitely a new experience."

He chuckles. "I bet it's a little more unsettling than meeting your boyfriends' parents."

I scrunch my face in confusion. "Aren't *you* my boyfriends' parent?"

Mal tilts his head. "I just meant a regular boyfriend, not your pairs."

"Oh, I see." A flush spreads across my face, and I can't believe I even said that out loud. "Well, I've never had one of those so…" I try to recover, but I think I made things more awkward.

"William," Mal calls, saving me from myself as he greets his pair—partner? I'm not sure what they call each other. I make a mental note to ask the guys.

"Thought I'd come say hi before Rosa gets hold of you."

My eyes bulge out at his announcement. "Not like that, I mean, once she has you, she's probably not going to let you go." William winces. I think he has a case of verbal diarrhea as well. "Hell…" William brushes his hand down his pant leg and extends it to me. I accept the shake, but he pulls me in and wraps his arm around my back. After a quick couple of pats, he releases me.

I blink up at him owlishly. Did that just happen? Is it possible that he is just as awkward as I am? William's brow is furrowed as he looks down.

"You're just standing there letting this happen?" Ares's voice floats over in our direction. I look over and see Malcolm with his hand covering his mouth, trying to hide his smile.

"Just be thankful you learned how to treat a lady from me and not him." Malcolm chuckles while pointing at William.

"Dad, did you really just give her a bro hug?" Ares sounds positively scandalized. That's the exact moment I can't hold in any more of the tension. A laugh bursts free from my mouth as my shoulders shake. Leaning forward, I laugh way too hard, but it's not just the bro hug, or his awkward words; it's everything.

"Great, now you broke her," Ollie chides, stepping over to my side. I swat him with the back of my hand, trying to calm my laugh, but every time I slow down, I imagine William's face after he hugged me.

"Quit giving your papa a hard time," Rosa admonishes, stroking her hand over William's shoulder. He looks down at her, and any residual awkwardness disappears when he gives her a saucy wink.

Clearing my throat as the last of the giggles melt away, I meet Rosa's gaze, and she scans my face before looking into my eyes. "You look very much like your mamma, Amanda."

"I never really thought so, she... she's had a tough few years."

Rosa takes my hand in hers and her grip is gentle as she asks, "Can you tell me about her?"

I was the one expecting to ask questions, so it catches me off guard. Opening my mouth, I catch Dante's gaze, and he nods.

Rosa insists on making eggs for the guys and me. Ares and Milo went and got a couple more chairs so we can all be in the kitchen while she prepares the food. I get my first taste of what Rosa calls a marocchino: it's coffee with chocolate and milk. Finding out how to recreate the drink has become a new priority 'cause, damn, it's delicious.

Rosa pushes a plate in front of me, and the eggs are soft and fluffy with a few pieces of thinly sliced meat off to the side. As the others begin eating, she turns so her rear is leaning against the counter. "Tell me about you, about your mamma. Where have you been all these years?"

That's a loaded question. I can't even remember all the places we've lived. "We traveled a lot," I tell her.

"Laura and her mother lived in a motor home," Ares interjects. Rosa tilts her head as she tries to envision what Ares is talking about.

Pulling the sleeves of my shirt over my fingers, I drop my hands to my lap. I haven't really talked about my mom much, not even with the guys. I don't really know where to begin. "My mom, she struggled with a lot of things, and it only got worse the older I got." I think back to the times when I was younger, when my mom would actually go out of the camper, get dressed in something other than sweatpants and a holey t-shirt.

"I can't believe she has been running this entire time," Rosa says almost to herself.

"Do you know why she was running, or from who?" I latch onto her words, needing to know the answers, especially if it will help me find her.

Rosa takes a deep breath. "How about I tell you about the Amanda I knew, and you can tell me about the one you know." Rosa smiles, but it doesn't reach her eyes.

"Yeah, okay," I agree easily. Seems like we both only know half of the story anyway.

I'M SITTING in a chair and Dante is on the arm of the chair next to me. The rest of the guys have taken seats around the room. We haven't been in here before, it's much more formal than the rooms we've hung out in so far. The furniture is heavy with thick patterned fabric and wood accents. There's a huge stone fireplace taking up almost one entire wall—you'd have to have a small mountain of wood to fill it—and the stone extends up to the ceiling, making it seem even larger. Several seating areas are dotted throughout the room. Ares and Milo are to my left on another sofa, while Ollie has opted to sit on the floor near my legs. He's not touching me, but he's close. I appreciate the support.

Rosa and her men are all on a couch across from my chair and they look completely at ease with each other, something I envy at this stage of our relationship. Before I can ponder too hard what it was like for them when they first met, Ares pipes up, "Who was Leon?"

Rosa closes her eyes but takes a deep breath. "Until recently I haven't thought about this in years." William places his hand over Rosa's, and she gives him a small smile in return. "I met Amanda by chance. I had taken Ares to the park one day, and there was this lovely young girl there. She was with a little boy herself. I still didn't have very many girlfriends here, especially one with a little boy. We chatted while the boys played, and by the end of the afternoon we had exchanged numbers and planned to meet again in a few days."

"Who was the little boy?" I can't help but ask. Do I have an older brother out there somewhere?

"I think his name was Teddy, it turns out she was just babysitting him for the summer while she was out of school, but we met up a few more times for playdates with the boys." The emotion that filters through me isn't quite relief, but it's something close. I don't know how I would handle finding out my mother hid even more from me.

"I don't remember him," Ares mutters.

"Well, you were young; you only played with him a few times before Amanda confessed to me that she was a Synergist." Rosa looks to the left, a frown falling over her features. "She had heard Ares talking about his papas—as in two—and asked if I had remarried. I didn't want to lose her friendship, but I wasn't willing to lie either, so I told her I had two husbands. Her face lit up, and she asked me if I were in an Infinity." Rosa's lips lift with a small smile.

"After that I knew why I was always drawn to her, our lives aren't always easy—especially when outsiders judge us. That's why so many groups choose to settle close together, so we have people around us we can share our lives with who won't judge us."

"So, she knew what she was?"

Rosa looks over at me, her eyes shrewd. "Yes, of course."

"Laura's mother never told her what she was, never told her about Infinities," Dante announces, brushing his hand over my back.

"But..." Rosa opens her mouth, her words failing her.

"My mom was... withdrawn at best, paranoid to say the least. She seemed to get worse as I got older. I wasn't allowed to have friends, or to do anything that would draw attention to myself. We moved around a lot, and it got to the point where she never even left the RV." I sigh as guilt for thinking she was crazy eats at me. If she would have only talked to me, told me the truth... I don't even know if I would have believed her. I probably would have thought it was just her delusions. Ares makes his way over to the chair, taking up a seat on the opposite arm of his brother.

"She probably thought she was protecting you," William adds.

"She always told me that there were bad people, people we were hiding from, but she never told me who. She made it like a game when I was little, but as I got older, I thought she had problems, you know…" I look down, not meeting any of their gazes. "Like mental problems, but I still loved her. I took care of her," I defend, but I can't even convince myself. Did I try hard enough; listen to her enough?

"We know you love her, *Cara*, no one blames you for not knowing." I let Ares's words settle over me, but they're not true. I blame myself. I should have tried harder to understand her.

"If there is anyone to blame, it would be me," Rosa tells me, looking right into my eyes. "I'm the one who convinced her to upload her information in the database; I'm the reason Leon found her."

Mal objects immediately and argues, "Rosa, you couldn't have known. Finding your Infinity is a blessing, you were trying to help her."

"Well, look how that turned out." I can hear the beginning of tears in her voice, but none fall from her eyes. Rosa's back is straight as she looks at me like she's ready to accept any punishment I have to give.

I look away. Could things have been different if she hadn't

interfered? I shake away the question as soon as it forms, there's no point in dwelling on the what-ifs.

"Why don't you tell us about the real person to blame for this, Leon." Ares leans down and grabs my fingers, placing them on his thigh.

"Leon Whitmore," Rosa says the name like it tastes bad. I expect to feel something hearing his name, but I don't. It's no more familiar than any stranger's. "He took less than twenty-four hours to track Amanda down after we uploaded the information about her and her identifier." Rosa pulls her hand out from under William's. "At the time, we thought it was amazing. Amanda had only turned sixteen a few months earlier, and here she was finding one of her partners. Leon was older, already in his early twenties, from a well-established family out West." Rosa stands then, like she can't bear to talk about this while she's sitting.

Walking over to the fireplace, she sets her fingers on the high mantle and looks into the empty hearth. "Amanda was smitten with Leon the moment she laid eyes on him, we all were." She looks over at her pair with a sad smile on her lips. "He seemed to be just as taken with her. I was sad that I was losing my new friend, but we made promises to talk to each other, even visit since her family was still near."

"I have a family?" I can't keep the shock from my tone, and maybe even a little hope is there, too. Maybe Mom is with them.

Rosa's shoulders fall, "You did, *bella ragazza*."

"Jesus Christ," Milo curses from the couch, his hands balled into fists over his thighs.

"What happened to them?" My voice sounds detached, but I can't help it. Until this moment I never even let myself believe in the possibility of a family. If we had them, then surely we would have been with them.

"Leon." Rosa spits the one word like it's enough of an explanation.

Mal looks over at Rosa then leans forward so his elbows are on his knees. "Amanda stopped returning Rosa's calls," he tells me, saving Rosa from speaking. "We didn't think too much of it at first. They were newly paired, and it can be overwhelming at first." He looks away clearing his throat.

"Anyway, after a few weeks with no word from Amanda, Will and I tried to get hold of Leon to see if we could get the girls together for a visit or something. Leon took our call, but he was... dodgy." Mal looks over at William who nods in agreement.

"He said it wasn't a good time, that Amanda had a lot going on with setting up their new house and getting to know everyone out there. We didn't like it, but we accepted it. We knew it would make Rosa sad, but what could we do?"

"Time passed, and I made new friends—Linda and Carolyn were new to the area, so I lost track of my old friend." Rosa's words are edged with guilt and I can hear the regret in her voice. She turns to face me then, her eyes wide, and she twists her hands together. "I should have known something was wrong."

In the next second, Mal is up from the couch with his arms wrapped around Rosa's shoulders. William watches them, longing in his eyes, but instead he turns to face me. He's letting Mal comfort Rosa so he can tell me more of the story. Voice pitched low, like he might spare Rosa from hearing, he says, "What we didn't know, was that Leon had tried to get his and Amanda's information removed from the directory. He didn't want to have a pair, but it was too late. There was another man, Wyatt, who had already found the information." I squeeze Ares's hand as I sit forward on my seat.

Rosa pulls away from Mal. "Let me," she tells William, returning to the couch. "Only Amanda and Leon know the whole story, and she never told me the details. But we know something happened between the three of them. Leon did something to Wyatt, something that was intended to take his abilities and get rid of him."

"I don't understand. Why would he want to do that?" I look at Dante, and then Milo and Ollie who are not far away on the couch. "I thought you said it was different, that pairs don't feel jealousy toward each other?" I don't mean for my words to come out like an accusation, but they do.

"We don't Laura; I've never met another pair that has ever felt that way," Ares tells me, his eyes searching mine to see if I believe him.

"Laura, it was Leon. I can promise you, nothing like that has ever happened before, or since," William adds.

"So, he was, like, crazy or something?"

"That's all we can assume." Rosa lifts her hands at a loss

for more answers. "I know Amanda called me one night, frantic about something that Leon had done. I could barely understand her, she was so upset." She looks at the fireplace, her eyes glazing over with the sheen of tears.

Taking a few moments to compose herself, Rosa wipes a delicate finger under her eyes and takes a deep breath. "She came to me for help, but there was only so much she would let me do. She was afraid of what Leon would do if he found out I was the one to help her. She wouldn't tell me where she was, or even what Leon had done, I just knew she was desperate to get away from him."

I sit forward on the chair, eager for any information she can give me. "So, what happened? Did she come back here? How did you help her?"

"Not much." Rosa looks over at William, and he gives her an encouraging nod. "I gave her money, but she would only take cash. I gave her everything I had, and she wouldn't stay until I could get more. I begged her to stay with us. I promised we would protect her, but she wouldn't. She was terrified of Leon by the time she ran away from him."

"So, she came back here then?" I mutter, almost to myself. Thinking back on how my mom said this was where we belonged, was she really ready to stop running?

"She did. She was only an hour away when she called, that's why I didn't have much time to gather anything for her. She wouldn't even stay the night with us." Rosa tips her head up to the ceiling before meeting my eyes again. "It was dark, but she looked horrible. She was too thin. She had dark circles under her eyes. I knew something bad had happened, but she only told me that Leon was dangerous, and made me promise I wouldn't ever go near him. I begged her to go home to her family, to stay with us, but she wouldn't. She said if she stayed, she would only put us in danger."

"Did she have a plan, or tell you where she was going?" Ares questions, running his palm over my back, reminding he's here with me, and so are the others.

Rosa is shaking her head before he can even finish the question. "No, if she hadn't been desperate for the cash, she wouldn't even have come to me. I told her I would get more money, that when she was safe to get hold of me, and I would get it to her, but I never heard from her, and then, your grandparents..." Rosa covers her mouth and buries her face against Mal's chest.

William pinches the bridge of his nose, a heavy sigh falling from him. "After Amanda disappeared, it was like nothing happened. We didn't hear from her again. Leon was still out West; I know because I checked up on him."

"It wasn't until the fire two years later that we learned what had really happened." William places his hand on Rosa's leg. "Leon had somehow managed to strip Wyatt of his abilities. Apparently, it killed Wyatt in the process, and Leon was injured as well, that was when Amanda came to us." The information isn't exactly new, but it's still shocking to hear.

"Leon hadn't given up looking for Amanda, he went to her family—your grandparents." He pauses and then cautiously continues, "They think it was an accident, that things got out of hand, but no one knows for certain. There was a fire, but it wasn't any normal fire, it was elemental fire. All we know is when the fire finally stopped burning, there wasn't anything left of your family home. Nothing. Just ash."

"How did you know it was Leon?" My voice is flat. Some unnamed emotion is simmering under the surface of my calm.

"The fire was unnatural, had to be investigated. Leon didn't make it a secret he was coming to visit the Carmichaels. Everything unraveled as soon as the Council looked into him. He had several norms working for him,"

Dante interrupts his father and informs me, "Norms, normal people like Mia." I figured, but it was nice of him to clarify.

"Leon had isolated himself from any other Infinities. No one had any idea that Amanda was missing or that Leon had already killed Wyatt. It was a simple matter of having someone with the right abilities questioning his employees. You can't keep secrets from someone who can get inside your head." William glances at Ares but looks away quickly.

"That's crazy," Ollie mutters from the floor near my legs.

Rosa's eyes are rimmed in red and she sniffles a few times before clearing her throat to speak. "Mal works with the Council; that's the only reason we know so much, and she was... is my friend. We looked for her after they presumed Leon was dead, but..."

"Presumed dead. You mean no one knows if he's actually dead?" I blurt before Rosa can finish.

William shakes his head slowly. "No one could have made

it out of that fire, Laura. No bodies were recovered, but everyone involved is confident that Leon is dead." His eyes lower, and what he's not adding is that my grandparents died with him.

I let my back fall against the chair behind me, feeling tired even though it's not even noon yet. "My mom never stopped running." The words just start to fall from my lips. "She either didn't believe Leon was dead, or she didn't know." I drop my elbows to my knees, cradling my head in my hands. "She never once mentioned her family, she didn't talk about the past at all, not even my dad." I look over at Rosa, and William has his arm around her while Mal has both of her hands folded in his. She doesn't look weak for taking their support, they look stronger together, a united front. "Was Leon my dad?"

Rosa flinches, but that's the only sign of discomfort she shows. "It had to be Wyatt. There are no other possibilities."

"But you don't know or can't tell which?" It's horrible to think, but I'd much rather Wyatt have been my father than Leon, he's a monster.

"It wouldn't matter." Ollie turns so he's kneeling in front of me. His clear green eyes search mine as he reaffirms, "Even if he were, it doesn't matter." I tip my lips in a sad replica of a smile.

"I don't know, *bella ragazza*; I never met Wyatt. But Oliver is correct," Rosa tells me.

Shaking away the thoughts of which of them might be my dad, I focus on what we need to do now. I still don't know what happened to my mom, and if Leon truly is dead, where would she have gone?

I peer up at Ares. "Something isn't right. My mom didn't just leave. They never even found Leon's body. I'm not so sure I'm ready to accept that he's dead, and he's not the reason my mom is gone."

"Me either, *Cara*."

CHAPTER 21

$\mathcal{I}$'m staring at the television in Ares's room, but I'm not paying attention to what's on. Dante told his parents we needed a little time to ourselves before shuffling me out of the fancy living room. Milo wrapped his arm over my shoulder while Ollie trailed behind us. Ares caught up with us in the hallway a few moments later.

I'm not ready to talk about what I learned, and I'm grateful that Dante got us out of there when he did. I'm even more thankful that none of them are pushing me right now. I need time to deal with everything I learned this morning before adding anything else.

Ollie and Milo have taken up residence as my constant companions. The mood isn't quite somber, but Ollie definitely isn't his normal, flirty self.

I let out a sigh for what feels like the hundredth time this morning. Milo's hand finds mine without taking his eyes from the TV. In truth, I don't think any of us are really paying attention, but the distraction is welcome.

Dante is having a hard time sitting still. He's gone to the kitchen no less than five times, and every time anyone even clears their throat, he offers to get a drink, a snack, anything to get out of the room for a few minutes.

I squeeze Milo's hand but release him. I feel like I need to be doing more than just sitting here. Scooting toward the end of the bed, I make my way over to Ares. He's been on his phone or laptop the entire time we've been back in the room. I don't know what he's working on, but it has to better than sitting here and wallowing in self-pity. "What are you doing?"

Ares turns to look at me, not answering while he takes his time running his eyes over me. Satisfied with whatever he sees, he says, "Now that I know who and what I'm looking for, I'm running down a few leads."

I settle next to him with my arm on his shoulder, so I can see the screen of his laptop. He has several windows open, each with a different search running. The one in the top left corner is for the State Police of South Carolina. I glance over at him, wondering, not for the first time, what exactly Ares does?

The name Leon Whitmore is in the search bar, and the window has lines of text scrolling faster than I can read. Another window has the name Amanda Carmichael running a similar search. "Find anything?"

Ares wraps his arm around my hip and pulls me against his

side. "Not yet, but I wasn't expecting it to be that easy. You doing okay?"

I open my mouth to tell him I'm fine but stop myself and take a moment to actually think about how I'm feeling. "A little numb, actually," I tell him honestly. I feel like I should be feeling more, especially considering the guy that killed my grandparents has a fifty-fifty chance of being my father.

Ares's eyes soften as he looks at me, and he tugs me closer so I'm draped over his lap, facing sideways. Without any false promises or trying to placate me, he lowers his chin to the top of my head and just holds me. I inhale, bringing the scent that is uniquely his within me. I'm more comforted by his presence than any words he could utter. None of us know what tomorrow might bring. But I know Ares, Dante, Ollie, and even Milo, will be with me every step of the way.

ALSO BY ALBANY WALKER

Completed Series Infinity Chronicles

Infinity Chronicles Book One

Infinity Chronicles Book Two

Infinity Chronicles Book three

Infinity Chronicles Book Four

Book 2 of the Monster Series

Friends With the Monsters

Some Kind of Monster

Havenfall Harbor Series

Havenfall Harbor Book One

Coming Soon

Havenfall Harbor Book Two

Standalone Books

Beautiful Deceit

Becoming His

ALBANY WALKER

I am, a mother, a wife, a reader and a writer. My truth, I believe in real life happily ever afters, but you have to work for them.

If you enjoyed my book, or any other consider leaving a review.

For updates:

Albanywalkerauthor@gmail.com

https://albanywalkerauthor.wixsite.com/mysite

Made in United States
North Haven, CT
07 December 2022

28105649R00186